THE BROTHER OF DAPHNE

CONTENTS

CHAPTER I

PUNCH AND JUDY

"I said you'd do something," said Daphne, leaning back easily in her long chair.

I stopped swinging my legs and looked at her.

"Did you, indeed." I said coldly.

My sister nodded dreamily.

"Then you lied, darling. In your white throat," I said pleasantly.

"By the way, d'you know if the petrol's come?"

"I don't even care," said Daphne. "But I didn't lie, old chap. My word is—"

"Your bond? Quite so. But not mine. The appointment I have in Town that day—"

"Which day?" said Daphne, with a faint smile.

"The fete day."

"Ah!"

It was a bazaar fete thing. Daphne and several others—euphemistically styled workers-had conspired and agreed together to obtain money by false pretences for and on behalf of a certain mission, to wit the Banana. I prefer to put it that way. There is a certain smack about the wording of an indictment. Almost a relish. The fact that two years before I had been let in for a stall and had defrauded fellow men and women of a considerable sum of money, but strengthened my determination not to be entrapped again. At the same time I realized that I was up against it.

The crime in question was fixed for Wednesday or Thursday-so much I knew. But no more. There was the rub. I really could not toil up to Town two days running.

"Let's see," I said carelessly," the fete's on-er-Wednesday, or Thursday, is it?"

"Which day are you going up to Town?" said Daphne. I changed my ground.

"The Bananas are all right," I said, lighting a cigarette.

"They only ate a missionary the other day," said my sister.

"That's bad," said I musingly. "To any nation the consumption of home produce is of vital—"

"We want to make sixty pounds."

"To go towards their next meal? How much do missionaries cost?"

"To save their souls alive," said Daphne zealously.

"I'm glad something's to be saved alive," said I.

Before she could reply, tea began to appear. When the footman had retired to fetch the second instalment of accessories, I pointed the finger of scorn at the table, upon which he had set the tray.

"That parody emanated from a bazaar," I said contemptuously.

"It does for the garden," said my sister.

"It'd do for anything," said I. "Its silly sides, its crazy legs—"

"Crazy?" cried Daphne indignantly. "It'd bear an elephant."

"What if it would?" I said severely. "It's months since we gave up the elephants."

"Is the kettle ready?"

"It boils not, neither does it sing."

"For which piece of irreverence you will do something on Thursday."

"My dear girl," I said hurriedly, "if it were not imperative for me to be in Town—"

"You will do something on Thursday." I groaned.

"And this," I said, "this is my mother's daughter! We have been nursed together, scolded together, dandled in the same arms. If she had not been the stronger of the two, we should have played with the same toys."

I groaned again. Berry opened his eyes.

"The value of a siesta upon a summer afternoon-"he began.

I cut in with a bitter laugh. "What's he going to do?" I said.

"Take a stall, of course," said Daphne.

"Is he? said Berry comfortably. "Is he? If motoring with Jonah to Huntercombe, and playing golf all day, is not incompatible with taking a stall on Thursday, I will sell children's underwear and egg cosies with eclat. Otherwise—"

"Golf," I said, "golf! Why don't I play golf?"

"I know," said Berry; "because—"

"Miserable man!" said Daphne.

"Who?" said her husband.

"You."

Berry turned to me. "You hear?" he said. "Vulgar abuse. And why? Simply because a previous engagement denies to me the opportunity of subscribing to this charitable imposition. Humble as would have been my poor assistance, it would have been rendered with a willing heart. But there!" he sighed-"It may not be. The Bananas will never know, never realize how-By the way, who are the Bananas?"

"The Bananas?" said I. "Surely you know the—"

"Weren't at Ascot, were they?"

"Not in the Enclosure. No. The bold, bad Bananas are in many ways an engaging race. Indeed, some of the manners and customs which they affect are of a quite peculiar interest. Let us look, brother, for a moment, at their clothing. At the first blush-I use the word advisedly-it would seem that, like the fruit from which they take their name—"

"I thought you'd better do some tricks," said Daphne, throwing a dark look in my direction.

"Of course," I said; "the very thing. I've always been so good at tricks."

"I mean it," said Daphne.

"Of course you do. What about the confidence trick? Can any lady oblige me with a public-house?"

"She means trick-cycling, stupid," said Berry. "Riding backwards on one wheel while you count the ball-bearings."

"Look here," I said, "if Berry could have come and smoked a cigarette, I wouldn't have minded trying to flick the ash off it with a hunting-whip."

"Pity about that golf," mused Berry. "And you might have thrown knives round me afterwards. As it is, you'll have to recite."

In a few telling sentences I intimated that I would do nothing of the kind.

"I will appear," I said at last, "I will appear and run round generally, but I promise nothing more."

"Nonsense," said my sister. "I have promised, and I'm not going to let you break my word. You are going to do something definite."

"Desperate?"

"Definite. You have three days in which to get ready. There's Jill calling me. We're going to run over to Barley to whip up the Ashton crowd. D'you think we've enough petrol?"

"I don't even care," said I.

Daphne laughed softly. Then: "I must go," she said, getting up. "Give me a cigarette and tell me if you think this dress'll do. I'm going to change my shoes."

"If," said I, producing my cigarette-case, "if you were half as nice as you invariably look—"

"That's a dear," she said, taking a cigarette. "And now, goodbye."

I watched her retreating figure gloomily.

Berry began to recite 'We are Seven.'

Thursday morning broke cloudless and brilliant. I saw it break. Reluctantly, of course; I am not in the habit of rising at cock-crow. But on this occasion I rose because I could not sleep. When I went to bed on Wednesday night, I lay awake thinking deeply about what I was to do on the morrow. Daphne had proved inexorable. My brain, usually so fertile, had become barren, and for my three days' contemplation of the subject I had absolutely nothing to show. It was past midnight before I fell into a fitful slumber, only to be aroused three hours and a half later by the sudden burst of iniquity with which two or more cats saw fit to shake the silence of the rose-garden.

As I threw out the boot-jack, I noticed the dawn. And as further sleep seemed out of the question, I decided to dress and go out into the woods.

When I slipped out of Knight's Bottom into the sunlit road to find myself face to face with a Punch and Judy show, I was not far from being momentarily disconcerted. For a second it occurred to me that I might be dreaming, but, though I listened carefully, I could hear no cats, so I sat down on the bank by the side of the road and prepared to contemplate the phenomenon.

When I say 'Punch and Judy show' I am wrong. Although what I saw suggested the proximity of a Punch and a Judy, to say nothing of the likelihood of a show, I did not, as a matter of fact, descry any one of the three. The object that presented itself to my view was the tall, rectangular booth, gaudy and wide-mouthed, with which, until a few years ago, the streets of London were so familiar. Were! Dear old Punch and Judy, how quickly you are becoming a thing of the past! How soon you will have gone the way of Jack-i'-the Green, Pepper's Ghost, the Maypole, and many another old friend! Out of the light into the darkness. The old order changeth, yielding place to new, and in a little space men shall be content to wonder at your ancient memory as their grandfathers marvelled at that of the frolics of my Lord of Misrule. However.

There was the booth. But that was all. It stood quite alone at the side of the white road. I walked round it. Nothing. I glanced up and down the road, but there was no one in sight. I had been feeling hungry, for it was seven o'clock; but this was better than breakfast, and I returned to the bank. The little red curtains fluttered, as a passing breeze caught them, and I marked how bright and new they looked. It was certainly in good condition-this booth.

"Well?" said a voice.

"Well?" said I.

A pause. A girl's voice it was: coming from within the booth.

"You seem rather surprised," said the voice.

"No, no," I said, "not really surprised. Only a little staggered. You see, I know so few booths."

"What are you doing here?"

"To be frank, booth, I'm waiting."

"I'm waiting, too."

"So?" said I. "I wait, you wait, let us wait, ye shall have been about to see, they would—"

"What are you waiting for?"

"Developments. And you?"

"My breakfast."

I looked up and down the road. "I don't see it coming," I said anxiously. "What's it look like?"

"Milk. You don't happen to have any, I suppose?"

I felt in my pockets.

"There, now," I said, "I must have left it on the piano. I got up rather hurriedly this morning," I added apologetically.

"Never mind."

"I'll tell you what, booth, I'll go and get some."

"No, thanks very much. Don't you bother; it'll come along presently."

"Are you sure? This isn't 'The Blue Bird.'"

"Yes, it's all right-really."

There was another pause. Then:

"Hadn't you better be getting back to breakfast?" said the girl.

"Not much," said I. "I don't run up against booths every day. Besides—"

"Besides what?"

"Well, booth, I'm awfully curious."

"What do you want to know?"

"You're very good."

"I didn't say I'd tell you."

"I'll risk that. In a word, why are you?"

"Ah!"

I waited in silence for a few moments. At length:

"Suppose," she said slowly, "suppose a bet had been made."

"A bet?"

"A bet."

"Shocking! Go on."

"Well? Isn't that enough?"

"Nothing like."

"I don't think much of your imagination."

I raised my eyes to heaven. "A prophet is not without honour," I quoted.

"Is this your own country?"

"It is."

"Oh, I say, you'd be the very man!"

"I am," I said. "Refuse substitutes."

It gradually appeared that, in a rash moment, she had made some silly wager that she could give a Punch and Judy show on her own in the village of Lynn Hammer and the vicinity. Of course, she had not meant it. She had spoken quite idly, secure in the very impracticability of the thing. But certain evil-disposed persons-referred to mysteriously as 'they'—had fastened greedily upon her words, and, waving aside her objection that she had no paraphernalia, deliberately proceeded to provide the same, that she might have no excuse. The booth was run up, the puppets procured. The gentle hint that she wanted to withdraw had been let fall at the exact moment with deadly effect, and-the wicked work was done. She had been motored over and here set down, complete with booth, half an hour ago. They were going to look back later, just to see how she was getting on. The ordeal was to be over and the wager won by six o'clock, and she might have the assistance of a native in her whimsical venture.

"Right up to the last I believe the brutes thought I would cry off," she said. "I very nearly did, too, when it came to it. Only I saw Peter smiling. It is rather a hopeless position, isn't it?"

"It was. But now that you've got your native—"

"Oh!" she said. Then: "But I've got one."

"Where?"

"He's getting the milk."

"I don't believe he is. Anyway, you can discharge him and take me on. I've been out of work for years. Besides, you've been sent. In your advent I descry the finger of Providence."

"I wish I did. What do you mean?"

"This day," I said, "I am perforce a zealot."

"A what?"

"A zealot-a Banana zealot. You, too, shall be a zealot. We will unite our zeal, and this day light such a candle—"

"The man's mad," she said. "Quite mad."

I explained. "You see," I said, "it's like this. Simply miles away, somewhere south south and by south of us, there are a lot of heathen.

They're called Bananas. I don't know very much about it, but there seems to be a sort of understanding that we should keep them in missionaries. So every now and then the 'worker' push here get up a fete thing and take money off people. Then they find one and send him out. Well, there's one of these stunts on this afternoon, and I've been let in to do something. That's why I look so pale and interesting. The last day or two I've been desperate about it. But now . . ."

"Now what?"

"If you'd let me help you today, we could take the show to the fete and simply rake it in. It's a splendid way of winning your bet, too. Oh, booth, isn't it obvious that you've been sent?"

"It certainly would be nicer than giving performances about the village," she said musingly. "If only I knew you—"

"You don't know the fellow who isn't getting the milk," I objected.

"That's different. He'd be only a servant."

"I would be the same."

There was a pause. A rabbit loped into the road and blinked curiously at the booth. Then he saw me and beat a hasty retreat.

"It is in a good cause," I urged. "You don't know the Bananas; they're absurdly-er-straight."

"It's all very well for you," she said; "you know everybody here. But it would be an impossible position for me; I don't know a soul. Now, if we were both strangers—"

"Well?"

"Well, then they wouldn't worry as to who we were and what we had to do with one another."

"Then let's both be strangers."

"How can you be strange to order?"

"Hush!" I said. "I will disguise me. At home I have put away a Pierrot dress not one of them knows anything about, and I think I can raise a mask. If I—"

A stifled exclamation from the booth made me look up. Framed in its mouth, her arms folded and resting on the ledge, was the girl. What I could see of her was dressed as a Pierrot. Her hair was concealed under a black silk cap, and the familiar white felt conical hat sat jauntily over one ear. A straight, white nose, and a delicate chin, red lips parted and smiling a little, such a smile as goes always with eyebrows just raised, very alluring-so much only I saw. For the rest, a strip of black velvet made an irritating mask.

I made her a low bow.

"I can see this is going to be a big thing," I said, "Won't you come down?"

"I haven't even said I'll take you,"

"Please."

"You're sure to be recognized, and then, what about me?"

"Oh, no, I shan't. If necessary, I'll wear a false nose. I've got one somewhere."

"Here's my milk."

I looked round and beheld a small boy approaching with a jug.

"Was that the best you could do in the native line?"

"You needn't sneer. I'm not over-confident about my second venture."

"Well, a knave's better than a fool, any day."

"I'm sure I hope so."

She slipped down out of sight into the booth again, to reappear a moment later in the road: and by her side a beautiful white bull-terrier, a Toby ruff about his sturdy neck.

"Good man," said my lady, pointing a finger at me. "Good man."

The dog came forward, wagging his tail. I stooped and spoke with him. Then I turned to his mistress. She had discarded her white hat and drawn on a long dust-coat, which reached almost to her ankles. She held it close about her, as she walked. It showed off her slim figure to great advantage. Below, the wide edges of white duck trousers just appeared above shining insteps and high heeled shoes.

When the urchin had come up, she took the jug from him with both hands.

"I shall have to drink out of it," she said, raising it to her lips with a smile.

"Of course. Why not? Only . . ."

I hesitated.

"What?"

"Hadn't you better-I mean, won't the mask get in your way?"

She lowered the jug and looked at me. "No; it won't get in the way. Thanks all the same," she said steadily. "Not all today."

"It's in the way now."

"Not my way."

I saw her eyes watching my face as she drank, and when she took the jug from her lips she was smiling.

We had some difficulty in persuading the boy to leave us; but at length, a heavy bribe, coupled with the assurance that we should be at the fete in the afternoon, had the desired effect, and he went slowly away.

Thereafter we took counsel together.

As a result, it was decided that we should fold the booth-it shut up like a screen-and convey it, puppets and all, a little way into the wood. It was early yet, but some people would be passing along the road, and we were not yet ready to combat the curiosity that the appearance of a Punch and Judy show would be sure to arouse. That done, she would lie close in the wood with Toby, while I made off home and changed.

As I started off, after settling her in the bracken, I heard the village clock strike the half-hour. Half-past seven. I gained the house unobserved. No one was abroad except the servants, but I heard Daphne singing in the bathroom.

I had worn the Pierrot dress two years ago at a fancy-dress ball.

There it lay with its mask at the bottom of the wardrobe. The change was soon completed, and I stood up a proper Folly, from the skull cap upon my crown to the pumps upon my feet. It took some time to find the nose, but luck was with me, and at last I ran it to earth in an old collar-box. Truly an appalling article, it stuck straight out from my face like a fat, fiery peg, but between that and the mask, my disguise would defy detection.

Suddenly I had a brilliant idea. Sitting down, I scribbled a note to Daphne to the effect that, owing to a sleepless night, my nerve had forsaken me, and that, unable to face the terror of the bazaar, I had fled to Town, and should not be back till late. I added that I should be with her in the spirit, which, after all, was the main thing.

I put on a long overcoat and a soft hat. The nose went into one pocket, the mask into another. Then I went cautiously downstairs and into the dining-room. It was empty, and breakfast was partially laid.

In feverish haste I hacked about a pound of meat off a York ham and nearly as much off a new tongue. Wrapping the slices in a napkin, I thrust them into the pocket with the nose. To add half a brown loaf to the mask and drain the milk jug was the work of another moment, and, after laying the note on Daphne's plate, I slipped out of the French windows and into the bushes as I heard William come down the passage. A quarter of an hour later I was back again in the wood.

She was sitting on a log, swinging her legs to and fro. When I took off my coat and hat, she clapped her hands in delight.

"Wait till you see the nose," said I.

When presently I slipped that French monstrosity into place, she laughed so immoderately that her brown hair broke loose from under the black silk cap and tumbled gloriously about her shoulders.

"There now," she said. "See what you've done."

"Good for the nose," said I.

"It's all very well to say that, but it took me ages to get it all under the wretched cap this morning."

"I shouldn't put it back again if I were you. You see," I went on earnestly, "everybody will know you're a girl, Judy dear."

"Why, Punch?" She drew aside the dust coat and revealed the wide Pierrot trousers she was wearing.

"Priceless," I admitted. "But what I really love are your feet." She looked concernedly at her little, high-heeled shoes.

I stooped to flick the dust from their patent leather.

"Thank you, Punch. What shall I do about my hair, then?"

"Wear it in a pig-tail. I'll plait it for you. It'll be worth another sovereign to the Bananas."

"If you put it like that—" she said slowly.

"I do, Judy." If the suggestion was not prompted by motives which were entirely disinterested, I think I may be forgiven.

"I say, Judy," I said a little later, pausing unnecessarily in my work, and making pretence to comb with my fingers the tresses as yet ungathered into the plait.

"Yes? What a long time you are!"

Well, there was a knot.

She tried to look round into my face at that, but I vigorously unplaited about two inches, which seemed to satisfy her. For me, I thought of Penelope and her web and the wooers, and smiled.

"Well, what is it, Punch?"

"About the mask."

"No good!"

"But, Judy—"

For the next two minutes I did a little listening. When she paused for breath:

"Have some ham," I suggested.

"Bother the ham! Do you hear what I say?"

"I heard you bother the ham."

"Before that?"

"Something about a mask, was it?"

"Give me back my hair," she demanded.

"No, no," I said hastily, "not that! I won't ask again."

"Promise."

"I promise."

When I had finished the plaiting, I tied the ends with a piece of ribbon which she produced, kissed them, and sat down in the grass at her feet.

We had oceans of time, for the fete did not begin till two. But we agreed there must be a rehearsal of some kind.

"What do you know about yourself, Punch?"

"I have a foggy recollection of domestic differences."

"You used to beat me cruelly."

"Ah, but you had a nagging tongue, Judy. I can hear your defiant 'wootle' now."

Her lips parted in a smile at the reminiscence, and before they closed again she had slipped something between them. The next instant the wood rang with a regular hurricane of toots and wootles.

"Oh, Judy!"

"Wootle?" she said inquiringly.

"Rather! But hush-you'll wake the echoes."

"And why not? They ought to be up and about by now."

I shook my head.

"They're a sleepy folk," I said; "they get so little rest. The day is noisy enough, but at night, what with dogs baying the moon, and the nightjars calling, when owls do cry—"

"When owls do cry—"

"-and the earnest but mistaken chanticleer, they have a rotten time. Poor echoes! And they wake very easily here."

"Don't they everywhere?"

"Oh, no! I know some that are very heavy sleepers. In fact, it's hopeless to try and wake them without the welkin."

"The welkin?"

"Yes, you make him ring, you know. They nearly always hear him. And if they don't the first time, you make him ring again."

For a little space she laughed helplessly. At last:

"I am an idiot to encourage you. Seriously," she added, "about the little play."

"Presently by us to be enacted?"

"The plot," I said, "is as follows. Punch has a row with Judy and knocks her out. (Laughter.) Various well-intentioned and benignant fools look in on Punch to pass the time of day, and get-very properly-knocked out for their pains. (Loud and prolonged laughter.) This is followed by the side-splitting incident in which a handy clown not only eludes the thirsty bludgeon, but surreptitiously steals the inevitable sausages. Exit clown. Punch, already irritated at having missed clown, misses sausages, and exit in high dudgeon. Re-enter Judy, followed by sausaged clown, who comforts her. (Oh, Judy!) Re-enter Punch. Justifiable tussle. Punch sees sausages and begins to find his length. Clown sees stars and exit. Punch knocks out Judy with a left hook. To him, gloating, enter constable. It seems Judy's knock-out more serious than usual. Constable suggests that Punch shall go quietly. Punch does not see it, and retires to fetch persuader. Constable protests and is persuaded. (Laughter.) Enter ghost-not clear whose ghost, but any ghost in a storm. Punch unnerved. Ghost gibbers. Punch more unnerved. Ghost gibbers again. Punch terrified. Exit ghost and enter hangman, to whom Punch, unstrung by recent encounter with apparition, falls an easy prey. Curtain. You bow from the mouth of the booth. I adjust nose and collect money in diminutive tin pail. How's that?"

"Lovely, Punch! But where does Toby dear come in?"

At the mention of his name the terrier rose and went to her.

His mistress stroked his soft head.

"In the background," said I. "Or the offing (nautical). I don't think he'd better act. Let him be stage-door-keeper."

"All right. Now open the puppet-box."

23

It was a nice set of puppets, and they were very simple to manipulate. They fitted easily on to the hand, the forefinger controlling the head, and the thumb and second finger the arms.

The old fellow's cudgel was a dream.

We decided that I had better stick to Punch and Punch alone.

For the others she would be answerable.

After rehearsing for half an hour, we stopped for breakfast. In the absence of cutlery, it was a ragged meal, but what mattered that? We were for letting the world slip-we should ne'er be younger.

People were stirring now. Carts rumbled in the distance, and cars sang past on the long, white road. Presently came one that slowed and slowed and stopped.

It was unfortunate that, but a moment before, I should have grown impatient of a large piece of crust and thrust it bodily into my mouth. But although articulation at this interesting juncture was out of the question, I laid an eloquent hand upon her arm and crowded as much expression as I could into a swollen and distorted visage. She glanced at me and collapsed in silent infectious laughter. And so it happened that, while we two conspirators lay shaking in the bracken, her friends turned their car wonderingly round and drove slowly back into the village away from her they sought.

Another hour and a half of somewhat desultory rehearsal found us 'wootle' perfect and ready for anything. So we laid the puppets by, fed Toby with brown bread and tongue, and rested against the labours of the afternoon.

The time passed quickly enough-too quickly.

It was a few minutes past one when, having adjusted my mask and slid my nose into position, I got the booth upon my shoulders and stepped out into the road.

"Come along," I said encouragingly.

"I'm afraid. Oh, there's something coming."

"Nonsense! I wish I hadn't packed that bludgeon."

"I'm nervous, Punch."

"Will you make me drag you along by the hair of your head? Of course, it'd be in the picture right enough, but I rather want two hands for this infernal booth. However, let me once get a good grip on that soft pigtail—"

"What-again?"

"Ah, that was in love, Judy."

The next second she had joined me on the white highway, the faithful Toby a short pace behind her. His not to reason why.

A good fellow, Toby.

It was rather a nervous moment. But, in spite of an approaching wagonette, she walked bravely beside me with the puppet-box under her arm. The occupants of the vehicle began to evince great curiosity as we drew nearer, but their mare caught sight of my nose at the critical moment and provided an opportune diversion.

"So perish all our enemies!" she said with a sigh of relief.

"Stage-fright, Judy, dear. You'll be all right in a minute.

We're bound to excite interest. It's what we're for and what we want. I'll keep it going. Give me your wootler."

She handed me the reed, and I held it ready between my lips.

"Buck up, lass!"

Ten minutes more and we entered the village. The grounds where the fete was to be holden lay three-quarters of a mile further on. The ball was opened by two small errand boys, on whose hands, as is usual with the breed, time was lying heavily.

They were engaged in deep converse as we came up, and it was only when we were close upon them that they became aware of our presence. For a few seconds they stared at us, apparently rooted to the spot, and as if they could not believe their good fortune.

Then one broke into an explosive bellow of delight, while the other ran off squeaking with excitement to find other devils who should share the treasure-trove. But, unlike his infamous predecessor, he was not content with seven. When he returned, it was but as the van of a fast-swelling rabble. His erstwhile companion, who had been backing steadily in front of me ever since he left, and had, after a hurried consideration of the respective merits of the booth and the box under Judy's arm, rejected them both in favour of my nose, kept his eyes fastened greedily upon that organ with so desperate an air of concentration that I was quite relieved when he tripped over a brick and fell on his back in the road.

And all this time our following grew. The news of our advent had spread like wildfire. Old men and maidens, young men and boys, the matron and the maid, alike came running. Altogether, Lynn Hammer was set throbbing with an excitement such as it had not experienced since the baker's assistant was wrongly arrested for petty larceny in 1904.

Amongst those who walked close about us, candid speculation as to the probable venue of the performance was rife, while its style, length, value, etc., were all frankly discussed. Many were the questions raised, and many the inaccurate explanations accepted as to the reason of our being; but though my companion came in for some inevitable discussion, I was relieved to find that my panache and a comic peculiarity of gait, which I thought it as well from time to time to affect, proved usefully diverting.

When the crowd had begun to assume considerable proportions, Judy had slipped her arm in mine, and an answering pressure to my encouraging squeeze told me that she was trying to buck up as well as she could. Good little Judy! It was an ordeal for you, but you came through it with flying colours, though with a flaming cheek.

When we reached the triangular piece of grass that lay in front of the village inn, I called a halt with such suddeness as to create great confusion in the swarming ranks that followed in our wake. But while they sorted themselves, I slipped the booth off my shoulders, gave one long, echoing call upon the reed, and, striking an attitude, made ready to address the expectant villagers.

After carefully polishing my nose with a silk handkerchief-an action which met with instant approval-I selected a fat, red-faced drayman, thanked him, and said that mine was a Bass, an assertion which found high favour with the more immediate cronies of the gentleman in question. Then I got to work.

After dwelling lightly on the renown in which the village of Lynn Hammer was held throughout the countryside, not to mention a gallant reference to the wit, beauty, and mirth which was assembled about me, I plunged into a facetious resume of recent local events. This, of course, came to me easily enough, but the crowd only saw therein the lucky ventures of a talkative stranger, and roared with merriment at each happy allusion. And so I came to the Bananas. Yes, we were for the fete. There should we be the livelong afternoon, giving free shows, and only afterwards soliciting contribution from such as could afford to give in a good cause. God save the King!

Then I called for mine host, and after ordering ginger beer for Judy and old ale for myself, slapped silver into his hand, and begged as many as would so honour her to drink the lady's health.

About that there was no difficulty, and when I had despatched the original boy-who all this while had never wavered in his constancy to my proboscis-for a small tin pail, I prepared to get my burden once more upon my back. But this was not to be.

Four good fellows insisted on constituting themselves booth-bearers, and the burly drayman gallantly relieved my fair companion of the box of puppets.

So we came in state to the grounds where the bazaar was to be held. The parley with the gatekeeper was of short duration, for the 'workers' scented money in our admission, and, with an eye to the Bananas' main chance, made us quickly welcome. On my explaining our intention to put our efforts at their service, and any increment that might result into their pockets, their expression of gratitude was quite touching.

The entrance fee deterred some, and their daily occupation more of those who had formed our kindly escort, from following us into the fete, but I believe that most of them contrived to return before six o'clock.

When I think of all that I said and did on that sunny afternoon, I get hot all over.

I could not go very far wrong during the actual performance, but it was afterwards, when Judy sat smiling in the mouth of the booth, and I went forth, pail in hand, seeking whom I might devour.

I drew my arm familiarly through that of a reluctant curate, and walked him smartly up and down, discussing volubly the merits of my nose in tones which suggested that I had no roof to my mouth, Did a lady protest that she had already contributed, I repeated "Oh, madam!" reproachfully and crescendo till the hush-money was paid, while in front of those who affected not to see my out-stretched hand, I stood as if rooted to the spot. I borrowed the vicar's wideawake, ostensibly for a conjuring trick, and wore it assiduously for the rest of the afternoon and, on his demurring to such use, I explained, in the voice of G.P.Huntley, that it went so well with the nose.

In short, I played the mountebank to a degree that astonished myself, but apparently to some purpose, for the money came in properly.

The performances went with a bang, and when, at the conclusion of the playlet, I lifted Judy to the rickety shelf, so that her head and shoulders were framed in the mouth of the booth, it was the signal for a burst of applause.

On one of these occasions:

"It's not fair that I should take every call," she said, looking down at my upturned face.

"My dear Judy, I have my reward."

"What?"

"Don't I lift you up every time?"

She laughed pleasedly.

"Gallant Punch, you're easily satisfied."

"Am I, Judy—am I?" I said gently, taking her hand.

"Yes," she said, snatching it away. "You are and will be. Go out and get the money."

I adjusted my nose thoughtfully. Daphne was, of course, in great evidence. Anxious to run no unnecessary risk, I avoided her when possible, and when I did find myself in her proximity, I at once indulged in some of my more extravagant behaviour.

"Where's your brother?" I heard a worker say.

"Brother!" said Daphne bitterly. "Coward! And I really thought we should have him this time. Fled to London before we were up this morning, thank you. From the amount of food he took with him, and the way he took it, anyone would have thought he was an escaped convict. Guilty conscience, I suppose. One hears a good deal about record flights nowadays, but I'd back my miserable brother against any aviator. My husband's promised to look in about five, if he's back from Huntercombe. That's something. But they're a wretched lot. Oh, here's one of the Pierrots!"

I hung the pail on my nose and looked at her.

"As one of the organizers of the fete," she said hastily, "I must thank you—"

"Nothing doing, madam," said I, in an assumed voice.

"But"

"Free list entirely suspended, madam," and I shook the pail mercilessly.

A small and grinning crowd had begun to collect, so Daphne parted up with a forced smile, and I went off chuckling to queer the animals' race.

Our penultimate performance was over, and I was in the midst of my vagaries again, when I saw Berry. Unanxious to tempt Providence, I retired precipitately to the shelter of the booth. My companion was sitting disconsolately upon the box on which she stood to work her puppets.

"Is it time for the next show?" she said.

"Not for a quarter of an hour."

I sat down at her feet and removed my mask and nose.

"I'm afraid I persuaded your hand last time, Judy."

"You touched it."

"Let me look."

"It doesn't show."

"Let me look."

After examining the knuckles carefully, I turned my attention to the soft little palm.

"Obstinacy," I said. "Obstinacy is clearly indicated by the dimple situate below Saturn and to the right of the watering-pot."

She tried to draw it away, but I tightened my hold and proceeded with my investigation.

"A gentle and confiding nature, characterized by a penchant for escapade, is denoted by the joy-wheel at the base of Halley's Comet. And so we come to the life-belt. This-my word, this is all right! Unrivalled for resistance to damp and wear, will last three to six times as long as ordinary paint-I mean life-of extraordinary durability. Now for the heart-line. The expert will here descry a curious mixture of—

Further investigation she cut short by so determined an attempt at withdrawal that I let her hand go.

"Oughtn't we to be beginning again?"

"You're very eager for the last show."

"No, I'm not, but I want to get it over."

"Oh, Judy!"

She laid her hand on my shoulder.

"No, Punch, no, I didn't mean that. It's been-great fun."

"It's sweet of you to say that."

"It's not. Don't you think I've liked it?"

30

I leaned forward.

"Dear Judy," I said, "very soon it will be over, and we shall go our several ways once more. And if we don't meet, as the months and years go by, when other cleverer, better men walk by your side, and glorious days crowd thick about you, throw a spare thought to the old time when you were a strolling player, and the poor fool you gave the honour of your company."

She turned her head away, but she did not speak.

"You'll not forget me, Judy?"

She caught her breath and slipped a hand under her mask for a second. Then:

"Next show, Punch," she cried. "No, of course, I shan't. You've been very good to me."

She was on her feet by now and busily arranging the puppets. I groaned. The next moment she had wound a long call upon the reed, which put further converse out of the question.

The last performance began. The first quarrel seemed to lack its wonted bitterness. Punch appeared halfhearted, and Judy was simply walking through.

I glanced at the girl and stroked her pig-tail-my pig-tail.

"Wootle," I said encouragingly. "Wootle, wootle."

She started at my touch. Then she seemed to remember, and flung herself into her part with abandon.

When the ghost was on, I had a brilliant idea.

"Leave the hangman out," I whispered, "and put up Judy instead. We'll have a reconciliation to finish with."

And so to Punch, sobered, shaking, cowering in the corner, with his little plaster hands before his face, came his poor wife. (Oh, but she did it well!) Gently, timidly, bravely, she laid a trembling hand upon his shoulder, and coaxed his hands from before his frightened eyes, then, backing, stood with outstretched, appealing little arms-a gesture at once so loving and pathetic that Punch was fain to thrust his sleeve before his eyes and turn his face in shame to the wall. Softly went Judy to him again, touched him, and waited. And as he turned again, to find two little arms stealing about his neck, and a poor, bare, bruised head upon his chest, he flung his arms about her with a toot of joy, and clasped her in the accepted fashion. Oh, very charming.

This was greeted with prolonged applause.

"Hold it," I said. "Hold the picture!"

As she obeyed I slid my left arm about her, ready to lift her up.

Suddenly Punch became limp and lifeless in his wife's embrace, and with my freed right hand I slipped her mask over her forehead, smiled into her eyes, and kissed them.

"I promised not to ask again."

"Punch!"

So for a moment we two let the world wag. Then the whole booth fell heavily over, mouth uppermost, and we within it. It was the final of the animal race that was responsible for our overthrow. The black pig, blind with jealous rage and mortification at being beaten on the tape by a cochin china, had borne violently down upon the booth and upset it, with wicked grunts of satisfaction.

"Hurt, dear?" said I.

"No."

As she slipped her mask into place, Berry put his head in at the mouth of the booth. Maskless, noseless, I looked at him. Slowly his astonished features relaxed in a grin.

"So!" he said softly. "I might have known."

CHAPTER II

CLOTHES AND THE MAN

"This," said Berry, "is all right. By which I mean—"

We assured him we knew what he meant, and that no explanation was necessary.

"All right," he said at last. "There. I've said it again now.

You're quite sure you do know what I mean? Because, if you've the least hesitation—"

"Will you be quiet?" said Daphne.

"Alright."

It was a beautiful August morning. After a roaring season in town, we had, all five-Berry, Daphne, Jonah, Jill, and myself-girded our jaded loins, packed, crawled into the car, and rolled down to Cornwall, there to build up the wasted tissues, go to bed at ten, and forget that there were such things as theatres and ballrooms.

We took a couple of days coming down by road, and our run was not without incident.

I wish cyclists would not hang on behind.

In Kingston a monger's boy, with some fish that were patently feeling the heat, took hold of the cape-hood. I spoke with him after a little.

"The use of this hood," I said, "for heavy and bulky packages involves risk of injury to passengers, and is prohibited. Didn't you know that?"

He regarded me with a seraphic smile, nearly lost his life by getting into a tram-line, and said I ought to know better than to talk to the man at the wheel.

"Friend," said I, "I perceive you are a humorist. Lo, here in this car are already three humorists. Under these unfortunate circumstances, I have no alternative but to ask you to withdraw."

It was just then that the near hind tyre burst exactly under him.

We gave him half a sovereign towards buying a new bicycle, but I believe he will always think we did it on purpose.

It had been arranged that we should spend the night at Salisbury and push on to Cornwall on the following day. We made the Cathedral city soon after five and slipped out to see Stonehenge. There were a few other people there, and one or two of them turned to watch our arrival. Berry left the car and went straight to the nearest-a fat tradesman, wearing a new imitation panama and a huge calabash.

"Can you tell me if this is Stoke Poges?" we heard him say. The rest of us alighted and walked hurriedly away in the opposite direction. Clearly my brother-in-law was in a certain mood and no fit companion for the sensitive. Memories of the unutterable torment, to which on like occasions we had been mercilessly subjected, by reason of Berry's most shameless behaviour among strangers, rose up before us. The fact that he called after us caused Daphne to break into a run.

Our luck was out. When we had completed the circle of the cromlechs, we came suddenly upon him. More to our dismay than surprise he had become the centre of a little knot of excursionists, who were listening to him eagerly. As we appeared:

"Ah," he said to the interested company, "here is my Aunt! She'll tell you. Aunt Daphne, wasn't it here that father lost the string bag?"

"Wretched fool!" said Daphne under her breath, turning hurriedly in the direction of the car.

Berry watched her retreat, and turned to his listeners with a sigh.

"I'm afraid I've gone and upset her now," he said. "I oughtn't to have reminded her of the untoward incident. It was the only string bag they had, and it was an awful blow to her. It upset him, too, terribly. Never the same man again. In fact, from that day he began to go wrong-criminally, I mean."

The little group grew closer to him than ever. Like a fool, I stayed to hear more.

"Yes," Berry went on, "in less than a month he was up at the Old Bailey, under the Merchandise Marks Act, for selling Gruyere cheese with too big holes in it. Five years his sentence was. Let's see, he ought to be coming out in about-oh, about-When does father come out, Cousin Albert?"

The excursionists gazed greedily at me-the felon's son. I approached Berry and laid a hand upon his arm. Then I turned to the little group.

"This fellow," I said, "has got us into trouble before. Those of you who have motor-cars will understand me when I refer to the great difficulty of securing a really trustworthy chauffeur. Now, this man is honest and a most careful driver, but when he is, so to speak, off duty, he is so unfortunate as to suffer from delusions, usually connected with crime and the administration of the criminal law. While we were having lunch at Whitchurch only this afternoon, he went off to the police-station and tried to give himself up for the Hounslow murder, didn't you?"

"Yes, sir," faltered Berry.

"And all the time," I went on, "I'm not at all satisfied myself that he did murder the woman, although things certainly looked rather black—"

"I did!" said Berry fiercely.

The crowd of excursionists recoiled, and a small boy in a green flannel blazer burst into tears.

"Anyway," I said, "there isn't anything like enough evidence against you, so we won't argue it. Now, then, we want to be going. Come along."

"Half a shake, sir," said Berry, feeling in his pockets. "You know that knife—"

The company began nervously to disperse. Some exhorted one another to observe some feature of the cromlechs which was only visible from some point of vantage on the side other to that on which we stood. Others agreed that they had no idea that it was so late, and the fat tradesman gave a forced shiver and announced that he must have left his coat behind "that big one."

"I'll get it for you, sir," said Berry, opening his knife.

I was forced to admit that Stonehenge looked far more impressive when apparently deserted, than with one or two tourists, however genial and guileless, in a high holiday humour in the foreground. At the same time, as we walked back to the car, I felt that I owed it to myself to lodge a grave protest against the indecent and involving methods my brother-in-law had seen fit to employ.

"After all," I concluded, "the fellow's your brother, and even if his panama wasn't a real one, that's no reason why he should be made to do the hundred in about twelve seconds. He wasn't in strict training either. You could see that. Besides, why rope me in? For yourself, if you must play the comic idiot—"

"He wasn't in the picture," said Berry. "None of them were. That kid's blazer absolutely killed the grass for miles around. Didn't you see how brown it had gone? That," he added coolly, "is the worst of having an artistic eye. One must pay for these things."

After spending the night at Salisbury, we pushed on to the Cornish coast. It was not until we were within three miles of our village that we lost the way. When we found it again, we were seven miles off. That is the worst of a car. However.

Stern is a place, where the coast-line is a great glory. The cliffs rise there, tall, dark, majestic-grave, too, especially grave. When the sky is grey, they frown always, and even the warm rays of the setting sun but serve to light their grand solemnity. Very different is the changing sea at their foot. At times it will ripple all day, agog with smiling; anon, provoked by an idle breeze's banter, you shall see it black with rage. In the morning, maybe, it will sleep placidly enough in the sunshine, but at eventide the wind has ruffled its temper, so that it mutters and heaves with anger, breathing forth threatenings. Yet the next dawn finds it alive with mischievous merriment and splitting its sides with laughter, to think how it has duped you the night before. The great grave cliffs and the shifting sea, and, beyond, woodland and pastures and deep meadows, where the cows low in the evenings, while the elms tower above them, their leaves unshaken by the wind-it is not difficult to grow fond of Stern.

And now we were sitting on the cliffs in the heat of the morning sun, half a mile from the village and another from the places where it was best to bathe.

After a while:

"Aren't you glad I made you come here?" said Daphne triumphantly.

I sat up and stared at her sorrowfully.

"Well?" she said defiantly.

"You have taken my breath away," I said, "Kindly return it, and I will deal with you and your interrogatories."

"I suppose you're going to say it was you—"

"It was. I did. I have. But for me you would not. You are.

I took the rooms. I drove the car nearly the whole way down. I got you all here. I sent the luggage on in advance."

"With the result that it got here two days after we did, and I had to wear the same tie three days running, and go down to bathe in patent-leather boots, thanks very much," said Berry.

Beyond saying that I was not responsible for the crass and purblind idiocy of railway officials, I ignored this expression of ingratitude and continued to deal with Daphne.

"You know," I said, "there are times when I tremble for you. Only yesterday, just before dinner, I trembled for you like anything."

"It's the heat," said my target, as if explaining something.

"And my reward is covert reflections upon my sanity. Need I say more?"

"No," said everybody.

"Thank you, ladies and gentlemen, for your kind attention. The next performance will be at four o'clock this afternoon, underneath the promenade pier."

I relapsed into comfortable silence and sank back into the bracken. My sister got up from the clump of heather in which she was ensconced, crossed to where I was, took my pipe out of my mouth and kissed me.

"Sorry, old boy," she said; "you're not such a bad sort, really."

"Dear love," said I, "what have you left behind?"

"My bathing-dress, darling."

In spite of the fact that I returned to the hotel and got it, they were positively rude about the bathing-cove I selected.

"Bathe there?" sneered Berry, as we looked down upon it, all smiling in the sun, from the top of the cliffs.

"Thanks awfully, I simply love the flints, don't you, Jill? Personally, my doctor bled me just before I came away. But don't let me stop you others. Lead on, brother-lead the way to the shambles!"

Of course, Daphne took up the running.

"My dear boy, look at the seaweed on the rocks! Why, we should slip and break our legs before we'd taken two steps!"

"That's all right," said Berry. "We have between us three shirts. Torn into strips, they will make excellent bandages, while for a splint—"

"The cove," I said, "is ideal. Its sand is a field of lilies, its sea perfumed, its boulders sweet-smelling cushions."

"Of course," said Berry. "Why do you tarry? Forward, friends all! This way to the drug department. To the lions, O Christians! For myself, if I start at once, I shall be able to get back with the coastguard's ambulance before you've been lying there more than an hour or two, and I can wire for your relatives at the same time."

"Anybody would think the place was an oubliette," said I. "As a matter of fact, the path down is an easy one, there are no flints, and there is a singular paucity of seaweed of any description. On the other hand, the sun is hot, the sand is soft, and I have already selected that rock, in the seclusion of whose shade I shall prepare myself for the waves. Sorry it's too dangerous for you. I'll write about some bathing-machines tonight. Do you like them with red or green doors?"

Without waiting for their reply, which would probably have been of the caustic and provocative type, I turned down the path I had not trodden for some three years. At one of the bends I looked up and saw them moving north along the coast-line.

I had the cove to myself, and was soon in my bathing-dress. The water was magnificent. I swam out about forty yards, and turned just in time to see Berry & Co. disappear in the distance, apparently descending into a neighbouring cove. After a rest on a rock, I set out to swim round and join them. It was further than I thought, and I was glad to wade out of the water and lie down on the sand in the sun. No sign of the others, by the way. But hereabouts the coast was very ragged. It must have been the next cove they were making for.

"Quite still, please," said somebody, and the next moment a camera clicked.

"You might have given me time to moisten the lips," said I.

"I doubt if it would have done any good."

"Thanks, very much. By the way, I suppose you're The Daily Glass? How did you find me out?"

"Rumour travels apace, sir."

"And I had been congratulating myself on eluding the Press since breakfast. Well, well! Only this morning—"

"Dry up!"

I apostrophized the sea.

"I don't want to have to report the chap," I said, "but if—"

The camera clicked again.

"I'm not sure this isn't an assault," I said. "That it is a trespass, I know. Who are your solicitors? And may I take it that they will accept service? "(Here I rolled over and leaned on my elbow.) "You do look fit. Just move your heel out of that pool-there's an anemone going to mistake it for a piece of alabaster. That's right! Oh, but, Mermaid, do tell me how you keep your hair so nice when you're bathing?"

"Like it?"

"I love it."

"I simply don't put my head under."

"A most dangerous practice, believe me."

"It's worth the risk."

"I belive it is."

She was sitting on a low slab of rock, clad in a bathing-costume of plain dark blue, and fashioned just like my own. Her dark hair was parted in the middle and divided at the back into two long, thick plaits which were turned up and hair-pinned round the top of her head. Her features were beautiful and her eyes big and dark as her hair. Her figure was slim and graceful, and her arms and hands and feet were very shapely. One brown knee was crossed over the other, and her left hand held the camera.

"I do have luck, you know," I said.

"What luck?"

"Well, honestly, it's a great pleasure to meet you like this, when I might have spent all day talking with my silly crowd and never have known of your existence. Don't be afraid. I merely mean that I am enjoying your society, and I'm glad I came round the corner. I'm not in love with you, and I don't want never to leave your side again, but-oh, you understand, Mermaid, don't you? You look as if you could if you liked."

My companion stared out to sea with a faint smile on her lips. I flung out an arm with a gesture of despair.

"Oh, if you knew how sick I am of the girl about town, the girl of today, who won't be natural herself, and won't let you be natural either, who is always bored, and who has no use for anyone who isn't forever making mock love to her, or-Why on earth can't a man tell a woman he likes her company, and mean it, without the woman thinking he wants to kiss her, or marry her, or something?"

I broke off and looked at her.

"Go on," she said. "You interest me."

"Oh, Heavens," I said falteringly. "Why have you got such big eyes?"

At this, to my discomfiture, she broke into peals of merriment.

"Before you looked at me like that, I was really enjoying your company without wanting to kiss you."

"Steady!"

"Besides your eyes, there's your-Look here, it isn't fair."

"That'll do. I'll race you to that rock out there."

She was in the water first, but I beat her easily. We swam back together, and she took her seat on the slab, while I stretched myself on the sand by her side.

"You're a very singular man," she said after a while.

"I have been told so of many."

"And rather dull."

I sat up.

"Don't say you want me to make love to you!"

"Not much!" This emphatically.

"Ah, glad of a change, I suppose."

There was a silence, while she eyed me suspiciously. At length:

"I shall ask you to leave my cove if you're not careful," she said.

"Mermaid," I said, "I apologize. I was unaware that I had the honour to speak to the lady of the manor."

"Well, if you didn't really know who I was—But you mustn't be dull."

I drew her attention to a sailing ship in the distance. "Now, that," I said, "is what I call a really good ship."

"Barque!"

"Barque, I mean. It must be—"

"About five thousand tons"

"Burthen. Exactly. By the way, I never know what that really means unless it means that, if you wanted to lift it, you couldn't."

"Try displacement."

"Thank you. It was off just such an one that I was cast away two years ago come Michaelmas. We were just standing by in the offing, when she sterruck with a grinding crash. There was a matter of seventy souls aboard, and I shall never forget the look on the captain's face as the ship's cat stole his place in the stern-sheets of the jolly-boat. I was thrown up on a desert island, I was. You ought to have seen me milking the goats on Spyglass Hill."

"Did you wear a goatskin cap?"

"Did I Not!" And two muskets. But my snake belt was the great thing. You see—"

"Which reminds me-I think it's about time I got civilized again."

"Not yet, Mermaid," I pleaded; "the sun is yet high."

"You don't suppose I'm going to stay here all day, do you? We're not on your precious island now."

"I only wish we were. I had my loaf of bread and jug of wine all right, but the one thing I wanted, Mermaid, was—"

"A woman to keep him company without thinking he wanted to kiss her, or marry her, or something. Whatever's that?"

I jumped to my feet and looked towards where she was pointing.

"It looks rather like-forgive me-a chemise."

"Good Heavens!"

Before I had time to move, she rushed into the surf and secured the floating garment, made another dart at something else, and was knocked down by a roller. I had her on her feet in a moment, but she dashed the water out of her eyes and looked wildly to and fro over the sea.

What is it, Mermaid?"

She tried to stamp her foot; but the four inches of water in which she was standing were against her.

"Can't you see, idiot? This is mine-this chemise-so's this shoe. The tide's come up into my cave while I've been making a fool of myself talking to you, and all my things are gone. There's the other shoe."

"All right-I'll get it."

I got it, and one stocking, but though I swam about till I was tired, and even climbed on to the rock, now almost submerged, to which we had raced, I could see nothing else. I returned temporarily exhausted to the cove. She waded out to meet me.

"Tell me exactly where your cave is," I said, as I handed her the flotsam.

She showed me, and, after a moment or two's rest, I swam out and round to the mouth, only to find the water too high to enter. I did try, but a wave lifted me up to the roof, and I only saved a broken head at the expense of a nasty cut on the back of my hand.

She was anxiously awaiting me, and listened to my report without a word. When I had finished, she deliberately wrung the last atom of water out of the derelict stocking, smoothed it out carefully by the side of the chemise in the sun, laid herself down on the sand, and burst into tears.

I tried to comfort her. I patted her shoulder and took her hand in mine.

"Don't worry, Mermaid dear," I said. "Trust me-I'll think of something. I know. I'll swim round to my cove and dress, and then go and get you some fresh clothes before anyone's the wiser. See? I'll go now," I added, getting up and licking the blood off my hand. "You wait here and—"

I broke off abruptly, and one of the more violent expletives, indicative of combined horror and amazement, escaped my lips before I could stop it.

"What is it?" wailed the Mermaid.

On the crest of a wave, some thirty yards from the shore, danced my grey hat. Beyond it, a little to the right, was something which might be a shirt.

Stammering incoherent sentences, I staggered into the water and swam for the hat. When I had caught it, I went on to get the shirt. I would have gone on round the headland to my cove, only the shirt was not my shirt. It was Berry's! Yes, it was-had his name on it and all. And not ten yards away floated Daphne's straw hat. For the next two minutes I was in imminent danger of drowning. At last I began to swim feebly, blindly back. When I reached the shore, I fell on my knees in the surf and laughed till the eighth wave knocked me head over heels and the ninth broke into my open jaws and choked me. The next moment the girl caught me by the arm, and I stumbled out and lay down on the dry sand with the shirt clasped to my breast. My hat had gone again ages ago. Then I looked at the girl kneeling anxiously by my side, and began to laugh again. She sat back on her heels, with one hand to her lips and a scared expression on her face.

"He's mad," she said, half to herself, "mad! Must have been stung by a jelly-fish or something. I've heard—"

I cut her short.

"Mermaid dear, I'm as sane as you are, only—"

"Only what?"

"Everybody's doing it"-she recoiled-"doing it! Listen to me. True, that is your chemise. True, that out there is my hat-there it is. But here is Berry's shirt, and miles out there is Daphne's straw hat. If I'd stayed long enough, I've no doubt I should have seen Jonah's trousers and Jill's chemisette, which means or mean-whichever you like-that . . ."

Hurriedly I explained, and then fell again into uproarious laughter. This time she joined me in my mirth. At length :

"But, after all," she said, "it doesn't make it any better for me, because I'm all alone, while you're a party."

"I admit it has been said that Unity is Strength," said I, "but I don't know that that exactly applies—"

"And I can't walk home like this, even with that on." She indicated the chemise.

"Certainly not with that on: it'd only make it more indec—"

"More what?"

"Er-unusual. Indeed, it would."

She regarded me suspiciously. Then:

"What about you?"

"Me? How d'you mean?" I said uneasily.

"Well, couldn't you slip back to the hotel somehow? Quite quietly, I mean, and—"

"I could slip all right," said I. "The short grass on the top of the cliffs would help me there. But, my dear girl, how on earth can I do anything quietly in this dress?"

"Everybody will be—"

"Just finishing lunch or sitting on the terrace. Thanks very much."

"There's a back door."

"I never thought of that. Splendid! Leading to the kitchen, of course. They'd never notice me there. And I could just drop in at the office for the key of my room, and see if there were any letters on the way up, and—My dear girl, how can I? I admit I've a good deal of nerve, but there is a limit. I know one can do most things nowadays, but—"

"But this is a special occasion."

"You seem to want to make it one."

"And it can't be helped. This sort of modesty's out of date."

"Not my date."

"Besides, everybody'd understand."

"I know they would. That's just what I'm afraid of."

"Well, we must do something, and if you—"

Suddenly there fell upon our ears the scrambling, clattering noise which invariably accompanies the descent of anybody rash enough to enter a Cornish cove with undue haste in leather-soled shoes. The Mermaid darted behind a rock, and I advanced gratefully up the foreshore to the fringe of stones. The noise grew louder, and the slips more frequent, until there was one long one, and then a thud. Up rose a fat oath. After a moment or two, there limped into sight-oh, blessed spectacle!-one of the hotel porters, conventionally hatless and coatless.

"Ah!" said I.

"The coastguard you sent hailed me, sir, across the fields yonder. Said something had happened-he didn't know what-but he heard the word 'hotel.' You see, you shouting to him from here, and he being up on top, he couldn't hear anything else rightly, so I came straight down."

"Why didn't be come down himself when-er-when I shouted?"

"He was taking a telegram to the post office sir. Said he told you so; but I suppose you didn't hear."

Berry's coastguard. Berry's porter.

I told him that my clothes had been washed away, and that the mermaid was in the same plight. I gave him implicit instructions and, with her assistance, the numbers of our respective rooms. He wrote it all down. He was to get some clothes for me himself, and enlist the services of a chambermaid for my companion.

"Be as quick as you can," I said, as he turned to go. "You're sure you'll know this cove again? They're all rather alike."

"That's all right, sir."

The next moment he was half-way up the path. If he had looked back, he would have beheld the singular and doubtless pleasing spectacle of the Mermaid and myself doing the real Argentine tango along the stretch of yellow sand.

She did not see the blood on my hand for a minute or two. Then:

"My dear lad, what have you done to your hand?"

"Cut on the rocks, "I said laconically. "Nothing of any consequence, I assure you. I shall be able to proceed home."

"After attention. Let me look at it."

And so it came about that, when the boots returned, my left hand was bound up with a strip of chemise, and the bandage was tied with the pale-pink ribbon that had lately lain upon the Mermaid's shoulder.

We received him delightedly. The Mermaid's garments had been placed by the thoughtful chambermaid in a little dressing-case. Mine were tied together with a piece of string, after the manner of costumes at Nathan's. But they were all right.

The girl started to dress behind a rock, and I told the fellow to wait at the foot of the path. "I have reason," I said, "reason to believe that there are others even now in the same or self-same plight as that in which you found us. Therefore remain within call. Don't investigate for yourself. This is my show. But don't go."

He promised.

Half an hour later he was once more on his way to the hotel with a note from me for Daphne's maid, and the promise of half a sovereign, while the Mermaid and I stood at the top of the path which led down to the cove where the rest of my party were chafing in exasperated idleness- with the exception of Berry, that is. Prior to our arrival, he had been hovering about on the top of the cliff, but the instant he descried us, and while we were yet a great way off, he had retired precipitately, and was now busy rejoining the others with Agag's walk and a profusion of embryo profanity. He explained afterwards that if he had been wearing his own bathing-dress, instead of a green and red striped one-his own was being mended—he should have remained, but that he did not like to be seen wearing the colours of the Redruth Rangers before he had been elected.

After waiting a minute or two to compose ourselves and settle finally our plan of action, we followed gaily in Berry's wake.

I was just saying in a clear voice that, perhaps, it was rather soon after lunch to bathe again, when we came upon them the other side of a large rock. One and all they sprawled easily on the sand in the hot sunshine, as if care were a thing of the past-forgotten, never known.

This was no more than I had expected of them. All of us hate to be caught bending. Berry especially. That artist was busily fashioning a miniature rampart of sand. He looked up at my greeting, and rose to his feet.

I introduced them all to the Mermaid.

"We made friends at lunch," I explained, "over the lobsters."

Jonah winced.

"And then, as we wanted a walk, we thought we'd come along to fetch you back to tea."

There was a polite murmur of appreciation.

"I must say," I went on, "it is glorious. I almost wish I'd given up my lunch, too."

The Mermaid stiffened, but none of the others noticed the error.

I felt myself colouring like a fool.

"Aren't you going to bathe again?" said Berry.

There was the note of eagerness in his voice, and I saw a vision of Berry in my clothes striding triumphantly homewards.

"I don't think so," I said carelessly. "Rather too soon after lunch. But I'm going to take off my coat and sit down in the sun."

After all, he couldn't do much with a coat.

The Mermaid was already seated between Daphne and Jill, talking vivaciously. Jonah pretended to be asleep. After a furtive glance at the top of the cliff, Berry resumed his building operations with awful deliberation.

After a while:

"Well, if you aren't going to bathe any more, aren't you going to dress?" said I.

"And leave this beauty spot?" said Berry. "Shame, shame on you, brother! Go your ways if you will. 'Then wander forth the sons of Belial.' You'll just be in time. But leave us here in peace. I have almost evolved a post-futurist picture which will revolutionize the artistic world. I shall call it 'The Passing of a Bathe: a Fantasy. It will present to the minds of all who have not seen it, what they would have rejected for lunch if they had. To get the true effect, no one must see it."

48

"But if some one does?"

"I shall have already left the country."

This was too much for Daphne, and she asked Jonah to come and help her to get some mussels. They walked away together.

"What on earth does she want mussels for?" said I.

"The garden paths," said Berry. "Our cobbles aren't wearing at all well."

I turned to the Mermaid. She was chattering away to Jill, with her back towards me. Over her shoulder, Jill's grey eyes regarded me wistfully. I made a rapid calculation. Yes, the porter ought to have arrived by now. I had told him to keep out of sight till I called him.

I waited until Daphne and Jonah came strolling back empty-handed. They had forgotten about the mussels. Daphne's brows were knitted, and Jonah was looking ruefully at the sun. It was getting on for half-past three. One could guess that much.

I rose and picked up my coat. "I say, aren't you ever going to dress any more?" I said.

Daphne swallowed before replying, and with the tail of my eye I saw Berry start and wreck six inches of architecture. Then :

"Presently," said my big sister. "You two go on and order a big tea at the farm, and by the time it's ready—"

"You can't have tea like that," I said. "There'll be a row."

In the dead silence that followed this remark, the Mermaid rose and brushed the sand from her dress.

I went up to Daphne and kissed her.

"Don't think I'm not proud of you, darling, and Jill looks lovely, too, but they wouldn't stand it, you know."

No one stirred except the Mermaid, and she, obedient to the instructions I had given her, strolled naturally enough towards the path up the cliff. The other four were looking at me straitly-I could feel their gaze-wondering whether, whether I knew.

I shaded my eyes with my hand and stared seawards.

"Do dress," I said absently.

"We shall dress when we want to," said Daphne sharply.

I turned to see the Mermaiden reach the path. A good start is everything.

"If you really mean that," I said slowly, "I'll send your other clothes back again. "Then I raised my voice:

"Porter!" I cried.

"Sir!" came from above us.

"Behold, now—"

I let the rest of the quotation go, as I wanted to rejoin the mermaid, looking as she had last seen me. Berry said afterwards that Jonah gained on me while the sand lasted, but the loose stones at the foot of the path were my salvation.

As I passed the porter, I told him to say that a square meal would be awaiting them at the farm. We ordered it generously enough, but, despite our hunger, the Mermaid and I decided to have our own tea at the hotel. Thither we set out to walk through the fields. Suddenly she stopped as we were crossing a deep lane.

"I don't know why you're here," she said.

"Try and think, Mermaid."

"You'd better go and have another bathe."

"Now, Mermaid, you know—"

"Afterwards you'll be wishing you had given up your tea, if you don't."

"I knew we should have this," I said.

"Well, it wasn't very polite of you, was it?"

"It wouldn't have been."

"She eyed me scornfully for a moment. Then:

"I'm disappointed in you," she said.

"You'll be more so in a moment," said I.

"Why?"

"You're not going to have a change, after all."

"Don't say you're going to make—"

"Love to you? Yes, I am."

She looked me up and down for a moment.

"And this is the man," she said slowly-"this is the man"

"Who said he was not in love with you, and that he didn't want never to leave your side again. Yes, it is. I might have known better than to say a thing like that. All the same, it wasn't meant for a challenge, Mermaiden."

She looked at me with a mischievous smile. "And now—"

I broke off and took her small, brown hand. Up went the dark eyebrows.

"I shouldn't like you to think that I thought you wanted to kiss me," she said.

"I think nothing," said I. "But one thing I know."

"And that is?"

"That it would be a crime if I didn't. The very stones would cry out."

"I don't think they would."

"I'm afraid they might," said I.

CHAPTER III

WHEN IT WAS DARK

Daphne pointed suddenly to the stile. "This is it," she said. "We get over here and go across the meadow, and there's the wood beyond the gate that we've got to-to-what's the word?"

"Encompass?" I hazarded.

"Skirt?" said Jonah.

"Skirt-thank you-till we come upon the carttrack."

"And then?" said I.

"Then we're all right," she said defiantly.

"Which means, that about two hours from now we shall, with a fine disregard for the highest traditions of British pugilism, strike the high road below the belt of firs, a good six miles from the roof-tree we should never have left. God forgive you."

"Am I," said Berry, "am I to understand in cold blood that, reckoning three miles to the league, some four leagues lie directly between me and the muffins?"

"You are," said I.

"To think that my wife is a bag," he said wearily.

It was an autumn afternoon in the county of Devon. There were we staying at a retired farmhouse, fleeting the time carelessly, simply, healthily. Sickened by forty-eight hours of continuous rain, we had fastened greedily upon the chance which a glorious October day at length offered, and had set out, complete with sandwiches, for one of the longer walks.

Daphne constituted herself guide. We never asked her to. But as such we just accepted her. We were quite passive in the matter. Going, she had guided us with a careless confidence which shamed suspicion. But coming back, she had early displayed unmistakable signs of hesitation and anxiety. Thereafter she had plunged desperately, with the result that at three o'clock we found ourselves reduced to a swine-herd who had been drinking. The latter detailed to us four several routes, and assured us that it was utterly impossible to miss any one of them.

To put it quite shortly, he was mistaken.

Within half an hour we had missed them all. Lost on a heath (which I have every reason to suppose was blasted) in a strange county, and not a soul in sight. That was the position.

We plodded in silence across the meadow.

"Didn't say anything about a bog, did he? said Berry, drawing his left leg out of some mire with a noise that made me shudder. Jill slid a warm arm into mine, and broke into long laughter.

"Don't encourage the fool," said Daphne.

We skirted the wood successfully to find that there never could have been a cart-track.

Berry leaned against a wall of stones." What a picture," he said ecstatically. "The setting sun, the little band, the matron and the maid, mist rising, shadows falling-subject for next year's Academy, 'The Walkers.'"

"Idiot!" said Daphne shortly.

"Do I hear aright?" said Berry.

"I said 'idiot.'"

Berry covered his face with his hat, and begged us to excuse his emotion. Daphne stamped her foot.

"I have an idea," said I.

"If it's one of your usual ones, we don't want it," said Daphne.

"Thank you, dear. We are undoubtedly lost. No, that is not my idea. But, as a would-have-been boy-scout, I recognize in this spot a natural camping-place. That water is close at hand, we know from Scout Berry.

Jonah can take the first watch, Berry the second, Jonah the third, and-and so on. My own energy I shall reserve for the dog-watch."

"Oh, stop him, somebody," wailed Daphne.

"I said dog-watch, dear, not stop-watch. Before we bivouac I will scale yon beetling mount if peradventure I may perceive one that will point us homeward. Scout Berry!"

"Sir," said Berry.

"You know your duties!"

"I do that, sir."

"'Tis well. If the worst comes to the worst, kill the women out of hand, or with your own hand-I don't care which. Age before honesty, you know."

With that I left them, and turned to climb the hill which rose sharply on our right, its side dotted with furze-bushes, and its crest hidden by a clump of trees.

Five minutes later I was back among them again.

"Well," said Daphne eagerly, "you haven't been right to the top, have you?"

"Oh, no. I only came back to say that when I said 'Age before honesty' just now, I really meant 'Death before dishonour,' you know," and I turned up the bank again.

I regret to say that Berry and Jonah thought it decent to attempt to stone my retreating figure. Ten minutes' walking brought me to a clearing on the top, which afforded a magnificent view. Hill and dale, woodland and pasture, stone wall and hedgerow, as far as I could see. The sinking sun was lighting gloriously the autumn livery of the woods, and, far in the distance, I could see the silver streak of the river flowing to the village on whose skirts stood the house that was our bourne. When I returned to the camp to find them gone I was rather bored.

The note that they had left made it worse:

"Regret compelled retire owing to serious outflanking movement on part of the Blues. Sorry, but that's the worst of being picket.

54

The natural intuition which characterizes all BSS will enable you to discern our route. So long."

Although I tried four times-mainly because Jonah had my matches-I was unable to discern their route. At last I came down to shouting, but only succeeded in arousing the curiosity of three cows and a well-nourished ram. The latter was so well nourished that when he had stamped for the second time, I thought it prudent to get over the wall. I did so with about four seconds to spare. Nothing daunted, the winning animal took a short run and butted the wall with surprising vigour. When three large stones had fallen for seven runs, I offered up a short prayer that Berry & Co. might return to look for me, and hastened to put two more walls between us. I suppose it was the river that I saw in the distance, from the summit of that fair hill . . .

Three and a half hours later I came upon the first signs of animal life as opposed to vegetable-since the ram. Up hill, down dale, along roads, along imitation roads, along future roads, along past roads, across moors I had tramped doggedly, blindly, and rather angrily. If I had had one match-only one match-it would have been different.

Yes, it was a dog-cart. And through the gloom I could distinctly see the shape of some one sitting in it, holding the reins.

I quickened my steps.

"I say, have you got a match?"

A girl's voice.

"That's about the worst thing you could have said." said I.

"Why?"

"Because a match is the one thing I've been wanting for the last four hours."

"Sorry. Swear for me, will you?"

"Certainly, madam. What sort of an oath would you like? We have a very large assortment in stock-fresh lot in only this afternoon. Let me see. Now, I've got a very nice thing in oaths—"

"I want a round one."

"Round? Certainly. And the usual black, I presume. We have been doing rather a lot in the way of blue oaths lately. No? Damn. How do you like that, madam?"

"That'll do."

"Much obliged to you, madam. Sign, please. Nothing else I can show you? Nothing in the curse line?"

"No, thanks. Good day."

There was a pause. Presently:

"I said 'good day,'" said the girl.

"Yes," said I; "but, then, we were only playing."

"Oh, were you?"

"Any way, you haven't paid yet," I said desperately.

"How much do you want? It was a very common oath."

"I've plenty more, if you like. For instance—"

"Hush! Not before the mare. What's your price?"

"The privilege of accompanying you on foot till we can get a light. You can't drive at more than a walking pace on this road without lamps. And it's not right for you to be alone."

"You are very good. But are you going my way?"

"I've not the faintest idea."

"Are you lost, then?"

"Hopelessly. Have been for hours."

"Where do you want to get to?"

"A farmhouse three miles out of Lorn."

"Which side of Lorn?"

"Well, if I'm the same side of Lorn as I was at one o'clock this afternoon, it's the other side."

"Well, but aren't you?"

"My dear girl, I don't know."

She laughed. "Well, I'm going to Lorn, any way," she said, "so come along."

"Heaven will reward you," said I, and climbed into the cart.

"You'd better drive."

I took the reins. We had to go very slowly, for it was one of the imitation roads, and when we were not scaling an ascent that positively beetled, we were going down a descent which I was glad it was too dark to see. After a minute or two, I took the near wheel eighteen inches up the bank.

"Sorry," said the girl, as she disengaged herself from my neck and arms and resumed her seat, "but it was your fault for taking it up the bank."

"I know. I hope you weren't frightened. I'm awfully sorry."

"You drive rather well, considering."

"Steady the Buffs. Considering what?"

"Considering it's your first shot."

In silence I gave her the reins.

"After that," I said icily," after that there is no more to be said. Was it for this that, at the age of four, I was borne by two reluctant goats along the Hastings strand? Pardon me, those last six words comprise an iambic line-a fact which is itself the best evidence of my agitation. It is a little winning way I have. Most criminals when charged make no reply. When I am arrested, I shall protest in anapaests. As I was saying, was it for this-?"

"Stop, stop," she said, laughing; "you drive all right-beautifully."

I took the reins again.

It was getting very cold, and I put the rug carefully about her.

"You're very good," she said, "but wait."

I felt her hand on my knee.

"Oh, you haven't got any of it."

She would have untucked it again if I hadn't caught her wrist.

"That's all right," I said. "I'm not allowed rugs."

"Nonsense."

"My dear, doctor's orders. The last thing the great Harley Street specialist said to me, as I pushed the two pounds two shillings beneath the current number of The Lancet, was, 'Now, mind, no rugs. Eat and drink what you like. Smoke in moderation, and get up as late as you please. But no rugs.'"

As the wrist felt unconvinced, I slipped it through my arm, where it lay comfortably enough.

"Do you often do this sort of thing?" I said presently.

"Get late coming home and have no lights? Not often."

"I'm glad of that-I'm sure it's very dangerous. Good whips like myself aren't as common as blackberries. And so few tramps one meets nowadays can drive really well."

"I don't look as if I'd got any money, do I?"

"Well, you don't look anything just now, as it's too dark to see; but you sound like a wrist-watch and a chain-purse."

"How did you know?"

"Intuition," I said carelessly. "You see I'm a boy-scout."

"Feel."

She laid a slim, warm wrist against my cheek. I distinctly felt the cold round glass of a wrist-watch.

"And I've got a chain-purse in my bag." "Ah!"

"Go on, boy-scout. Tell me what I look like in the daytime."

"You have ear-rings and your face is rather cold. About the kind of ear-rings I am not certain."

"How did you know that?"

"I found that out, when-er-when we went up the bank."

"Oh!"

"Yes," I went on hurriedly," and—"

"Am I dark or fair?"

Ilooked hopelessly at where I knew my companion was sitting. Then:

58

"Dark," I said, after a minute. "Dark, with long eyelashes and two brown eyes."

"Two!"

"Yes, I think so. You sound extravagant."

"Dimples?"

"I think not."

"Nose?"

"Yes."

"Yes, what?"

"Yes, please, teacher."

"Nonsense. What did you mean by 'yes'?"

"Sorry. I thought you were asking me if you'd got a nose, and I think you have. That's all. Sorry if I'm wrong, but when you're in the dark—"

"Yes, but what sort of nose?"

Here I got the near wheel up the bank again with great effect. When we had sorted ourselves:

"If you do that again," she said severely, "I'll leave you in the road—"

"In the what?"

"In the road to find your own way home as best you can."

"You have a hard nose," I said doggedly. I was almost sure that the ear-rings were pearl ear-rings.

There was a pause. The cold was making us silent. My fingers were getting numbed, but I dared not chafe them. I was afraid of the rug.

"You're not doing much for your drive," she said presently. "Do say something."

"You want to converse?"

"Yes."

"Very well, then. I didn't see you at Blackpool this year."

"That's curious."

"Yes, isn't it? What's your recreation? Forgive my seeming inquisitiveness, but I've just joined the staff of Who's Who."

"What?"

"No, who?"

"Recreation?"

"Yes. Hobby, amusement. Don't you collect cats or keep stamps or motor-boat or mountebank, I mean mountaineer, or anything?"

"No."

"Never mind. I expect you know Oldham rather well, don't you?"

"Not at all."

"Oh, I'm sorry."

"Why?"

"Because I don't know it either, and I thought—"

"What?"

"Well, you know, we ought to know Oldham-one of us ought to. It was a Unionist gain last time."

"Are you a Unionist?"

"My dear, you see in me-at least you would see in me, if it were not so dark-a high Tory."

"I thought you were a boy-scout."

"The two are not incompatible. Did you see that thing in Ally Sloper last week?"

"No, I didn't. Here's a gate."

I got down and opened it, and she drove carefully through.

It was the first of seven gates. By the time we had done six, I was becoming good at getting up and down, but rather tired.

As I resumed my seat for the sixth time, I sighed. For the sixth time she returned me the reins.

"You don't take much care of your clothes, boy-scout," she said. "Nearly all the men I know hitch up their trousers when they sit down."

"Perhaps they're sailors."

"No, they aren't."

"My dear girl, I don't know how you can see I don't, but I don't because I haven't got any on. I mean, I'm wearing breeches."

"Would you hitch them up if you had got on trousers?"

"Let's see, today's Thursday. Yes, I should."

"Why do men always bother so about their knees?"

"Take care of the bags, and the coats will take care of themselves," I observed sententiously.

"But why-?"

Here we came apon the seventh gate.

I groaned.

"Six gates shalt thou labour, and do all that thou hast to do, but the seventh—"

"Out you get, boy-scout."

I laid a hand on my companion's shoulder. "Are you an enchantress?" I said. "At least, of course you are. But I mean, is this the way to your castle, Circe? And am I going to be turned into a herd of swine presently? They always have seven gates and a dense forest through which I cut a path with my sword, which, by the way, I have left in the tool-shed, unless perchance, maiden, thou hast filched it from my side this last half-hour. Note the blank verse again. I may say I am looking at you narrowly."

"Fret not for thy sword, Sir Scout." she replied, "neither flatter thyself that Circe wastes her spells on all who come her way. Those only will she lure who—"

"I simply love your voice," I said.

"Get down and open the gate."

I did so, and climbed slowly back.

"It's all right," she said, "We haven't got much further to go."

"I'm sorry for that."

"Sorry?"

"Certainly. I've enjoyed this awfully. It's rather funny, isn't it? Our meeting in the dark like this and driving all these miles together and not being able to see each other once."

"Unique, I should think."

"Yes, it's rather like being in a cell next to some one and talking by rapping against the wall."

"Is it?"

"Yes, it reminds me awfully of my young days at Brixton."

"Were you at school there?"

"Yes, for five years, before I went to Dartmoor."

"Oh, were you at Dartmoor? I had a cousin there a year or two ago. But he's out now. His name was Taber."

"What! Not Billy Taber?"

"That's right."

"This is very strange, Circe."

"Yes, boy-scout. Round to the left here. That's right. Only three more miles. This is Dilberry Farm."

"Dilberry! Why, that's—"

"Where you're staying?

I gulped, and laid the whip over the mare's shoulders.

"No," I said doggedly," it's not."

She laid two firm little hands on my left and pulled the mare up.

"Anything the matter? "said I.

"Say 'goodbye' like a good boy-scout and thank the kind lady for giving you a lift, and then run along home," she said sweetly.

"What are we stopping for?" I said. "You can't get a good view from here today. It's too hazy."

"Go on."

"But, Circe—"

"Be quick. I'm awfully cold."

"Won't you come in and get warm before you go on, or borrow another rug, or—"

"No, thanks awfully, I must get home."

"Mayn't I see you there? I can easily walk back."

"No, thanks awfully, boy-scout."

"You mean it?"

"I do."

"I gave her the reins and got heavily out of the dog-cart. She moved on to the seat I had vacated and I put the rug carefully round her feet. Suddenly I remembered.

"Stop," I said. "Let me get some matches. At least your lamps shall be lighted."

Not a bit of it. Said she didn't want them lighted. Simply wouldn't have it.

While I was speaking, my fingers had mechanically strayed to the ticket pocket of my coat, where I sometimes carry my matches loose.

"By George !" I said.

"What is it?"

"I've just found a bit of a match—with the head on."

"Oh, boy-scout, and you've had it all the time."

"Yes, but it wouldn't be enough to light the lamps with."

"Oh!"

"Not the lamps."

"What would it be enough for?"

"A face, Circe."

"Goodbye."

"Stop, Circe. Two faces."

"How?"

"Well, I'11 strike it on the tire, and then hold it between us.

"All right."

"It'll only last a second-it's not a quarter of an inch long. You'll have to bend down."

"Go on."

"Nerve yourself for the shock, Circe. Think you can stand it?"

"I'll try. Keep your back to the mare."

"Thank you."

I heard her lean over and struck the match on the tire, I raised it cautiously, sheltering it with my hands. Just as I was about to raise my eyes:

"Thank you," she said, very softly, and blew it out.

I laid my hands on her shoulders.

"I won't say 'damn,'" I said. "I'll say 'goodbye' instead, like-like a good boy-scout."

"Say it then."

I said it.

"Oh, but that isn't—"

"Yes," I said. "It's a new rule."

When the clatter of the mare's hoofs had died away in the distance, I walked slowly up to the farm. I was quite sure about the ear-rings this time. At least, about the one in her left ear.

"Ah," said Daphne, as I entered the room, "where have you been all this time?"

All things considered, I thought that was rather good.

"I don't think I've been into Cornwall," I said, "but I've done Devon pretty thoroughly."

"We went back for you."

"Ah!"

"Why do you say 'Ah!' ?"

"Oh, I don't know. Didn't see anything of a ram, did you?" I added carelessly.

There was a pause.

"Not until after he'd seen Berry," said Jonah.

"Ah, where is Berry?"

"Upstairs," said Daphne.

"He did-er-see Berry then?"

"Yes."

"Er-how did he see him? I mean-hang it, I didn't bring the beastly ram there."

64

"You left him there," said Daphne.

"I know: but you can't pick up every tame ram you meet. Besides—"

"Tame!" said Jonah. "Good Lord!"

He saw Berry, you say? Did he see him well?"

"I think he'd have seen him home, if it hadn't been for the brook."

"Courteous beast. He saw him as far as that, did he?"

"He saw him half-way across."

I regret to say I laughed so immoderately that I never noticed that Berry had entered the room, until he clapped me on the shoulder.

"It was a neat revenge," said that gentleman; "very neat, my boy. But you deserve six months for it."

"Hang it," I said, "you seem to think I—"

"I should certainly have haunted you," said Berry.

Six weeks had sloped by.

The train ran slowly into the station. I got out. Then I remembered my umbrella and got back. Then I got out again. "Porter," I said.

The individual addressed turned round, and I saw it was the station-master. For a few moments he regarded me with indignation, obviously wondering whether he would be exceeding his duty if he ordered me to be flung to the engine. Two inspectors hovered longingly near him. Then he said "Chut!" and turned away.

I fought my way the length of the platform to the vicinity of the luggage van. Four porters were standing looking moodily at the luggage already upon the platform.

I touched one on the shoulder.

"Yes," I said," it's a nice bit of luggage, isn't it?"

He said it was.

"Don't you think it's that dressing-case that does it? Lends an air of distinction to the rest. Bucks it all up, as it were, eh?"

Before he could reply:

"So you're down for the week-end too," said a voice I should have recognized amid the hubbub of the heavenly choir. "Staying at Watereaton?

It was she.

Such a pretty girl. Very fair, very blue eyes, a beautiful skin, and-yes, a dimple. She was wearing a long, fur coat, while a little black felt hat with a ghost of a brim leaned exquisitely over one of the blue eyes. Her hands were plunged into deep pockets, but a pair of most admirable legs more than made good the deficit.

I sighed.

"Disappointed?" she said.

"Not in you-you're beautiful. But in myself. Yes, I shall resign."

"Resign?"

"My scout-hood."

"You were wrong about my hair, but—"

"But what?"

"You knew me again, at any rate."

"But of course. You've the same voice and the same dear laugh, and-yes, you've got—"

"What?"

"The same ear-rings," said I.

CHAPTER IV

ADAM AND NEW YEAR'S EVE

Jonah rose, walked to the window, pulled the curtains aside, and peered out into the darkness.

"What of the night?" said I.

"Doth the blizzard yet blizz?" said Berry.

"It doth," said Jonah.

"Good," said Berry. Then he turned to Daphne. "Darling, you have my warmest Yuletide greetings and heartiest good wishes for a bright New Year. Remember the old saying:

"You may have move pretentious wishes,
But more sincere you can't than this is."

"Do you believe it's going on like this?" said his wife.

"Dear heart-two words-my love for you is imperishable. If it were left at the goods station for a month during a tram strike, it would, unlike the sausages, emerge fresh and sweet as of yore. I mean it."

"Fool," said Daphne. "I meant the weather, as you know."

"A rebuff," said her husband. "Do I care? Never. Strike me in the wind, and I will offer you my second wind for another blow. I did not forget everything when I married you. But to the weather. This berlizzard-German-has its disadvantages. A little more, and we shan't be able to bathe tomorrow. Never mind. Think of the Yule log. Noel." Here he regarded his empty glass for a moment. "Woman, lo, your lord's beaker requires replenishing. I ought not to have to tell you, really. However."

Daphne selected one of the harder chocolates, took careful aim, and discharged it in the direction of her husband's face. It struck him on the nose.

"Good shot," said I. "That entitles you to a vase. If you like, you can have another two shots instead." "I'll take the vase," said my sister. "For all the area of the target, I mightn't hit it again."

"A few years ago," said Berry, "you would probably have been pressed to death for this impious display. In consideration of your age, you might instead have been sent to a turret."

"What's a turret?" said Jill.

"Old English for bathroom, dear, and kept there till you had worked the murder of Becket in tapestry and four acts. I shall be more merciful. When you can show me a representation of the man who drew Slipaway in the Calcutta Sweep trying to believe that it wouldn't have won, even if it hadn't been knocked down when it was leading by nineteen lengths—"

"Very brilliant," said Daphne, "but the point is, what are we going to do about tomorrow night?"

"If it goes on like this, we can't go."

"Oh, but we must," said Jill.

"My dear, I'm not going out in this sort of weather without Sjvensen, and he may be too busy to leave town. Besides, the blubber hasn't come yet."

"Couldn't we get hold of Wenceslas?" said I. "He's getting five million a week at the Palliseum. Makes footprints there twice daily in real snow. The audience are invited to come and tread in them. They do, too, like anything. Happily, Wenceslas is famed for the size of his feet. But you can't expect a man to leave—"

"But it can't go on like this," said Daphne

"My dear, English weather is like your dear self-capable of anything. Be thankful that we have only snow.

68

If it occurred to it to rain icebergs, so that we were compelled willy or even nilly to give up sleeping out of doors, it would do so. Well, I'm tired. What about turning out, eh? Light the lanthorn, Jonah, and give me my dressing-gown."

"If you want to make me really ill," said Daphne, "you'll go on talking about bathing and sleeping out of doors.

"Berry laughed a fat laugh. "My dear," he explained, "I was only joking."

We were all housed together in an old, old country inn, the inn of Fallow, which village lies sleeping at the foot of the Cotswold Hills. We knew the place well. Few stones of it had been set one upon the other less than three hundred years ago, and, summer and winter alike, it was a spot of great beauty-comparatively little known, too, and far enough from London to escape most tourists. The inn itself had sheltered Cromwell, and before his time better men than he had warmed themselves at the great hearth round which we sat. For all that, he had given his name to the panelled room. Our bedrooms were as old, low-pitched and full of beams. The stairs also were a great glory. In fact, the house was in its way unique. A discreet decorator, too, had made it comfortable. Save in the Cromwell room, electric light was everywhere. And in the morning chambermaids led you by crooked passages over uneven doors to white bathrooms. It was all right.

Hither we had come to spend Christmas and the New Year. By day we walked for miles over the Cotswolds, or took the car and looked up friends who were keeping Christmas in the country, not too many miles away. The Dales of Stoy had been kind, and before the frost came I had had two days' hunting with the Heythrop. And tomorrow was New Year's Eve. Four miles the other side of the old market town of Steeple Abbas, and twenty-one miles from Pallow, stood Bill Manor, where the Hathaways lived. This good man and his wife Milly were among our greatest friends, and they had wanted us to spend Christmas with them. Though we had not done so, we had motored over several times and they had lunched with us at Fallow only the day before. And for New Year's Eve the Hathaways had arranged a small but very special ball, to which, of course, we were bidden. Indeed, I think the ball was more for us than for anyone else. Anyway, Jim and Milly said so.

The idea was that we should come over in the car in time for dinner with the house-party, the ball would begin about ten, and when it was over, we should return to Fallow in the ordinary way. Nobody had anticipated such heavy weather.

And now it was a question whether we should be able to go. Also, if we went, whether we should be able to get back. The dispute waxed. Daphne and Jill insisted that go we must, could, and should. I rather supported them. Berry and Jonah opposed us; the latter quietly, as is his wont, the former with a simple stream of provoking irony. At length:

"Very well, ghouls," said Berry, "have your most wicked way. Doubtless the good monks of the Hospice will find my corpse. I wish the drinking-trough, which will be erected to my memory, to stand half-way up St.James's Street. How strange it will sound in future."

"What'll sound?" said Jill. "The new Saint's Day, dear-Berrymas."

When order had been restored, Jonah suggested that we should adjourn the debate till the next morning, in case it stopped snowing during the night. As it was nearly one, the idea seemed a good one, and we went to bed.

The morning was bright and cloudless. The cold was intense, but the sun glorious, while the clear blue sky looked as if it had never heard of snow. In a word, the weather was now magnificent, and, but for the real evidence Upon the country-side, no one would ever have believed such a cheery, good-natured fellow guilty of a raging blizzard. But the snow lay thick upon the ground, and it was freezing hard.

"We can get there all right," said Jonah, "but I don't see the car coming back at four o'clock in the morning. No, thanks, I'll have marmalade."

"There's almost a full moon," said I.

"I know," said Berry, "but the banjo's being painted."

"We'd better stop at the inn at Steeple Abbas," said Jonah.

"If we can get as far as Steeple, we can make Fallow," said I. "Remember, I'm driving."

"We are not likely to forget it, brother," said Berry. "If you knew the difference between the petrol-tank and the gear-box—

"But I do. Petrol in one, tools in the other. However."

"Jonah's right," said Daphne. "We'd better stop at Steeple."

"Not I." said I.

"Nor me," said Jill. "Boy and I'll come back to our dear Fallow and our nice big grate and our own beds."

"Good little girl," said I. Berry emptied his mouth and began to recite "Excelsior."

At twenty minutes past three the next morning I drove out of the courtyard of 'The Three Bulls', Steeple Abbas. Alone, too, for it had begun to snow again, and although I was determined to sleep that night, or what remained of it, at Fallow, I would not take Jill with me for such an ugly run. As a matter of fact, I had started once with her in the car, but before we had got clear of the town, I had turned about and driven her back to the inn. The people had evidently half expected her back, for, as we stopped at the door, it was flung open and the landlord stood ready to welcome her in. The next moment I was once more on my way. In spite of the weather, the car went well, and I had soon covered more than half the distance. I was just about to emerge from a side-road on to the main highway, when a dark mass right on the opposite corner against the hedgerow attracted my attention. The next second my head-lights showed what it was, and I slowed down. A great limousine, if you please, standing at an angle of twenty degrees, its near front wheel obviously well up the bank, and the whole car sunk in a drift of snow some four or five feet deep. All its lights were out, and fresh snow was beginning to gather on the top against the luggage rail.

I stopped, took out one of my side oil lamps, and, getting out of the car, advanced to the edge of the drift, holding the light above my head. The limousine was evidently a derelict.

"You look just like a picture I've seen somewhere," said a gentle voice.

"And you've got a voice just like a dream I've dreamed some time or other. Isn't that strange? And now, who, what, where, why, and how are you? Are you the goddess in the car, or the woman in the case? And may I wish you a very happy New Year? I said it first."

"Try the woman in the car."

"One moment," said I. "I know."

"What?"

"I know who you are. Just fancy."

"Who am I?

"Why, you're New Year's Eve."

A little laugh answered me.

"I know I've dreamed that laugh," said I. "However, where were we? Oh, I know. And your father, Christmas, has gone for help. If I know anything, he won't be back again for ages. Seriously, how did what happen?"

"Chauffeur took the turn rather late, and next moment we were up the bank and in this wretched drift. It wasn't altogether the man's fault. One of our head-lights wouldn't work, and you couldn't see the drift till we were in it."

"He might have known better than to run so close to the hedge these days."

"He's paying for it, any way, poor man. He's got to walk till he finds a farm where they'll lend him horses to get the car out."

Considering the hour and the climatic conditions, I don't suppose the farmers will come running. I mean they'll wait to put some clothes on."

"Probably. Besides, he doesn't know the district, so he's up against something this little night."

"Of all nights, too, Eve! But what about her, poor lass?"

"Oh, I'm all right."

"You must be. But don't you find it rather hot in there? Can I turn on the electric fan?"

"I've been making good resolutions to pass the time."

"Hurray! So've I. I'm going to give up ferns. And you can tell me yours as we go along."

"Go along?"

"Yes, my dear. Didn't I tell you I was a highwayman? I only left York two hours ago."

"Quick going."

"Yes, I came by the boat train, with Black Bess in a horse-box. And now I'm going to abduct you, Eve. Your soul's not your own when you're up against High Toby. I have a pistol in my holster, a cloak on my back, and a price on my head. My enemies call me Red Nat, me friends—"

I paused.

"What do your friends call you?"

"Adam," said I. "Let's see. You'll have to get out on the near side, won't you? Wait a moment."

I plunged round the back of the car and opened the door. Certainly it was terribly cold. While we had been talking, she had been leaning against the side of the tilted car, with her face close to the inch and a half of open window. Except for an occasional flash, which had showed where her eyes were, I had not seen her at all. Expectantly I raised the lamp and peered into the limousine. Out of a huge fur rug a solitary eye regarded me steadily.

"Only one eye?" I said. "How sad. How did it happen?"

The solitary eye went out, and then reappeared with a fellow.

"You remind me of the North Foreland," said I. "That's an intermittent light, isn't it? Two winks and a blink every ten seconds."

"I didn't wink." This in a plainly indignant, if muffled tone-too muffled for me. So:

"I beg your pardon," said I. A little hand appeared and pulled the rug away from a small white nose and a mouth whose lips were paler than they should be. But it was a dear mouth.

"I said I didn't wink."

"So you did. I don't mean you did, you know. I mean, I know you said you didn't. I'm not sure I've got it right now."

"Never mind. I've only one brain, and at this hour of night—"

"The vitality of the human frame is at its lowest ebb. Exactly. That's why you must let me get you out of this as quick as possible."

"Oh, but I don't think-I mean—"

"My dear Eve, I know you come of an old-fashioned family-look at your father-but Convention's going by the board tonight. I'm staying at an inn about nine miles away. We'll be there under the half-hour. There's supper and a fire waiting for us, Why, yes, and you can have Jill's room. Of course, there'll be a fire there, too, and everything ready. You see—"

Hurriedly I explained the situation. When I had finished:

"But what'll the inn people think?" she said, with big eyes.

"Oh, hang the inn people?"

"And supposing it got out?"

"I think the proceedings at the inquest would read worse, my dear. Get up and come along at once."

"Oh, but you know I can't."

"You must. I'm serious. You'll die if you stop here much longer, my dear child. Do you realize how cold it really is?"

A faint smile came over the gentle face, set in its frame of fur.

"Poor lass," I cried. "What a fool I am. Give me her hand, and I'll help her up."

"But what about Falcon?"

"The chauffeur?"

She nodded. I thought for a moment, then I looked for the companion. There, happily, were tablets and a pencil.

"We'll write him a note," said I. "Wait a minute."

With difficulty I scrawled a few words. Then:

"How will this do?" Falcon, I have been found and taken to shelter. If possible, bring the car to 'The Three Bulls,' Steeple Abbas, by noon tomorrow. Will you sign it?"

I put the pencil into her hand and held the lamp for her to see. She wrote quickly. When she had finished, I laid the tablets on the seat, where they must be seen at once. When I looked at her again, I saw she was smiling.

"So there's something in the nickname, after all?"

"What nickname?" said I. "Red Nat?"

"No. 'Gentleman of the road,' Adam."

"Thank you, Eve. If I could feel my mouth, I'd kiss your hand for that. As it is—"

I helped her to her feet and set the lamp on the front seat. Then I bade her stand in the doorway while I wrapped the rug about her.

"I'm afraid I can't dig you a pathway, so I'm going to carry you to my car. I used to be able to delve once—"

"When Who was a gentleman?"

"Exactly. And you span. But I'm out of practice now. Besides, I left my niblick in London. Come along. Don't be frightened if I slip. I shan't go down. Yes, I'll come back for your dressing-case."

The next moment she was in my arms, and three minutes later we were making for Fallow at nearer thirty than twenty miles an hour.

As we an into the village, I heard the church clock chime the half-hour. Half-past four. We had come well. A moment later I had stopped at the old inn's door. Except for a flickering light, visible between the curtains of the Cromwell room, the place was in darkness. I clambered stiffly out and felt for the key I had asked for. A Yale lock in the studded door! Never mind. This door is only a reproduction. The original probably shuts off some pantry from some servants' hall in New York City. However. When I had switched on a course of lights, I went back to the car and opened the door. Have I said that it was a cabriolet?

"Eve," said I. No answer, I took the lamp once more and flooded the car with light. In the far corner, still wrapped in the rugs, my lady lay fast asleep. With some difficulty I got her into my arms. On the threshold I met Thomas, our waiter. He had little on but a coat and trousers, and there was slumber in his eyes.

"I didn't wait up, sir," he explained, "but, hearing the car, I just come down to see you'd got everything. Miss Mansel asleep, sir?"

I stared at him for a moment and then looked down at the charge in my arms. A corner of the rug had fallen over her face. Thomas, naturally enough, thought it was Jill.

"Er-yes," said I. "She's tired, you know. And you'd better not let her see you. She'll be awfully angry to think you got up for us. You know what she said."

Thomas laughed respectfully. I passed up the stairs, and he followed. "I'll only open the door and see that the fire's all right, sir," he said. I placed my burden gently on the sofa, away from the light of the fire.

"You'll let me light the candles, sir?"

"Not a farthing dip, Thomas. Miss Mansel may wake any moment. You can come and open the coach-house door, if you like."

"Very good, sir."

"You can get to it from the inside, can't you? Because you're not to go out of doors."

"Oh, yes, thank you, sir."

Two minutes later the car was in the garage, and Thomas and I were making our way back past the kitchens. Outside the Cromwell room I stopped.

"You may take Miss Mansel's dressing-case to her room and see to her fire, then you are to go back to bed."

"It won't take a minute to serve you, sir."

"Thomas, you are to do as I say. It was very good of you to come down. I'm much obliged. Good night."

"Good night, sir. Oh—"

"Yes?"

"I forgot to tell you, sir, there's a temporary maid will wait on Miss Mansel in the morning, sir. Susan's had to go away sudden. I think her father's ill, sir."

"I'm sorry for that. All right. I'll tell Miss Mansel. Good night."

"Good night, sir."

As I closed the door of the Cromwell room:

"So I'm Miss Mansel," said Eve.

"Quite right, my dear," said I. "One of our party-my cousin, in fact. When did you wake?"

"Just as you were lifting me out of the car."

I took off my cap and shook its snow into the fire.

"I uncover," said I. "In other words, I take my hat off to you. Eve, you are an artist. I only wish I were."

"Why?"

"I'd paint you-here, now, just as you are."

"I know I look awful."

"You look perfectly sweet."

"I can't help it."

"I shouldn't try."

She did look wonderful. I had put her upon the sofa, but she had moved from there, and was sitting on the hearth in front of the great fire. Plainly she had kept her long grey fur coat on, when she had first sat down but now she had slipped out of it, and it lay all tumbled about her on the rug. She was in evening dress, and might have returned, as I had, from a ball. All blue, it was, blue of a wonderful shade-periwinkle,

I think they call it, Her stockings were flesh-coloured and her shoes of gold: these she had taken off, the better to warm her little shining feet. White arms propped her towards the fire, and she sat sideways, with one leg straight by the warm kerb, the other drawn up and bringing her dress tight and a little away from a silk knee. Her dark hair had worked loose under the weight of the rug, and was lying thick about her smooth shoulders. Save in her face, she wore no jewels, but two great brown stars smiled at me from either side of a straight nose. The lips were red now, and her throat soft and white as her shoulders. I gazed down at her.

"No jewels, you see, Adam," she said suddenly. "I'm afraid you've struck a loser this time. You'll have to stick to the Great North Road in future."

"No jewels?" said I. "You have a wealth of hair, and what about the pearls behind your lips? They're worth a king's ransom."

"They're not made to take out, though, and there's no gold with them."

She put up the red mouth and showed two rows of teeth, white and even.

"Tempt me no more," said I. "Oh, Eve, you're just as bad as ever. After all this time, too. However. I hesitate to mention supper, because you look so lovely sitting there, but—"

She stretched out a warm hand, and I lifted her to her feet. For a second I held the slight fingers.

"Tell me one thing," said I. "Is there anyone who doesn't love you?"

The fingers slipped away. "Yes, stacks of people. You wouldn't like me a bit, only I'm not myself tonight. I'm just-just Eve. See? New Year's Eve."

"Thomas thinks you're Jill-Miss Mansel."

"To him I am. To the temporary maid in the morning, too. As for breakfast-oh, you and my high collar must get me through breakfast and out of here and over to Steeple Abbas somehow. Funny, your telling

Falcon to go to 'The Three Bulls.' It's where we were making for. I'd taken a room there."

"By Jove," said I. "Then, when I went back with Jill, they thought it was you arriving."

And I related what had occurred. When I had finished, she threw back her head and laughed.

"Then you're not a robber, after all, Adam?"

"Certainly not. But why?"

"I mean, assuming the exchange is a fair one."

"Fair?" said I. "It's exquisite. Why, just to look at you's as good as a feast, and—"

"Which reminds me I'm awfully hungry. Oh, no, no, I didn't mean that, Adam, dear, I didn't really."

And my companion leaned against the chimney-piece, laughing helplessly.

"That's torn it," said I, laughing too.

"And now," said Eve, recovering, "take off your coat. You must be so tired."

I drew my pumps out of the great pockets, and threw the coat off me and across the back of a chair. Then I kicked off my great high rubber boots, stepped into my pumps, and looked ruefully at my dress trousers.

"They're only a little creased," said the girl.

"You must forgive them," said I.

"Jill wouldn't have minded, would she?"

"Jill wouldn't have mattered."

"Nor does Eve. Remember my hair."

"I shall never forget it," said I. Then I picked up her little shoes and stooped to fit them on to their feet.

"You are looking after me nicely, Adam," she said, laying a hand on my shoulder to keep her balance. I straightened my back and looked at her.

"My dear," I said, "I-oh, heavens, let's see what we've got for supper."
And I turned hurriedly to the dishes in front of the fire.

When I looked round, she was lighting the candles.

"You mustn't go to bed at once," I said, pushing back my chair. "It's
bad for the digestion. Sit by the fire a little, as you did before. Wait a
moment. I'll give you a cigarette."

I settled her amid cushions, put out the candles, and struck the red
fire into flames.

"But where will you sit, Adam?"

"I shall lean elegantly against the chimney-piece and tell you a fairy
story."

"I'm all for the story, but I think you'd better be a child and sit on the
hearthrug, too. There's plenty of room."

"A child," said I, sitting down by her side. "My dear, do you realize
that I'm as old as the Cotswold Hills."

"There now, Adam. And so am I."

"No," I said firmly, "certainly not."

"But—"

"I don't care. You're not. Goddesses are immortal and their youth
dies not."

"I suppose I ought to get up and curtsey."

"If you do, I shall have to rise and make you a leg, so please don't."

For a moment she smiled into the fire. Then:

"I wonder if two people have ever sat here before, as we're sitting
now?"

"Many a time," said I. "Runaway couples, you know. I expect the old
wood walls think we're another pair."

"They can't see, though."

"No. Born blind. That's why they hear so well. And they never forget. These four"-with a sweep of my cigarette-"have long memories of things, some sweet, some stern, some full of tears, and some again so mirthful that they split their panelled sides with merriment whenever they call them to mind."

"And here's another to rnake them smile."

"Smile? Yes. Wise, whimsical, fatherly smiles, especially wise. They think we're lovers, remember."

"I forgot. Well, the sooner they find out their mis—"

"Hush!" said I. "Walls love lovers. Have pity and don't undeceive them. It'd break the poor old fellows' hearts. That one's looking rather black already.

"She laughed in spite of herself. Then:

"But they haven't got any hearts to break."

"Of course they have. The best in the world, too. Hearts of oak. Now you must make up for it. Come along." I altered my tone. "Chaste and beautiful one, dost thou realize that at this rate we shall reach Gretna next Tuesday week?"

"So soon, Jack?"-languishingly.

"Glorious," said I: "that is, aye, mistress. Remember, I have six spare axles disguised as golf clubs."

"But what of my father? His grey hairs—"

"When I last saw thine aged sire, pipkin, three postboys were engaged in sawing him out of a window, through which he should never have attempted to climb. The angle of his chaise suggested that one of the hind wheels was, to put it mildly, somewhat out of the true. The fact that, before we started, I myself withdrew its linchpin goes to support this theory."

"My poor father! Master Adam, I almost find it in my heart to hate you."

Believe me, fair but haughty, the old fool has taken no hurt. Distant as we were, I could hear his oaths of encouragement, while the post-boys sawed as they had never sawed before. From the way they were doing it, I shouldn't think they ever had."

"But they will soon procure a new linchpin. Is that right? And, oh, Adam, they may be here any moment."

"Not so, my poppet. To get a linchpin, they must find a smith. All the smiths within a radius of thirty miles are drunk. Yes, me again. A man has to think of all these little things. I say, we're giving the walls the time of their life, aren't we? Have another cigarette?"

"After which I must go to bed."

"As you please, Mistress Eve," said I, reaching for a live coal to give her a light.

For a little space we sat silent, watching the play of the flames. Then she spoke slowly, half her thoughts elsewhere:

"You never told me your fairy tale, Adam."

"I expect you know it," said I. "It's all about the princess a fellow found in the snow, and how he took her to his home for shelter, and set her on her way in the morning, and then spent his poor life trying to find her again. Anyway, one doesn't tell fairy-tales to fairies, and-and I'd rather you watched the fire. He'll tell you a finer story than ever I could. At least—"

"Yes?"

"Well, he's a bold fellow, the fire. He'll say things that I can't, Eve. He'll praise, thank, bless you al] in a flash. See what he says for a moment. Remember he's speaking for me."

"Praise, thank, bless," she repeated dreamily. "Does he ever ask anything in return?"

"Never," said I.

For a full moment she sat gazing into the flames. Then she flung her cigarette into the grate and jumped to her feet before I had time to help her.

"Bed-time," she cried. "Mine, at any rate.

"I'll see you to your room," said I, lighting one of the candles. Then I picked up her grey fur coat and laid it over my arm.

"Adam, said Eve.

I looked up and across at her, standing straight by the other side of the hearth, the leaping flames lighting her tumbled hair. One foot was on the kerb, and her left hand hitching her dress in the front a little, as women do. The other she held, palm downwards to the blaze, warming it. I marked the red glow between its slight fingers, making them rosy. Her eyes still gazed into the fire.

"Yes," said I.

"If Jill were here, Adam, would you kiss her good night?"

The next morning, with the help of the high collar and a little strategy, my companion's incognito was preserved, and by half-past eleven we had breakfasted and were once more in the car. It was another brilliant day, and at five minutes past twelve we ran into Steeple Abbas. Eve was sitting in front by my side this time. As we turned into the main street, I slowed down. Outside 'The Three Bulls' stood the limousine, weather-beaten a little and its nickel work dull, but seemingly all right. In the middle of the road stood a chauffeur, his cap pushed back and a hand to his head. As we approached, he looked away from the little writing-block and stared up at the signboard of the inn. When he heard the car approaching, he made for the pavement, turning a puzzled face in our direction. At that moment I heard Jill's voice.

"Berry, Berry, I can hear a car coming. I expect it's Boy."

There was not a moment to lose. Quick as a flash I drew alongside the limousine, which stood on our left between us and the hotel. Then I stopped, stood up, leaned across my companion and opened the big car's door.

"Goodbye, dear," I said.

The next moment she had changed cars. To thrust her rug and dressing-case after her was the work of a second. For a moment I held her hand to my lips. Then I shut the door, slipped back into my seat, and drove on and in to the kerb. As I pulled up, Jill came running down the steps of the inn.

"Then you got home all right, Boy?

"Before I had time to answer, Berry appeared in the doorway. "Aha," said he, "the brave's return! Skaul! You are late, but never mind. Skaul again, my pathfinder. I thought of you when I was going to bed. Was the snow-hut comfortable? I hope you didn't find that coat too much? It isn't really cold, you know. Now, when I was in Patagonia—"

"Are you all ready?" said I. "I'm just coming in to warm my hands." I followed Jill up the steps. In the doorway I turned and took off my hat. The chauffeur was starting up the limousine. And Eve was leaning forward, looking out of the open window. As I smiled, she kissed her hand to me.

Ten minutes later we left 'The Three Bulls.' I had thrown my gauntlets on to the front seat before I entered the inn. As I drew on the right one, I felt a sheet of paper in its cuff. I plucked it out, wondering. It had been torn from the writing-block, and bore the message I had written for Falcon the night before. The signature was Evelyn Fairie, and underneath had been added, "Castle Charing, Somerset. With my love."

I slipped it into my pocket and started the car.

"And how did Jilly get on?" I said abstractedly, as we rolled down the street.

"Oh, Boy," she cried, "it was so funny. I'm sure they took me for somebody else. There was a lovely big room all ready and everybody kept bowing and calling me 'my lady.' They couldn't understand my connection with the others at first and when they asked about the car, and I said it

84

had gone back to Fallow, they nearly fainted. They were going to make out my bill separately, too, only Berry—"

"And you didn't enlighten them?"

"I couldn't make out what was wrong till I was undressing."

"And the real one never turned up?"

"I don't think she can have. The landlord stammered something about 'your ladyship,' as I said 'Goodbye.'"

"How strange," said I. Jill chattered on all the way to Fallow. Fortunately I remembered to tell her about the new chambermaid. I was rather uneasy about the girl, as a matter of fact. She must have seen Eve properly. But my luck was holding, for on our arrival we found that Susan had returned.

The following day, January the second, after breakfast, a wire for Jonah arrived. When he had read it:

"That's curious," he said. "I wonder how he knew we were here?"

"Who's it from?" said Jill.

"Harry Fairie, the man I met at Pau last Easter. Wants us to go over to his place in Somerset before we go back to town."

"All of us?"

"Apparently. 'You and party,' the wire says."

"I believe I met his sister once," said I.

"You wouldn't forget her if you had," said Jonah. "She's a wonderful creature. Eyes like stars."

"Where did you meet her?" said Daphne.

"I seem to associate her with winter sports.

"Switzerland?" said my sister. "What year? Nineteen-twelve?"

I walked to the door and opened it. "If I told you," I said, "you wouldn't believe me. "Then I went out.

CHAPTER V

THE JUDGEMENT OF PARIS

"I suppose," said Daphne." I suppose you think you're funny."

Her husband regarded his cigarette with a frown." Not at all," he replied. "Only there's nothing doing. That's all. My mind is made up. This correspondence must now cease. For myself, as bread-winner and—"

"Never did a day's work in your life," said Jonah."

"And one of the world's workers (so you're wrong, you see)—"

"Of course he's going," said I, looking up. "Only what as?"

"Why not himself?" said Jill.

"M, no," said I. "We must find something out of the common. A mountebank's too ordinary. I want our party to be one of the features of the ball."

"Would it be asking you too much to shut your face?" said Berry. "Nobody spoke to you. Nobody wants to speak to you. I will go further. Nobody—"

"Could he go as a cook, d'you think?" said Daphne. "A chef-thing, I mean. They had cooks, of course. Or a wine-butler? They must have had—"

"Or a birthright?" said Berry. "We know they had birthrights. And I'd sooner be a birthright than a wine-cooler any day. Besides, Jonah could go as a mess of pottage. There's an idea for you. Talk about originality!"

"Originality!" said his wife contemptuously." Studied imbecility, you mean. Anyone can originate drivel."

"It's in the blood," said Jonah. "One of his uncles was a Master in Lunacy."

I laid down my pen and leaned back in my chair.

"It comes to this," said I. "Whatever he goes as, he'll play the fool. Am I right, sir?"

"Yes," said every one."

"(A voice,'Shame')," said Berry.

"Consequently he must be given a part which he can clown without queering the whole scene."

"Exactly," said Daphne."

"What d'you mean, talking about parts and scenes?" said Berry. "I thought it was going to be a ball."

"So it is," said his wife. "But people are taking parties, and every party's going to represent some tale or picture or play or a bit of it. I've told you all this once."

"Twice," corrected her husband. "Once last night with eclat, and once this morning with your mouth full, Jilly's told me three times, and the others once each. That's seven altogether. Eight, with this. I'm beginning to get the hang of the thing. Tell me again."

His voice subsided into the incoherent muttering, which immediately precedes slumber. This was too much. In silence Jonah handed Daphne his cigarette. By stretching out an arm, as she lay on the sofa, my sister was just able to apply the burning tobacco to the lobe of her husband's ear. With a yell the latter flung his feet from the club-kerb and sat up in his chair. When he turned, Jonah was placidly smoking in the distance, while Daphne met her victim's accusing eye with a disdainful stare, her hands empty in her lap. The table, at which I was writing, shook with Jill's suppressed merriment.

"The stake's upstairs," said Berry bitterly. "Or would you rather gouge out my eyes? Will you flay me alive? Because if so, I'll go and get the knives and things. What about after tea? Or would you rather get it over?"

"You shouldn't be so tiresome," said Daphne. Berry shook his head sorrowfully.

"Listen," he said. "The noise you hear is not the bath running away. No, no. My heart is bleeding, sister."

"Better sear that, too," said his wife, reaching for Jonah's cigarette.

It was just then that my eyes, wandering round the library, lighted on a copy of "Don Quixote." "The very thing," said I suddenly.

"What?" said Jill.

"Berry can go as Sancho Panza."

The others stared at me. Berry turned to his wife.

"You and Jill run along, dear, and pad the boxroom. Jonah and I'll humour him till you're ready."

"Sancho Panza?" said Daphne." But we're going to do The Caliph's Wedding out of the Arabian Nights."

"Let's drop the Eastern touch," I said, getting up from the table. "It's sure to be overdone. Give them a page of Cervantes instead. Jonah can be Don Quixote. You'll make a priceless Dorothea in boy's clothes, with your hair down your back. Jilly can be-Wait a minute."

I stepped to the shelf and picked out the old quarto. After a moment's search:

"Here you are," said I. "Daughter of Don Diego. Sancho Panza strikes her when he's going the rounds at night. 'She was beautiful as a thousand pearls, with her hair inclosed under a net of gold and green silk.' And I can be the Squire of the Wood, complete with false nose."

"I rather like the idea," said Daphne, "only—"

"Wait till I find the description of Dorothea," said I, turning over the pages." Here it is. Read that, my dear," and I handed her the book.

In silence my sister read the famous lines. Then she laid the book down, and slipped an arm round my neck.

"Boy," she said, "you flatter me, but I can sit on my hair."

Then and there it was decided to illustrate Cervantes.

"And Sancho can wear his governor's dress," said Jill.

"Quarter of an hour back," said Berry, "-I told you that it was no good ordering the wild horses, because nothing would induce me to go. Since then my left ear has been burned, as with a hot iron. Under the circumstances it is hardly likely that—"

"Oh dear," said Daphne wearily.

I reached for the telephone and picked up the receiver.

"Number, please."

"Exchange," I said, "there is here a fat swab."

"What?"

"Swab," said I. "I'll spell it. S for soldier, W, A for apple, B for Baldwin."

"Have you a complaint to make?"

"That's it," said I:

"About this swab. You see, he won't go to the ball. His ticket has been bought, his role chosen, his face passed over. And yet—"

"Mayfair supervisor," said a voice.

"That's done it," said I.

"I mean-er-Supervisor."

"Speaking."

"I want to complain about our swab here."

"Oh yes. Can you tell me what's wrong with it ?"

"I think its liver must be out of order."

"Very well. I'll report it to the engineers. They'll send a man down tomorrow."

"Thanks awfully."

"Goodbye."

I replaced the receiver and crossed to where Berry was sitting, nursing his wounded ear.

"They're going to report you to the engineers," I said shortly. "A man will be down tomorrow."

"As for you," said my brother-in-law, "I take it your solicitors will accept service. For the others, what shall I say? Just because I hesitate to put off my mantle of dignity and abase this noble intellect by associating with a herd of revellers and-er—" "Libertines?" said Jonah.

"Toss-pots, my ears are to be burned and foul aspersions cast upon a liver, till then spotless. Am I discouraged? No. Emboldened rather. In short, I will attend the rout."

"At last," sighed Daphne.

"My dear. I ordered the supper yesterday. We're sharing a table with the Scarlets. But you needn't have burned my ear."

"Only means some one was talking about you," said Daphne. "Why did you say you weren't going?"

"A passion for perversity," said I.

Berry stole a cautious glance at the time. The hands stood at a quarter past three. A slow grin spread over his countenance.

"Didn't you say something about a sacred concert?" he said. "Good Heavens," cried Daphne, jumping up. "I forgot all about it. It begins at thr—"

Arrested by her husband's seraphic smile, she swung round and looked at the clock.

Berry apostrophized the carpet.

"Sweet are the uses of perversity," he said, with inimitable inflection. For a moment his wife eyed him, speechless with in-indignation. Then:

"I hope you've got ear-ache," she said.

Berry settled himself among the cushions."

"I have," he said, "But back-ache would have been worse."

I sank back in my seat with an injured air. The coach swayed slightly, as it rattled over the points. The train was gathering speed. In the far corner of the compartment the brooch of a gay green hat winked at me over the top of The Daily Glass.

"That's a nice thing," said I.

"What?" said the girl, laying down her paper.

"Oh, nothing. Only the train's run through the station I was going to get out at. That's all."

"How tiresome for you!"

"There are consolations. You would never have opened your small red mouth, but for my exclamation. And I should never have exclaimed, but for—"

"It's very rude to make personal remarks." This severely.

"Only when the person's plain or the remark rude. Note the alliteration."

"What are you going to do?

"Obey orders, I suppose." said I, pointing to the door.

"'Wait until the train stops?'"

"I think so," said I, looking at the flashing hedgerows.

"You see, I've given up acting for the pictures. Otherwise, I should adjust my handcuffs, run along the foot-board, and dive in the direction of the nearest pond."

"While I-?"

"Lay perfectly still. You see, I should be carrying you in my teeth."

"Thanks awfully."

"Not at all. It's a great life."

"It's a rotten death."

"Possibly. Otherwise, you emerge from the infirmary to find that A Jump for Life has already left the Edgware Road for Reading and is eagerly expected at Stockton-on-Tees, that the company for which you work is paying twenty-seven percent and that rehearsals for Kicked to Death begin on Monday. However."

I stopped. The girl was leaning back in her corner, laughing helplessly.

"It's all very fine to laugh," said I. "How would you like to be carried a county and a half beyond your station?"

"You should have asked before you got in."

"Asked?" said I. "The only person I didn't ask was the traffic superintendent himself. They said he was away on his holiday."

"They can't have understood what you said."

"I admit my articulation is defective-has been ever since a fellow backed into my car at Brooklands, did it twenty pounds' worth of damage, and then sent in a bill for a new tail-lamp. At the same time—"

Here another station roared by. I was too late to see the name. "I shall swear in a minute," said I. "I can feel it coming. I suppose we do stop somewhere, if only to coal, don't we?"

"Well, we may stop before, but I know we stop at Friars Rory, because that's where I get out."

I turned to her open-mouthed. She was consulting a wrist-watch and did not see the look on my face. Friars Rory was where I was bound for. We had run through the station ten minutes ago. I knew the place well. I had just time to recover, when she looked up.

"We're late now," she said." I expect that's why we're going so fast."

"You know," I said, "I don't believe you asked either."

"If this was the right train? Well, I've used it, going down to hunt, for two seasons. Besides, I told a porter—"

"Can't have understood what you said," said I, producing my cigarette-case. "Will you smoke? There's plenty of time."

"What d'you mean?"

"I was going to Rory, too. My dear, if this train really stops there, there must be the very deuce of a hairpin corner coming, or else we're on the Inner Circle. We've passed it once, you know, about nine miles back, I should think. No, twelve. This is Shy Junction." We roared between the platforms. "Wonderful how they put these engines along, isn't it?"

But my companion was staring out of the window. The next moment she swung round and looked at me wildly. Gravely I offered her a cigarette. She waved me away impatiently.

"Have we really passed Rory?" she said.

"Ages ago," said I. "Your porter can't possibly have under—"

She stamped a small foot, bright in its patent-leather shoe.

"Aren't you going to do anything?" she demanded.

"I am already composing a letter to the absent traffic superintendent which will spoil his holiday. I shall say that, in spite of the fact that the dark lady with the eyes and the seal-skin coat asked the porter with the nose—"

"Idiot. Can't you do anything now?"

"I can wave to the engine-driver as we go round a bend if you think it's any good, or, of course, there's always the communication cord, only—"

I broke off and looked at her. There was trouble in her great eyes. The small foot tapped the floor nervously. One gloved hand gripped the arm of her seat. I could have sworn the red lips quivered a moment ago. I leaned forward.

"Lass," I said, "is it important that you should be at Friars Rory this morning?"

She looked up quickly. Then, with a half-laugh, "I did want to rather," she said. "But it can't be helped. You see, my mare, Dear One-she's been taken ill, and-and-oh, I am a fool," she said, turning away, her big eyes full of tears.

"No, you're not," said I sturdily, patting her hand.

"I know what it is to have a sick horse. Buck up, lass! We'll be there within the hour."

"What d'you mean?" she said, feeling in her bag for a handkerchief.

"I have a plan," said I mysteriously. "Can't you find it?"

She felt in the pocket of her coat and turned to the bag again.

"I'm afraid my maid must have—"

I took a spare handkerchief from my breast-pocket.

"Would you care to honour me by using this to-er—"

"Go on," she said, taking it with a smile.

"To brush away some of the prettiest tears—"

She laughed exquisitely, put the handkerchief to her eyes, and then smiled her thanks over the white cambric. I let down the window nearest me and put out my head. A long look assured me that we were nearing Ringley. My idea was to pull the cord, stop the train in the station, pay the fine, and raise a car in the town, which should bring us to Rory in forty minutes by road.

"But what are you going to do?" said the girl.

"Wait," said I over my shoulder. Again I put out my head. In the distance I could see red houses-Ringley. I put up my right hand and felt for the chain. As I did so, there seemed to be less weigh on the train-a strange feeling. I hesitated, the wind flying in my face. We were not going so fast-so evenly. Yet, if we had run through Shy Junction, surely we were not going to stop at—The next moment I saw what it was. We were the last coach, and there was a gap, widening slowly, between us and the rest of the train. We had been slipped. I took in my head to find my companion clasping my arm and crying.

"No, no. You mustn't, you mustn't. You're awfully good, but—"

"It's all right," I said. "I didn't have to. We're in the Ringley slip."

"And we're going to stop there?"

"Probably with an unconscionable jerk-a proper full stop. None of your commas for a slip. But there! I might have known. It's a long train that breaks no journey, and there's many a slip 'twixt Town and the North of England. However. If there isn't a train back soon, I'm going to charter a car. May I have the honour of driving you back to Rory and the mare? I'm sure the sight of her mistress will put her on her legs again quicker than all the slings and mashes of outrageous surgeons. I take it you know your Macbeth?"

She laughed merrily. I looked at her appreciatively, sitting opposite and perched, as I was, on one of the compartment's dividing arms.

"Sunshine after rain," I murmured. Sweet she looked in her gay green hat and her long seal-skin coat. Beneath this, the green of a skirt above the slim silk stockings and the bright shoes. Gloves and bag on the seat by her side. The face was eager, clear-cut, its features regular. But only the great eyes mattered. Perhaps, also, the mouth—"

"You're a kind man," she said slowly." And it was sweet of you to think of pulling the cord. But I should have been awfully upset, if you had."

The coach ran alongside of the platform and stopped with a jerk that flung me backwards and my lady on to my chest. I sat up with my arms full of fur-coat, while its owner struggled to regain her feet.

"Infants in arms need not be paid for," said I, setting her upright with a smile." I hope the station-master saw you, or he mightn't believe— Where were we? Oh, I know. You'd have been upset, would you? More upset than this?"

"Oh, much," she said, her eyebrows raised above a faint smile." You see, then I should have been upset properly."

As she spoke, she laid a hand on my shoulder, to steady herself, while she peered into the mirror above my head. I looked round and up at the smiling face, six inches away.

"Then I wish I had," said I. One hand was settling her plumed hat. Without looking down, she set the other firmly upon my chin, and turned my face round and away.

"Open the door and hand me out nicely," she said.

I rose and put on my hat."

Do you ever play the piano?" I said suddenly.

"Why?"

"I was thinking of the fingers. You have such an exquisite touch."

The evident pleasure the chestnut mare evinced at her mistress's arrival was a real tribute to personality. Also the vet's morning report was more satisfactory. It seemed that Dear One was mending. Greatly comforted, my lady let me give her lunch at the Duck Inn. Afterwards-there being no train till four o'clock-she came with me to choose a spaniel pup. It was to purchase him that I had started for Friars Rory that sunshiny day.

"What shall you call him?" she said, as we made our way to the kennels." I really don't know," said I. "What about Seal-skin? Must be something in memory of today."

She laughed merrily. Then:

"Why not Non-Stop?"

"I know," I said. "I'll call him Upset."

Three black and white urchins gambolled about us, flapping ears, wagging ridiculous tails, uncertainly stumbling about upon baby legs.

"Oh, you darlings," said the girl, stooping among them, caressing, in turn caressed. She raised a radiant face to me.

"However will you choose which you'll have?"

I leaned against the wall and regarded the scene before me.

"I like the big one best," I said.

"The big one?" she said, standing up. "Aren't they all the same—"

"The one on its hind legs," said I. "With the big eyes."

"Ah," she said, smiling. "But that's not for sale, I'm afraid. Besides, its temper's very uncertain, as you know."

"I'd risk that. The spaniel is renowned for its affectionate disposition. And what dog wouldn't turn, if it was put in the wrong train? Besides, your coat's so silky."

But I'm sure my ears don't droop, and I've never had distemper. Then there's my pedigree. You don't know—"

"Don't I? By A Long Chalk, out of The Common's good enough for most people."

"Oh, you are hopeless!" she said, laughing. She turned to the scrambling pups. "Who's for a mad master?" she said.

Suddenly a bulldog appeared. She stood regarding us for a moment, her massive head a little on one side. Then a great smile spread over her countenance, and she started to sway in our direction, wagging a greeting with her hind quarters, as bulldogs do. Two of the puppies loped off to

96

meet her. The long-suffering way in which she permitted them to mouth her argued that she was accustomed to being the kindly butt of their exuberance. The third turned to follow his fellows, hesitated, caught my lady's eye, and rushed back to his new-found friend.

That's the one for me," said I. "Give me good judgment. I shall call him Paris."

"Appropriately. Off with the old love and on with the new. I'm sure he's faithless, and I expect the bulldog's been awfully kind to him, haven't you, dear?" She patted the snuffling beauty. "Besides, I gave him the glad eye, which wasn't fair."

"I'll bet that's how Venus got the apple, if the truth were known. Any way, I'm going to choose him for choosing you. You see. We shall get on well."

"Juno, Juno!" cried a woman's voice from the house. Immediately the bulldog started and turned towards the doorway.

"What did I say?" said I. "Something seemed to tell me you were a goddess, when—"

"When?"

"When you were upset this morning. I saw you very close then, you see. Well! What sort of weather have you been having in Olympus lately? And how's Vulcan? I suppose Cupid must be getting quite a big boy?"

She laughed. "You wouldn't know him if you saw him," she said."

"Don't be too sure. When does he go to the 'Varsity? Or shan't you send him?"

"He's there now. Doing awfully well, too!"

"Taken a first in the Honour School of Love, I suppose? Is he as good a shot as ever?"

"He's a very good son."

"Ought to be," said I.

"Yes," she said steadily, gazing with eyes half-closed, over the fields and hedgerows, away to the distant hills, the faintest smile hung on her parted lips. "He's never given me a day's trouble since he was born. I don't think he will, either, not for a long time, any way,"

Thoughtfully I pulled on my gloves. Then:

"My dear," said I, "for that boast you may shortly expect a judgment."

"More judgments?" she cried with a laugh, turning to look at me, the straight brews raised in mockery. "Which will cost you more, my fair Olympian, than a glad eye."

A quarter past five. The train was passing through the outskirts of London. A bare ten minutes more, and we should arrive. I looked anxiously at the girl, wondering where, when, how I should see her again. For the last half-hour we had spoken but little. She had seemed sleepy, and I had begged her to rest. Dreamily she had thanked me, saying that she had had little sleep the night before. Then the eyes had smiled gently and disappeared. It was almost dark now, so swift had been the passing of the winter's day. Lights shone and blinked out of the darkness. Another train roared by, and we slackened speed. Slowly we crawled over a bridge spanning mean streets. One could not but mark the bustling scene below. The sudden din compelled attention. I looked down upon the writhing traffic, the glistening roadway, the pavements crowded with hurrying, jostling forms. An over-lighted public house made the cheap shops seem ill-lit, poorer still. Its dirty splendour dominated everything: even the tall trams took on a lesser light. The lumbering roar of wheels, the insistent clamour of an obstructed tram, the hoarse shouts of hawkers crying their wares-all this rose up above the rumble of the slow-moving train. I was glad when we had left the spot behind. It would not do after the country-side. It occurred to me that, but a little space back-some seventy rolling years-here also had stretched fair green fields. Perchance the very ones poor dying Falstaff had babbled of. We slunk past an asylum-a long mass, dark, sinister. By this even the trams seemed to hasten. I could just hear their thin song, as they slid forward.

Enough. Already I was half-way to depression. Resolutely I turned, giving the window my shoulder. My Lady had not stirred. Wistfully I regarded her closed eyes. In five minutes we should be in, and there were things I wanted to say . . . A smile crept into the gentle face.

"Go on," she said quietly. "I'm listening."

"I was wondering, goddess, if I should ever see you again."

"Oh, probably! The world's awfully small. Not for some time, though. I leave for Cannes tomorrow, to join my people."

"Cannes!" I exclaimed.

"Yes. You must have heard of it. Where the weather comes from."

"Where it stays, you mean," I growled, as the rising wind flung a handful of raindrops against the windows. For a moment I sat silent, looking out into the night, thinking. Except for a luncheon, tomorrow was free. And I could cut that. A network of shining rails showed that the terminus was at hand. I turned to my lady.

"Then we shall meet again tomorrow," I said gravely. "I have to go down to Dover, too."

"What for?" This suspiciously.

I rose and took up my hat. "Another dog," I said shortly.

She broke into silvery merriment. At length:

"Nonsense," she said, rising.

"Not at all," said I. "The Dover dogs are famous."

"Sea-dogs, perhaps," she murmured, setting one knee on the cushions to look into the glass. "Well, you've been awfully kind, and I'm very grateful. And now—" she swung round-"goodbye." She held out a slim hand.

The train drew up to the platform.

"Goodbye?" said I, taking the cool fingers. She nodded.

"And I hope you'll get a good dog at Dover," she said, smiling. "I shall think of you. You see, I'm going by Folkestone and Boulogne."

In silence I bent over the slight fingers. Slowly they slipped away.
I opened the door. Then I turned to the girl.

"You know," I said, "the Folkestone dogs."

"At last," said Berry, as the car swung into line in Kensington Gore, about a furlong from the doors of the Albert Hall. "A short hour and a quarter, and we shall be there. Can anyone tell me why I consented to come?"

"To please yourself," said Daphne shortly.

"Wrong," said her husband. "The correct answer will appear in our next issue. Five million consolation prizes will be awarded to those who, in the opinion of—"

"Have you got the tickets?" said his wife.

"Tickets!" said Berry contemptuously. "I've had to put my handkerchief in my shoe, and my cigarette-case has lodged slightly to the right and six inches below my heart. You'll have to make a ring round me, if I want to smoke."

"Have you got the tickets?" said Daphne.

"My dear, I distinctly remember giving them to—"

A perfect shriek went up from Daphne and Jill. The footman slipped on to the step and opened the door.

"Did you call, madam?"

"Yes," said Berry. "Give Mrs. Pleydell the tickets."

Our party was an undoubted success. Jonah looked wonderful, Daphne and Jill priceless. With her magnificent hair unbound, her simple boy's dress, her little rough shoes at the foot of legs bare to the knee, my sister was a glorious sight. And an exquisite Jill, in green and white and gold, ruffled it with the daintiest air and a light in her grey eyes that shamed her jewellery. Berry was simply immense. A brilliant make-up, coupled with the riotous extravagance of his dress, carried him half-way. But the pomp of carriage, the circumstance of gait which he assumed, the manner of the man beggar description. Cervantes would have wept with delight, could he have witnessed it. The Squire of the Wood passed.

And did little else. And that somewhat listlessly, till he saw my lady. That was just after supper, and she was sitting on the edge of a box, scanning her programme. All lovely, dressed as Potpourri.

"You were right," said I. "The world is small." We floated into the music. "So is your waist. But, then I learned that this morning. So. When you were upset."

"Do you like my dress?"

"Love it. Where did it come from?"

She mentioned a French firm.

"Ah!" said I, "Give me the judgment of Paris."

CHAPTER VI

WHICH TO ADORE

"I suppose you think I'm going to swear," said Berry defiantly.

Jill and Daphne clasped one another and shrieked with laughter. Berry stopped addressing the ball and gazed at them.

"Go on!" he said, nodding sardonic approval. "Provoke me to violence. Goad me in the direction of insanity."

His caddie sniggered audibly. Berry turned to him.

"That's right, my boy. Make the most of your time. For you I have already devised a lingering death."

"Look here, old chap," said I, "there's some mistake. I said I'd give you a stroke a hole, not a divot a stroke."

Jonah strolled up. "Hullo!" he said, "making a new bunker, old man? Good idea. Only a cleek's no good. Send the boy for a turf-cutter. Quicker in the long run."

My brother-in-law regarded us scornfully. Then:

"What I want to know," he said, "is how the Punch office can spare you both at the same time."

Daphne, Berry and I were playing a three-ball match. while Jill and Jonah-who had sprained his wrist-were walking round with us. Berry is rather good really, but just now he was wearing a patch over one eye, which made him hopeless.

It was glorious spring weather on the coast of Devon. A little village is Feth. Over and round about it the wind blows always, but the cluster of white cottages and the old brown inn themselves lie close in a hollow of the moorland, flanked by the great cliffs. Only the grey church, set up on the heights, half a mile distant, endures the tempests. The wind passes over Feth and is gone. A busy fellow, the wind. He has no time to stop. Not so the sunshine. That lingers with Feth all day, decking: the place gloriously. It is good to be a pet of the sun. So are the gardens of Feth bright with flowers, the white walls dazzling, the stream, that scrambles over brown pebbles to the little bay, merry water.

Except for the natives, we had the place to ourselves. But then Feth sees few visitors at any season. Sixteen miles from a station is its salvation. True, there is Mote Abbey hard by-a fine old place with an ancient deer-park and deep, rolling woods. Ruins, too, we had heard. A roofless quire, a few grass-grown yards of cloister and the like. Only the Abbot's kitchen was at all preserved. There's irony for you. We were going to see them before we left. We were told that in summer at the house itself parties assembled. But the family was away now.

The round of golf proceeded. "How many is that?" said Berry, as he sliced into the sea.

"Seven," said I. "Not seven into the sea, you know. Seven strokes. You've only hit three into the sea altogether."

"Isn't he clever with his sums? Here, give me another ball. Where's Henry?"

I handed him the last-named-a favourite cleek. The caddie had gone to collect the flotsam.

"Now then. Ladies and gentlemen, with your kind permission I shall now proceed to beat the sphere into the sky."

It was a tremendous shot, and we could see that it must have reached the green; but when we came up and found the ball in the hole nobody was more surprised than Berry. Of course, he didn't show it. Berry doesn't give things away.

"Ah!" he said pleasantly. "That's better. I'm beginning to get used to playing with one eye. You know, all the time I-er-seem to see two balls."

"Nonsense," said Daphne.

"If you said you'd been seeing two holes all day, I could believe it," said Jonah. "Anyone might think so from the way you've been playing."

Berry smiled ecstatically. "My recent-er-chef d'oeuvre-(note the Parisian accent)-has ipso facto-(Latin of the Augustan Age)-placed me beyond the pricks of criticism. The venom, brother, which you would squirt upon me, bespatters but yourself. Boy, place me the globe upon yon pinnacle of sand. So. Now indicate to me the distant pin. Thank you. Do I see it? No. Natheless (obsolete, but pure), I say nameless it beckons me. And now give me-yes, give me Douglas."

The caddie handed him a brassie. He had caddied for Berry before.

"Don't breathe for a moment, anyone," said Daphne.

Her husband frowned and silently sliced into the sea.

"How many balls did you see that time?" said Jonah.

"Three," said I. "That's why he's going to pawn his clubs."

"The aftermath of gluttony." I spoke disgustedly. It was after luncheon, and Daphne was already asleep. Jill and Jonah drooped comfortably in huge chairs. Berry sprawled upon a sofa.

"I suppose we outrage what you call your sense of decency." murmured the latter.

"You do. Incidentally, you also irritate me, because I shall have to go round alone."

"Friend, your foul egoism leaves me unmoved. Go forth and harry your balls. I am about to slumber like a little child. Do you think I shall dream, brother?"

"Probably," said I. "About fried fish shops."

Jill shuddered in her chair, and Berry sat up.

"After that most offensive allusion," he said pompously, "I have no option but to ask you to withdraw. The touts' room is downstairs.

Before leaving you may give me what cigarettes you have in your case."

I smiled grimly. Then: "I'm afraid I don't approve of-ah-children smoking," I said, moving towards the door. "Besides, a little exercise 'll do you good. There is a box in my room-you know where that is?"

"Where?" snarled my brother-in-law.

I put my head round the door and looked at him. "Immediately above the touts'," said I.

The breeze of the morning had died away, and though the month was the month of April, it might have been a midsummer afternoon. I started on my solitary round, well enough pleased, really, to be alone. The weather was excellent company. My clubs I carried myself.

The fourth hole lies in a little valley, under the lee of a steep, rock-studded hill, whose other side falls sheer into the tumbling waves. On an idle impulse I left my clubs at the fifth tee and scrambled on up the green slope to gaze upon and over the sea below. I have a weakness for high places on the edges of England. I cannot match the dignity of them. Where yellow sands invite, these do not even stoop to challenge. They are superb, demigods, the Royalty of the coast.

As I breasted the summit, I heard a child's voice reading aloud.

"And the people told him of all the splendid things which were in the city, and about the King, and what a pretty Princess the King's daughter was."

'Where can one get to see her?' asked the soldier.

"'She is not to be seen at all,' said they, all together 'she lives in a great copper castle, with a great many walls and towers round about it; no one but the King may go in and out there, for it has been prophesied that she shall marry a common soldier, and the King can't bear that.'"

"'I should like to see her,' thought the soldier . . ."

"The reading came from beyond and below me. I fell on my knees, crawled forward, and peered over the top of a slab of rock. On the warm grass, twenty paces from the edge of the cliff, sat a little boy, his brown knees propping a book. By his side, facing the sea, lay a girl of nineteen or twenty years, her hands clasped behind her head. Her eyes were closed. She seemed to be asleep. The reading continued.

"And all his friends knew him again, and cared very much for him indeed."

Once he thought to himself,' It is a very strange thing that one cannot get to see the Princess. They all say she is very beautiful; but what is the use of that, if she has always to sit in the great copper castle with the many towers? Can I not get to see her at all? Where is my tinder-box?' And so he struck a light, and whisk! came the dog with eyes as big as teacups.

"'It is midnight, certainly, said the soldier; 'but I should very much like to see the Princess, only for one little moment.'"

Here the child shaded his eyes and looked down at the sands of a creek, quarter of a mile away.

"There they are," he exclaimed, dropping the book and scrambling to his feet. He waved delightedly to two specks on the sands below. Then:

"Goodbye, Cousin Lallie," he cried. "I'll be home by six," and tore away down the green slope like a mad thing. But his cousin never waked. I watched her meditatively.

A skirt of grey-blue tweed, and the fresh white of a blouse beneath a smart coat to match. Her small grey hat lay on the grass by her side. Her slim legs were crossed comfortably, and the bright sun lighted a face at once strong and gentle, clear-cut under its thick black hair, which was parted in the middle and hung low over each temple. Her brews were straight, and on the red mouth was a faint smile.

I looked away over the glittering waves. Then I came quietly down, picked up "Hans Andersen," and took my seat by her side. I found the place and continued the story aloud:

"And the dog was outside the door directly, and, before the soldier thought it, came back with the Princess. She sat upon the dog's back and slept; and every one could see she was a real Princess, for she was so lovely. The soldier could not refrain from kissing her, for he was a thorough soldier."

Here the girl stirred, opened her eyes, saw me, and sat up.

"Who on earth-"she began. "It's all right," said I. "It's only a fairy tale. Besides, I'm not a soldier, although I don't see—"

"How long has this been going on?"

"Only just begun," said I." Listen.

"Then the dog ran back with the Princess. But when morning came—"

"Where's Roy?"

"He had to go and join his friends," said I. "Fortunately I happened to be here to take his place. He asked me to say he should be home not later than six. Where were we? Oh, I know.

"But when morning came—"

She raised a slim hand for me to stop. Then she clasped her knees and regarded me with her head on one side.

"A bad end," she said laconically.

"A good beginning, anyway," said I.

"I might be a sorceress."

"I believe you are."

"Or an adventuress, for all you know."

"Or a Princess," said I.

"What made you do this?"

"I'll tell you," said I. "Whilst you were asleep, a little smile was playing round your lips. And this smile told me that he had two twin sisters who dwelt In your eyes. And, like the soldier, I wanted to see them, Princess."

"Well, you have now, haven't you?"

I looked at her critically. "I'm afraid they must be out," said I. In spite of herself she laughed. "No,there they are. Besides—"

"What?"

"The little smile said he had a big brother living in your heart."

"Yes," she said softly.

"Yes. And that made me very brave, Princess. Otherwise I should never have dared. Honestly, it was all the little smile's fault, bless him. Isn't it glorious here?

"The bright eyes swept the horizon.

"Yes," she said slowly," it is. In fact, every prospect pleases."

"And only golf is vile."

"Byron never said that."

"I know he didn't," said I. "Nor, in fact, did Heber. He said 'man.' All the same, I'm not vile. I'm rather nice, really. At least, so one of the smaller birds told me."

"Not really?"

"I mean it."

"Perhaps it was a skylark."

"As a matter of fact," I said stiffly, "it was an owl. A breed famous for its wisdom."

"Ah, but you shouldn't believe everything you're told."

"It isn't a question of what I believe, but of what other people believe," said I. "But if you don't believe it yourself, how can you expect—"

"I never said I didn't believe it myself. Besides, I don't want to argue. I want to watch the smiles playing 'Here we go round the mulberry bush.'"

The girl broke into peals of silvery laughter. "Is my nose as bad as all that?" she said presently.

"Your nose is the nose of dainty Columbine," said I. "Dream noses, they call them. And you know that mulberry bushes don't figure in that game any more than the bells of St. Clement Danes are ever used by children playing 'Oranges and lemons.'"

"Admit it was a floater on your part, and I'll let you play a round with me."

"I-er-confess, upon consideration, that the allusion—"

"That'll do," she said, laughing.

108

I rose. She put out a hand, and I drew her to her feet.

"My clubs are just by that rock there. Do you think you can manage Hans Andersen?"

"Every time," said I, picking up the book. I shouldered her clubs and together we scrambled over the rise and down towards the fifth tee.

"Oh, I told you I adored you, didn't I?" I said suddenly.

"I don't think so."

"Surely I did. Perhaps you were asleep."

"Asleep!" she said scornfully. "I was awake all the time. I nearly died when you began to read."

I stopped short and looked at her. "You are a deceitful witch." I said.

"A what witch?"

"The which to adore," said I.

After the fourth hole the course lies inland. For the next ten holes you play directly away from the sea. Then the fifteenth takes a sharp turn to the left, skirting the deer-park of Mote Abbey, while the sixteenth bears to the left again, heading straight for the club-house and the coast once more.

My lady was a pretty player. I gave her two strokes a hole and led till the fourteenth, but on that green she holed a ten-foot putt which made us all square.

If she hadn't sliced her drive from the fifteenth tee, it would have been a beautiful shot. We watched it curl over the grey wall into the sunshot park.

"Out of bounds, I suppose," said I. "What a pity, pretty Princess."

"Not at all," she replied. "It was a lovely shot. You can't do better than follow that line."

"Into the deer-park?"

"Why not? It's much prettier."

"I'm sure it is," said I.

"But what of that? Unless somebody's moved it since this morning, the green's about a hundred and twenty yards away from the wall on this side. To say nothing of the fact that the park's private property, while there's a notice-board about three feet square, beginning 'Golfers are requested to remember,' at the one place where a giant might effect an entrance."

"Yes," she said quietly, "I got brother to put that board there. We tried to make it polite. The caddies used to frighten the deer so."

I just stood and looked at her. The three smiles blazed back at me. In silence I turned and teed up. Then I drove after her ball into the fair park.

When we reached the place where the board was posted, she touched my hand and pointed to her little brown shoe. For an instant she rested on my palm. The next moment she was on the top of the wall. She smiled her thanks before disappearing. I followed with the clubs. There was a ladder on the other side. She was awaiting my descent. In silence we walked forward together. Presently I touched her arm and stood still. She turned and looked at me, the sun making all manner of exquisite lights in her glorious hair.

"If I had a hat on," I said simply, "I should uncover."

The little bow she gave me would have launched another "thousand ships." In the slight action all the charm of her was voiced exquisitely. Grace, sweetness and dignity-all in a bow. So it was always. Helen's features would not have fired a sheepcote: the charm that lighted them blotted out a city. Cleopatra's form would not have spoiled a slave: the magnetism of her ruined Marc Antony. Elizabeth's speech would not have sunk a coracle: the personality behind it smashed an Armada.

We came to her ball first. As I handed her her brassie:

"Tell me one thing," said I. "If I had not been there, how would you have got over the wall?"

She looked at me mischievously. "I have a way," she said.

"I know," I said, patting her golf-bag. "These aren't really clubs at all."

"What are they, then?"

"Broomsticks."

It was the best part of a mile to the fair lawn, where we holed out underneath the cedars. I won with fourteen, which wasn't bad, considering I was bunkered in a bed of daffodils. She gave me tea in the old library, sweet with the fragrance of pot-pourri. Out of its latticed windows I could see the rolling woods, bright in their fresh green livery. For nearly an hour and a half we sat talking. I told her of Daphne and the others. She told me of her mother and sisters and how her brother had cared for the Abbey since her father's death. It was true that the family was away. She was alone there, save for her eldest sister's child-Roy. Next month she would go to London.

"Where I may come and see you?"

"I should be very hurt if you didn't. It's going to be rather nice."

"It is," I said with conviction.

"I meant the season. I'll enjoy it all. The dances and theatres, Ranelagh, Ascot, Lord's, the Horse Show and everything. But—"

"How glad and happy she'll be to get back to the Abbey with its deep woodland and its warm park, its gentle-eyed deer, its oaks and elms and cedars, its rose-garden and its old paved court. How grateful to lean out of her bedroom window into the cool, quiet, starlit nights. How pleased to watch the setting sun making the ragged clerestory more beautiful than did all its precious panes."

I stopped. She was sitting back in her chair by the window, chin in air, showing her soft, white throat, gazing with half-closed eyes up at the reddening sky.

"He understands," she murmured, "he understands."

For a little space we sat silent. Then I rose.

"Goodbye." I said. "You have been very kind. Perhaps I may come again."

She did not move. Only her eyes left the window and rested on mine. "Ring the bell," she said. "I am going to take you to see the ruins. They are at their best, as you said, at sundown."

"Thank you," I said, and stepped to the fireplace. A footman entered the room. "I want the key of the Abbot's kitchen," said my hostess.

"Some visitors have it, madam. A gentleman called to ask for it ten minutes ago."

"Oh, all right." She rose and turned to me. "Let's go, then. We'll probably meet them bringing it back."

The half-light lent the old quire's walls a rare beauty. A great peace hung over them. Perhaps it was of them. For a little we strolled, talking, upon the greensward. Then:

"Now you shall see the kitchen," she said.

"If you please, Princess."

The kitchen stood away from the ruins, in the middle of a fair meadow: a circular building of grey stone, very lofty and about sixty paces in circumference. Its great oak door was closed. I could see one tiny window-glassless, of course-some sixteen feet from the ground.

"Why!" said the girl, stopping suddenly, "the door's shut,"

Yes," said I; "but what of that?"

"Well, the people must have gone."

"Why?"

"Well, you can't see inside if you shut the door. Besides, if you do, you can't open it again. Not from within I mean. It's a spring lock."

"Perhaps they're locked in."

"They can't be."

"They might," said I. "Come on."

I was right. As we drew near, a confused murmur fell upon our ears. People talking excitedly. Then came the sound of blows upon the door.

"O-o-oh," said my companion. "So they are."

At that moment feminine tones were raised in a wail of expostulation.

"Yes, I shall! It's silly not to. Help! He-elp!"

Daphne's voice.

I fell on the green grass and writhed in silent laughter. When the girl recoiled in horror, I caught her by a warm ankle.

"Don't move!" I whispered. "Don't speak! Don't make a sound! Listen! It's my own party in there-Berry and Co. It's the most perfect thing that ever happened. Hush! We're going to have the time of our lives."

Again I rolled in an ecstasy of mirth. As the comedy of the situation dawned upon the girl, she began to laugh helplessly.

The knocking began again. I got up, and together we approached warily. As we reached the door:

"I'm glad I had four cups of tea," said Berry. "How many did you have?"

"Two," said Jill tearfully.

"Ah, I shall survive you, then. Very likely I shall be alive, if insane, when found. At any rate, with the aid of artificial respiration—"

"Rubbish!" said Daphne. "Some one must hear us soon."

"My dear, the noise we can make wouldn't flush a titlark at twenty paces. No, no!" he went on airily, "a lingering death awaits us. I only wish my caddie was here, too. Is anyone's tongue swelling? That's a sure sign. Directly you feel that, you know you're thirsty."

"Fool!" said his wife, "Besides, they'll miss the key soon."

"Where is the key?" said Jonah. "If we once lose that, we shall never find it again."

There was an awful silence. Then:

"Er-didn't I give it to you?" said Berry.

His words were the signal for a general uproar. The others fell upon Berry and rent him. As it died down, we heard him bitterly comparing them to wolves and curs about a lion at bay. Then a match was struck and there were groping sounds.

"When you've quite finished with my feet," said Daphne in a withering tone.

"Sorry, dearest. I thought it was a bag of meal," said her husband. "My thoughts run on food just now, you see." Here he gave a yell of agony. "Get off!" he screamed. "You're on my hand."

"That's more like it," said Jonah. "That ought to carry."

"Meal-bags don't hurt, do they?" said Daphne coolly. My sister is proud of her dainty feet.

"Vixen," replied her spouse.

I slipped my arm into that of the girl, who was leaning against the wall shaking with laughter. Tears were coursing down my cheeks. I drew her away from the door and whispered brokenly in her ear. She nodded and pulled herself together. Then she went to the door and knocked. Silence.

"Hullo," she said.

"Er-hullo," said Berry.

"I thought I heard somebody calling," said the girl.

"Er-did you?" said Berry.

"Yes, but I'm afraid I must have been mistaken. Perhaps it was some boys calling. Goodbye."

There was a perfect shriek of "Don't go" from Daphne and Jill. Then:

"You idiot!" said Daphne. "Let me." We heard her advance to the door.

"I say," she purred, "it's awfully sweet of you to have come. We did call. You see, it sounds awfully silly, but we're locked in."

"Oh, how dreadful for you," said the girl.

"Yes, isn't it? There's no key-hole this side."

"How awfully tiresome. Have you been there long?"

"Oh, no. Only a few moments. We just came to see the place."

"Well, do you think you can manage to throw the key out of the window? Then I could unlock the door for you, couldn't I?"

"Oh, thank you so very much. If you don't mind waiting a minute-er-it's so dark in here and so confusing that—"

114

"You don't mean to say you've lost the key?" said the girl.

"Oh, it's not lost," said Daphne. "It's just here somewhere. One of us laid it down for a moment and, really, in this darkness you can't see anything. If we only had some more matches—"

"I've got a box," I said. A long silence followed my words. Then:

"My dear lady," said Berry. "Are you still there?"

"Yes," said my companion, her voice shaking a little.

"Then I beseech you to have no dealing with the being whose vile accents I heard but a moment ago. A man of depraved instincts and profligate ways, he is no fit companion for a young and innocent girl. Moreover, viper-like, he bears malice towards us, who have shielded him for years."

"How awful," said the girl.

"Yes," said Berry, "for your own sake, dear lady, beware of him. And for ours, too, I beg you. On no account accept his proffered assistance-in the matter of the key, I mean. If he really has matches, tell him to throw them in. Adopt a hectoring tone and he will fear you. But, remember, he is as cunning as a serpent, Let but that key fall into his hands—"

"Wait till it's fallen into your own hands, old cock," said I.

"Dear lady," said Berry, "you hear his ribald—"

The rest of the sentence was drowned in the peals of laughter to which my companion at last gave vent. I joined her, and the meadow resounded with our merriment. When we had recovered a little:

"Will you have the matches?" said I, standing beneath the window, "or shall I send for the battering ram?"

"Throw them in, fathead," said my brother-in-law.

"Ask nicely, then."

"I'll see you—"

"Please, Boy, dear," cried Jill.

I laughed and pitched the box into the kitchen. The next second we heard a match struck, and the groping sounds recommenced. The girl and I strolled a little back from the window and stood, awaiting the key.

"So it's all come true," said I, looking at her.

"What has?"

"The fairy tale." I pointed to the kitchen. "There is the copper castle, and here"-with a bow-"the pretty Princess. The tinder-box I have just thrown to my companions."

"And I suppose you're the soldier," she said slowly.

"Yes," I said, "the common soldier."

"Common?"

"Yes, dear," I said, taking her hand. "Common, but thorough; thoroughly common, but uncommonly thorough. And now look at me, pretty Princess."

She turned a laughing face to mine. Suddenly, as I bent forward, the eyes flashed.

"I suppose this is the little smile's fault, too," she said quietly.

Instantly I released her hand and stood up, smiling.

"No," I said gently. "It would have been the soldier's."

For a moment she smiled back. Then she slipped an arm round my neck.

"Let's call it Hans Andersen's," she whispered.

A perfect Babel arose suddenly from the kitchen. In the midst of the turmoil I seemed to discern Berry's fat laugh. The next second a large key hurtled through the window.

I picked it up and strode to the door. When I had put it into the keyhole, I paused.

"Buck up, Boy!" said Berry.

"One question," said I. "Where was the key?"

"Where d'you think?" said Jonah bitterly.

"In his pocket all the time?" said I.

"Right," said Berry. "Now do your worst."

"I'm going to," said I. "I'm going to let you out."

CHAPTER VII

EVERY PICTURE TELLS A STORY

The front door banged. Followed quick steps on the steep, uncarpeted stairs, and a knock on the studio's door.

"Come in," said I.

The door opened and a girl in a lilac dress swept into the room.

"I'm afraid I'm awfully la-O-o-oh!" she said.

"If it isn't her!" said I.

For a moment we stood looking at one another with big eyes. Then:

"Where's Mr. Larel?" she demanded.

"He'll be here in a moment. Won't you sit down? He and I are old friends."

She smiled.

"I know," she said.

"He's told me—"

"The devil he has," said I.

A little peal of laughter.

"As I feared," said I.

"My dear, you've been misled. Yes. That over there is a chair. It cost three and ninepence in the King's Road. Local colour, you know. He's putting it in his new picture, 'Luxury'"

Still smiling, she took her seat. Then:

"He said you were awful," she said.

Till a fortnight ago, I had not seen George Larel for quite five years. Not since we had been at Oxford together. When he went down, he left England, to study, I understood. He always drew rather well. Then one spring morning I struck him in Piccadilly, by the railings of the Green Park. He was standing still, a large, blue air-ball in his hand, steadfastly regarding the Porters' Rest. Our greeting was characteristic.

"Well, George," said I. He looked round.

"Hullo, old chap." He pointed to the Rest. "Rather nice, that. Pity there aren't more. Why didn't they keep the Pike at Hyde Park Corner?"

I shrugged my shoulders. "I begged them to," said I. "But you know what they are."

George looked at me critically. Then:

"That's a good hat," he said. "I'd like to paint you just as you are." He stepped back and half closed his eyes. "Yes, that'll do. When can you come? I always said I would, you know," he added.

"You're very good, George. Come to the club and—"

He shook his head. "We'll talk, when you come. I've got to go to Richmond now." He pointed to the air-ball. "There was a child there yesterday, playing in the Park, with eyes-I've only seen their like once before. That was in Oporto." He sighed. "Will you come tomorrow at eleven? Cheyne Row. I forget the number, but it's got a green door."

"I'd love to."

He hailed a taxi.

"That's right, then." He turned to the driver. "Go to Richmond," he said, opening the door.

As it moved, he put his head out of the window.

"Mind you wear that hat, old boy."

The next morning I had my first sitting. It was a great success. There was much to say, and we talked furiously for three hours. And all the time I sat still upon the throne, and George painted. About his work he said little, but I gathered that be had begun to do well. He mentioned that he had had two or three commissions.

"I'm on that now," he said carelessly, during one of my rests. He was pointing to a canvas, which leaned-face inwards-against the wall. I walked across the studio, and turned it round. A girl's picture. A girl in a flowered dress and a shady hat, her slight shining legs crossed at the knee. Sitting square in the high-backed chair, he was painting her, one small hand on each of its rosewood arms. The face was most of all unfinished.

"You've got those legs well," said I, "And I like the dress. She looks rather lovely, as far as one can tell without seeing the face."

George laughed.

"She's all right," he said.

At the end of my second sitting George picked up a knife and began deliberately to scrape out all the work he had done that morning. I watched him, petrified with horror.

"Sorry, old chap," he said, smiling.

"Stop," I cried. "I like that curve of the nostril. It denotes the force of character which has made me what I am."

George went on ruthlessly.

"I want it to be good of you," he said simply. Half way through my third sitting George gave a cry and flung off his coat.

"What's the matter?" said I. "Something biting-?"

"Talk, man," he said, seizing his palette. "Just talk. Don't mind how I answer. I'm going to paint. By Jove, how I'm going to paint!"

Clearly the fit was upon him. These artists! Not daring to disobey, I talked and talked. Heaven knows what I said. After an hour my tongue clove to the roof of my mouth, but I talked on. And all the time George alternately bent his brews upon me, and hung himself at the canvas, uttering strange, smothered cries and oaths, but painting, painting . . . At a quarter past two he laid down his palette and cried to me to descend. Stiffly I did so.

For a long moment I looked at the portrait. Then I turned to George and clapped him on the back.

"I think you're going to make a name," said I.

"That's right," he said. "And now give me a cigarette."

Before we went to lunch, he showed me the picture of the girl. It was almost finished. Such a fine, brave face. Not a bit pretty-just beautiful. Dark hair showing under the brim of the hat, steady brown eyes, the mouth exquisite . . .

That was three days ago. And now-pleasedly I regarded the original.

"May I offer you a cigarette?" I said.

When I had lighted it for her:

"Today is Thursday, isn't it?" she said.

"That's just what I was going to say."

"Yes, I'm sure it is, because last night brother left—"

"The light on in the kitchen garden, with the result that this morning all the cocks were two hours fast. I know. But of course it is. Hasn't Thursday always been my lucky day?"

She blew out a little cloud of smoke and smiled at it. Then:

"I don't know you at all, you know," she said gravely, "and Aunt Prudence always used to say—"

"I know. 'Beware of pickpockets. No smoking.' They quote her in the lifts on the Tube. But then I'm not a pickpocket, and you are smoking. Besides, your picture knows mine very well. They've seen quite a lot of each other lately.

"Yes, but—"

"And then you know my picture a little, and I know yours by heart."

"You're quick to learn."

"Perhaps. But I do. I know every eyelash, long as they are. I believe I could say them. But then I was always good at poetry." This with a bow.

She rose and made the daintiest curtsey. "Would have been better," she said, resuming her seat in the depths of 'Luxury.' "But the skirts of today don't help."

"And my bow would have been deeper: but the braces I bought yesterday afternoon—"

120

"That'll do," she said, laughing. "Seriously, where is Mr. Larel, and why are you here?"

"George is probably scouring Battersea for a child he saw there last autumn with ears such as he has never beheld outside Khartoum. I am here, as you are, in the interest of Posterity."

"Did he tell you Thursday, too?"

"Certainly. I remember it perfectly. We were standing in St. James's Square, near where I get my shirts. Nobody recognized us. George had a cigar in his mouth, and his exact words were, 'Wottabow Hursday?' I had some of the wood pavement in my eye, and my exact words were therefore excusable."

"And now he's forgotten us both."

"On the contrary, he's probably remembered."

"And is consequently afraid to come himself?"

"Exactly. Well, we couldn't very well overlook the insult, could we?"

"It might be wiped out in paint."

I shook my head. Then:

"French polish might do," I said. "But then, he hasn't got any of that. However. To tell you the truth, I don't know that I'm very angry with him. I shall pretend to be, of course. But, now that from admiring the imitation, I find myself face to face with the real thing, I—"

"And the rest. I like these cigarettes rather."

"Dear Sir or Madam," said I, "what is it about our cigarettes that so appeals to your palate?"

She laughed. "I don't know anything about cigarettes, really, but these seem so fresh."

"My dear," said I," you could have said nothing more calculated to warm the cockles of my heart. You are a connoisseurs (very good indeed). These cigarettes are actually straight from the stable, I mean the Ottoman Empire. I shall send you a box this afternoon by Carter Paterson."

"You're very kind. But tell me, why is their paper brown?"

"Berry says it's swank. But then he would. As a matter of fact, it's maize. I like it myself: it's so nourishing. Besides, it goes so well with a blue suit. Talking of which, with a flowered dress and dark hair, it's absolutely it."

She stretched out a shapely hand, reflectively settling her frock. "White ones would match my gloves, though."

"They would. And the whites of your eggs-I mean eyes. I know. Oh, and your soft throat. But—"

"He said you were awful."

"You see, my dear, we live in an age of contrast. Women no longer play for safety in dress. They have begun to dare. And contrasts show imagination. Sometimes they're actually striking."

"While matches have to be struck."

"Like bargains. Exactly. They're passive, while contrasts are active. We're rather clever this morning, aren't you?"

"It's the coming of summer in my case. I was in the Row at half-past seven this morning, and the air—"

"I know. It was like hock-cup out of a stone jar, while the others are on the bank looking for a place to tie the punt up. I noticed it too. I was in the bathroom—"

"Lazy."

"Taking off my riding boots. You see, you don't give me time."

"I don't believe you."

"Hush. I feel that my tie is not straight. This must be rectified. Is there a mirror in the room? No, there is not a mirror in the room. The room is mirrorless. Very well, then. Either I must use the patent-leather of your little shoes, or perhaps you will lend me one of your large eyes. Of the two, I'd rather have the eye. There's more room."

"Sorry the line's engaged. Shah I call you?"

"If you please. My pet name is Birdie, short for Bolingbroke. Meanwhile, may I have a nail? Only one little nail?"

"You'll have a whole palm in a minute."

"Which will be quite in order. I have frequently borne the palm."

"How many biscuits have yon taken?"

"Seven, and two buns. My sister's awfully proud of them. But about this tie."

"You shouldn't wear made-up ties," she said severely.

I sat up and looked at her. Mischievously she regarded the ceiling. Presently:

"Note the awful silence," I said.

"And dickeys are going out too."

"Look here," said I, "I shall undress in a minute. Just to show you. These are matters touching the reputation."

With that I gravely untied my tie.

To my indignation she clapped her small hands with delight, and gave way to quiet laughter. I nodded solemnly.

"Very good," I said. "Now I shall simply have to have an eye. No mere nail will suffice."

"You will have nothing of the kind."

I rose and walked to the window in some dudgeon. After considerable focussing, I managed to locate the environs of my collar in a dusty pane. While the work of reconstruction was proceeding:

"Once upon a time," said I, "there was a queen. She was very beautiful from the crown of her little head, which the dark hair kept always, to the soles of her shining feet. And people loved to look at her and hear the music of her laughing. Only, it was no good going on Thursday, because that was early-closing day in her realm, and she and The Mint and The Dogs' Cemetery, and all the other places of interest were closed. You weren't allowed to see the crown jewels, which she wore in her eyes . . ."

Outside a taxi slowed down and stopped. Cautiously I peered out of the window. George.

I turned to the girl. "Here he is," I said.

As I spoke, an idea came to me. Hurriedly I glanced round the studio. Then:

"Quick," I said, pointing to a little recess, which was curtained off. "You go in there. We'll punish him."

A smile, and she whipped behind the curtain.

"Are you all right?" I whispered.

"Yes."

"Put your hand out a second. Quick, lass!" I spoke excitedly.

"What for?" she said, thrusting it between the curtains.

"Homage," said I, kissing the slight fingers.

The next moment George burst into the room. "Thank heaven," he said, as soon as he saw me.

"What d'you mean?" I said stiffly.

"I'm so thankful," he said with a sigh of relief. "I knew it was you. I was a fool to worry. But, you know, I suddenly got an idea that I'd fixed Thursday for Margery Cicester."

"That would have been awful," I said bitterly.

"Yes," said George, "it would, wouldn't it?"

I could have sworn I heard smothered laughter in the recess.

"But, George," I said, "how did you know I liked waiting?"

George laughed and clapped me on the back.

"I forgot." he said. "I'm sorry, old man. But you see—"

"One hour and ten minutes," said I, looking at my watch. George took off his coat, and began to draw a blind over the sky-light.

"I was very late last night," he said.

I gasped.

"D'you mean to say you've only just got up?" I roared.

"Oh, I've had breakfast."

I picked up my hat and turned to the door.

"Where are you going?" said George.

"There are limits," I said over my shoulder. "If it had been Miss Cicester, you would have crawled about the room, muttering abject apologies and asking her to kick you. But as it's me—"

"No, I shouldn't. I should have said that my housekeeper 'd been taken ill suddenly, or . . . "

"Go on," said I.

This was better.

"Or that the Tube had stuck, or something."

"Why not tell her the truth, and fling yourself—"

"You know what women are?"

"George, you surprise me. Would you deceive an innocent girl?"

"Women are so narrow-minded. They can't understand . . . Nice kid, though, this."

This was splendid. "You mean, Margery-er-What's-her-name?"

"Yes. She's taken rather a fancy to you-your picture, I mean."

I laughed deprecatingly. Then:

"What's she like?" I said carelessly. "To look at, I mean?"

"Like!" roared George. "What d'you mean?"

"Like," I replied coolly. "You know. Similar to."

"Well, she's like that, you fool!" said George heatedly, pointing to the picture.

"Ah, of course. Is she really?"

"Look here," said George. "If you can't—"

"Wait a bit," said I. "When was she due here? I mean to say, supposing you had fixed today for her to come?"

"Eleven o'clock. Why?"

"There now," I said musingly. "It must have been just about then."

George seized me by the arm. "Has she been and gone?" he cried.

"Well, I don't know. But about an hour ago a girl did come here. Now I come to think, she was something like the picture. I thought she was a model, and—"

George flung up his hands with a cry. I stopped and looked at him.

"Go on," he said excitedly. "What did she say?"

"Yes, I know it was about then, because a van had just gone up the street. You know. One of those big vans with—"

"Damn the van!" said George. "What did she say?"

"She didn't say anything. I tell you, I thought she was a model. I just said you didn't want one this morning."

George literally recoiled.

"What's the matter?" said I. "Aren't you well?"

"Had she a lilac dress on?" he cried, with the air of one hoping against hope.

"Er-yes," said I.

At that, George uttered a terrible cry, snatched up his coat, and before I could stop him, rushed out of the studio. I put my head out of the window. As he dashed hatless out of the front door:

"Where are you going?" I said.

He threw me a black look. Then: "To wire an apology," he said.

I turned to find my lady at my shoulder.

"He's gone to wire you an apology," I said.

"You are wicked," she said. "Poor Mr. Larel. I feel quite—"

I put my head on one side and regarded her. "Nice kid, though," I said.

"I know," she said severely. "But the poor man—"

"She's taken quite a fancy to me," said I.

She drew back, biting a red lip and trying hard not to smile.

"He'll soon be back," I went on, "and then you're going to have your show. Kindly ascend the throne. All queens do sooner or later."

"Really, I think he's had enough," she said, settling herself in the high-backed chair.

After a little argument:

"All you've got to remember," I said, "is that you're awfully sorry you're so late, and that the truth is you forgot all about the sitting, and that, by the way, when you got here, you met a man going out, and that you don't know who he was, but you suppose it was alright. Only you thought Mr. Larel ought to know."

"I've never met anyone like you before."

126

"My dear, you never will. I am unique. And remember you've taken rather a fancy—Here he is. Yes, queens always have their hands kissed. All real queens . . ."

I seized my hat, stick, and gloves, and faded behind the curtains. She was really wonderful. "Mr. Larel, will you ever forgive me? I'm most awfully sorry. D'you know I quite forgot. I suppose you'd given me up? And now it's too late. Oh, yes. I only came to apologize. I can't think—"

George couldn't get a word in edgeways. I watched him through the crack of the curtains. His face was a study. Of course, he was mentally cursing himself for sending the wire so precipitately, and wondering how the deuce he could explain its arrival without revealing the true state of affairs. Apparently in the end he decided for the moment, at any rate, to say nothing about it, for, as soon as she let him speak, he assured her it didn't matter at all, and passed, somewhat uneasily, direct to the weather.

"By the way," said Margery suddenly, "there was a man here when I came. I suppose it was all right."

George started. "You mean him?" he said, pointing to my portrait.

"That?" cried Margery. "The man you're painting? Oh, no. It wasn't him. At least," she added, leaning forward and looking carefully at the picture, "I don't think so."

"But it must have been," cried George. "He was here five minutes ago, and no other man-it must have been him."

"But the one I saw was clean-shaven," said Margery.

George pointed to my portrait with a shaking finger. "Isn't that one clean-shaven?" he wailed.

"So it is," said Margery. "For the moment, the shadow—"

"I'll never paint again!" said George fiercely. "They've hung over each other's portraits for a week—""Oh!" cried Margery. "And the first time they see one another, they don't know one another from Adam."

"Did you find the post office all right?" said I. Then I came out.

"One thing," said Margery. "Did the Tube stick?"

George stared at her. "Then you were here," he gasped.

"All the time," said I. Margery broke into long laughter.

George regarded us darkly. "You two," he said.

"One hour and ten minutes," said I. "To say nothing of asking us both on the same day."

"You two," said George.

"We two give you five minutes," I said. "Of these, three may be conveniently occupied by your full and abject apology, and two by the arranging of our next sittings. Then we two are going to lunch. It is, ah, some time since we two breakfasted."

I made a careful note of Margery's sittings-to-be, as well as of my own.

As we were going: "You know, old chap," said I, "you've never apologized."

"Miss Cicester knows that I am her humble servant."

"At any rate," said I," there'll be the telegram."

"Half-way down the stairs Margery turned and ran back to the studio. When she came back, she was smiling.

"What new mischief . . . ?" I began.

She turned to me with a maddening smile and opened her mouth. Then she changed her mind and raised her eyebrows instead.

"This isn't fair," I said. "You can't ride with the herring and run with the beagles too."

But she would not tell me. Neither would she let me give her lunch.

"But the telegram," said I desperately. "You might let me—"

"I don't suppose you have tea, but if you do happen to be in St. James's Street about a quarter to five . . . "

That afternoon she showed me the wire. It was as follows:

"Thousand apologies housekeeper's sudden illness detained me just learned my fool of servant misunderstood hasty instructions and refused

you admission another thousand apologies two thousand in all writing."
We thought it was rather good.

The next morning I glanced at the clock and pushed back my chair.

"I must be off," I murmured.

Jonah raised his eyes and then looked at Berry. The latter's eyes were already raised. He had begun to sigh.

"What's the matter with you?" said I defiantly.

"One moment," said Berry. "My flesh is creeping. Now then. How many more of these sittings?"

"Wednesdays be the last, I think."

"Which means that she's leaving Town on Thursday."

I looked at him sharply. Then:

"What d'you mean, 'She'" I said shortly.

"I have known you for—"

"Less of it," said I. "Much less."

"You know, old chap," said Daphne lazily, "you do seem suspiciously keen about this portrait business, don't you?"

I looked at her. She returned my indignant gaze with a steady smile, her chin propped on her white hands, her elbows upon the table.

"Yes, said Jonah. "Afraid of being a minute late, and all that sort of bilge."

"This is an outrage," I gasped. This was nothing but the truth. It really was, They were simply drawing a bow at a venture.

"Don't tell me-"Berry began.

"I shan't," said I.

"Naughty temper," said my brother-in-law. "Has she shell-like ears?"

"Look here," I said, "all of you."

"Must we?" said Berry. "We've only just finished a heavy meal, and—"

"I have been five times to George's studio, each time solely with the object of affording him an opportunity, if possible, of perpetuating upon canvas my gripping personality." This was the whole truth.

"Guilty upon your own confession of felony," said Jonah. "Have you anything to say why the Court—"

"With the same object I am going today." This was the truth. George was going to give me an hour before Margery came.

"Perhaps we're wronging Boy," said Jill.

"Thank you, dear," said I.

"You can't wrong outlaws," said Berry. "Never mind. Some day we shall know the ter-ruth."

"I believe you're jealous," said I. "Just because you can't find an artist sufficiently dauntless to reproduce your brutal physiognomy—"

"He means to be rude," Berry explained.

I walked to the door.

"Don't forget our lunch, old chap," said my sister.

"You've taken away my appetite," said I.

"Oh, Boy, you know we love you."

I opened the door.

"I say," said Berry.

"What?" said I, pausing.

"Tell George to put in the warts."

Six weeks had hurried away. And then, one morning, I got a note from George, saying that he had had my picture framed and was sending it along. I broke the news to the others after breakfast.

"Oh, Boy!" cried Jill excitedly.

"I want to see it awfully," said Daphne.

"Why rush upon your fate?" said her husband.

"I hope you'll like it," said I nervously.

"Where are we going to bury-I mean, hang it?" said Jonah.

"What about the potting-shed?" said Berry. "We can easily move the more sensitive bulbs."

"If it's good," said Daphne, "we'll have it in the library."

"I object," said her husband. "I don't want to be alone with it after dark."

130

I smiled upon him. Then:

"Bur-rother," said I. "I like to think that I shall be always with you. Though in reality harsh leagues may lie between us, yet from the east wall of the library, just above the type-writer, I shall smile down upon your misshapen head a peaceful, forgiving smile. What a thought! And you will look UP from your London Mail and—"

"Don't," said Berry, emitting a hollow groan. "I am unworthy. Unworthy." He covered his face with his hands. "Where is the Indian Club?" he added brokenly, "I don't mean the one in Whitehall Court. The jagged one with nails in it. I would beat my breast. Unworthy."

"Conundrum," said Jonah. "Where were the worthy worthies worthy?"

"I know," said I. "They were worthy where they were."

"Where the blaze is," said Berry.

"The right answer," said Jonah, "is Eastbourne."

Daphne turned to Jill. "Is the trick-cycle ready, dear? We're on next, you know."

Here a servant came in and announced that a picture had come for me. We poured into the hall. Yes, it had come. In the charge of two messenger-boys and a taxi, carefully shrouded in sackcloth. Berry touched the latter and nodded approval. Then he turned to the boys.

"Are there no ashes?" he said.

We bore it into the dining-room and set it upon a chair by the side of a window. I took out my knife and proceeded to cut the string.

"Wait a moment," said Jonah. "Where's the police-whistle?"

"It's all right," said Berry. "James has gone for the divisional surgeon."

I pulled off the veil. It was really a speaking likeness of Margery.

Two hours later the telephone went. I picked up the receiver. "Is that six-o-four-o-six Mayfair?"-excitedly.

Margery's voice.

"It is," said I.

"Oh, is that you?"

"It is."

"Oh, d'you know, the most awful thing has happened."

"I know," I said heavily.

"Then you have got mine?"

"Yes."

"I suppose you guessed I've got yours?"

"You don't sound very sympathetic,"-aggrievedly.

"My dear, I'm—"

"You don't know what I've been through."

This tearfully.

"Don't I?" I said wearily.

CHAPTER VIII

THE BUSY BEERS

"They never sting some people," said Daphne.

"Perhaps," said I, "perhaps that is because they never get the chance. It doesn't offer, as they say."

"Oh, yes, they do. They simply don't sting them."

"'M. During Lent, I suppose?" I murmured drowsily. A May afternoon can be pleasantly hot.

"It's a sort of power they have," said Daphne mercilessly.

I opened my eyes. "The bees? It's a very offensive power."

"No, Boy, the people. They simply swarm all over some persons, and it's all right."

I shuddered.

"Perhaps," said Berry, looking at me, "perhaps you have that power. Who knows?"

"Who will ever know?" said I defiantly.

"We can easily find out," said Berry eagerly.

I sat up. "It is," I said, "just conceivable that I have that power. I do not recollect my immersion in the Styx, but it is, I suppose, not impossible that, although I am not actually invulnerable, my sterling qualities may yet be so apparent to the bee mind that, even were I so indiscreet as to lay hands upon their hive, they would not so far forget themselves as to assail me. At the same time, it is equally on the cards that the inmates of the hive I so foolishly approached would be a dull lot-shall we say,

Baeotian bees? Or an impulsive lot, who sting first and look for qualities afterwards. In short, mistakes will occur, and, as an orphan and a useful member of society, I must refuse to gratify your curiosity."

"I think you might try," said Daphne. "We want them to swarm awfully, and they might actually swarm on you. You never know."

"Pardon me, I do know. I have no doubt that they would swarm on me. No doubt at all."

"Well, then—"

"Disobliging of me not to let them, isn't it? And we could have the funeral one day next week. What are you doing on Tuesday?"

"Well, we've got to move them from the skep into the new hive tonight somehow," said my sister, "and you've got to help."

"Oh, I'll help right enough."

"What'll you do?"

"I'll go up the road and send the traffic round by West Hanger. We don't want to be hauled up for manslaughter."

Daphne turned to Berry.

"He'd better hold the skep, I think," she said simply.

"Yes," said her husband. "Or keep the new hive steady while we shake the bees out of the skep into it. We've only got two veils, but he won't want one for that."

"Of course not," said I with a bitter laugh. "In fact, I think I'd better wear a zephyr and running shorts. I shall be able to move with more freedom."

"Ah, no," said Berry. "You must keep the trunk covered. The face and hands don't really matter, but the back and legs . . . That might be dangerous."

"Nonsense, nonsense," said I. "I'm not afraid of a bee or two. How many are there in the hive?"

"Twenty or twenty-five thousand," said Daphne. "Where are you going?"

134

"To set my house in order. Heaven forgive you, as I do. I have already forgiven Berry. I should like Jonah to have my stop-watch."

As I walked across the lawn, I heard the wretched girl reading from The Busy Bee-Keeper:

"Toads are among the bees' most deadly enemies. They will sit at the mouth of a hive and snap up bees as fast as they emerge . . .

Till then I had always been rather against toads.

I well remember the day on which I learned of the purchase of the bees. It had been raining the night before and all day the clouds hung low and threatening. Misfortune was in the air. Their actual advent I do not recollect, for when I had heard that they were to arrive on Saturday night, I had made a point of going away for the week-end.

On my return I avoided the kitchen garden assiduously for several days, but after a while I began to get used to the presence of the bees, and their old straw home-I could see it from my bedroom-looked rather pretty and comfortable.

Then Daphne, who never will leave ill alone, had announced that they must be moved into a new hive.

In vain I characterized her project as impious, wanton, and indecent in turn.

A new hive, something resembling a Swiss chalet was ordered, and with it came two pairs of gauntlets and some veils which looked like meat-safes. Oh yes, and a 'smoker'.

The 'smoker' was the real nut.

At a distance of five paces this useful invention might have been mistaken for a small cannon. As a matter of fact, it consisted of a pair of bellows, with the nozzle, which was very large, on the top instead of at the end. As touching the 'smoker' the method of procedure was as follows:-One lighted a roll of brown paper, blew It out again and placed it in the nozzle. Then, telling the gardener's boy to stand by with the salvolatile, one began to blow the bellows. Immediately the instrument belched forth clouds of singularly offensive smoke.

One might think that, if this were done in the vicinity of a hive, such a proceeding would tend to irritate the bees into a highly dangerous, if warrantable, frenzy, and that they would take immediate steps to abate the nuisance in their own simple way. But that, my brothers, is where we are wrong. Where bees are concerned, the 'smoker's' fumes are of a soporific and soothing nature. Indeed, before a puff of its smoke a bee's naughty malice and resentment disappear, and the bee itself sinks, gently humming, into the peaceful, contented slumber of a little che-ild.

At least, that was what the books said.

Seven o'clock that evening found us huddled apprehensively together outside the kitchen garden, talking nervously about the Budget. All was very quiet. A fragrant blue smoke stole up gently from the 'smoker,' which I held at arm's length. Berry and Daphne were arrayed in veils and gauntlets. They reminded me irresistibly of Tenniel's Tweedledum and Tweedledee.

"Mind you're ready with the 'smoker' when I want it," said Berry shortly.

"I-er-I thought you'd take it with you," I said uneasily.

"Nonsense," said Daphne. "We can't do everything. You must be ready to hand it to Berry if the bees get infuriated."

Thank you.

"Look here," said I, "I'm sure I shall do something wrong. You'd much better have the gardener's boy."

"And have to pay him hundreds of pounds compensation. I don't think," said Berry.

At the mention of compensation I started violently and dropped the 'smoker'. When I had picked it up:

"Look here," I said, "I'll stand on the path and keep the beastly thing smoking and if-if they should get-er—excited, well-er-there it'll be all ready for you."

"Where?" said Daphne suspiciously.

"On the path."

136

"And you?"

"I shall probably be just getting my second wind."

They looked at one another and sneered into their veils.

"It's murder," I said desperately, "sheer murder. You ask my death."

The stable clock chimed a quarter past seven.

We entered the kitchen garden in single file.

The hive was as silent as the tomb. It seemed almost wicked to—

All went well until Berry was on the point of lifting the skep. Suddenly something jumped in the wallflowers by Daphne, and she started against her husband with a little scream. It was a toad. I felt braver. We were not alone. But my pleasure was shortlived. Berry's hand had been upon the skep and the jolt had aroused the bees.

Uprose an angry murmur. I felt instinctively it was an angry one.

My brother-in-law had the 'smoker' in his hand. They told me afterwards that I had gone and given it him. That shows the state I was in. I was not responsible for my actions.

With all speed he applied the nozzle to the mouth of the skep. He was in time to stop the main body, but a few had already emerged.

I stood as if rooted to the spot.

Immediately seven bees alighted on Berry's left hand. I saw them black against the white of his gauntlet. Spellbound I watched him train the 'smoker' upon them one by one. Three rolled slowly off before as many puffs, intoxicated, doubtless, with delight and drunk with ecstasy. The fourth one he missed. The fifth moved as he was shooting and he missed again. Then he got nervous and tried to please two at once. The sixth began to buzz and four more arrived.

Berry lost his head and began to shoot wildly. One settled on Daphne's veil and she screamed. The hive began to hum again. With mistaken gallantry, Berry left the bees on his gauntlet and turned to the one on his wife's veil. The next moment she was reeling against the wall in a paroxysm of choking coughs. Some more of the twenty-five thousand began to emerge from the skep, and a moment later I was stung in the lobe of the right ear.

The pain, I may say, was acute, but it certainly broke the spell, and I turned and ran as I have never run before.

Across the garden, down the drive, out of the lodge gates, over a hedge, with eighteen inches to spare, and across country like a thoroughbred.

At last I plunged into a roadside wood almost on the top of a girl. She stared at me.

"Lie down," I gasped.

"Why?"

"Never mind why. Lie down for your life."

She lay down wonderingly beside me, as I sobbed and panted in the undergrowth.

At last, after cautioning her to keep quiet, I listened long and carefully. The result was satisfactory. My escape was complete.

I turned my attention to the girl. She was sitting up now regarding me with big eyes.

Her hair was almost hidden under a big-brimmed garden hat, but I could see her face properly. Her features were delicate and regular, and her mouth was small and red. Steady grey eyes. She was wearing a soft blue dress of linen, and her brown arms were bare to the elbow. In her hand she had a posy of wild flowers. Little shoes of blue, untanned leather, I think it is. She was slender and lithe to look at, and the flush of health glowed in her cheeks.

"I'm sorry," I said. "It all comes of beeing. If we hadn't been beeing—"

"And yet he doesn't look mad," she said musingly.

"I'm not mad," I said. "I admit that if I had on a bonnet, I should have several bees in it. Happily I lost it at the water jump. I'm a beer."

"A what?" she said, recoiling.

"A beer. At least I was one. Two other beers were with me-busy beers. Stay," I went on, "be of good beer-I mean cheer. I do not refer to the beverage of that name. By 'beer' I mean one actively interested in bees."

She looked more reassured.

"Why were you running?"

I spread out my hands.

"The beggars were at my heels."

"By which you mean—"

"That the inmates of the hive in which I was just now actively interesting myself, resented such active interest and endeavoured to fall upon me in great numbers."

"And you escaped unhurt?"

"Except that at the outset I was winged in the ear, I have baulked them of their prey. Selah!"

"I had an idea that the person of a beer was sacred."

"So it is, my dear. But these were impious bees, dead to all sense of right and wrong. They've done themselves in this time. Guilty of sacrilege and brawling, they may shortly expect a great plague of toads. It will undoubtedly come upon them. I shall curse them tomorrow morning directly after breakfast."

"Have you really been stung?"

"Every time."

"How exciting."

"Perhaps. But it's very overrated, believe me."

"Let me look."

I submitted readily. After a brief scrutiny my lady announced that she could see the sting. Her fingers dealt very gently with the injured lobe, and by dint of looking out of the far corners of my eyes, I just managed to command a prospect of one grey eye and half the red mouth. Her lips were parted and she was smiling a little.

"If I didn't love your mouth when you smile, I should be inclined to suggest that it was nothing to laugh about," I said reprovingly.

The grey eye met mine. Then she laid a small cool hand firmly on my chin and pushed it round and away.

"Otherwise I can't see properly," she explained. Then, "I believe I can dig it out," she said quietly.

I broke away at that and looked round. She was quite serious and began to unfasten a gold safety-pin.

"Look here," I said hurriedly." You're awfully kind; but, you know, as it is in, don't you think perhaps it had better stay in?

I mean, after all, a sting in the ear—"

She just waved my head round and began.

"Police," I said feebly. "Assault and wounding stalk in your midst. Police."

She really got it out very well . . .

"And so you live here?" she said, after a while.

"In the vicinity," said I. "About a mile and a half away as the crow flies or a beer runs-the terms are synonymous, you know. Large, grey, creepered residence, four reception, two bed, six bath, commands extensive views, ten minutes from workhouse, etc., etc."

"Is it 'White Ladies?'"

"It is. From which you now behold me an outcast—a wanderer upon the face of the earth. But how did you know?"

"They'll be quiet by now," she said, ignoring my question. "The bees, I mean."

"I'm not so sure."

She rose to her knees, but I laid a hand on her shoulder.

"What are you going to do, lass?"

"I shall be late for dinner."

"Your blood be upon your head. The bees certainly will."

"Nonsense."

"I have no doubt they are at this moment going about like raging lions seeking upon whom they may swarm."

"Must I pass your house?"

"To get to the village you must."

"Well I'm going, anyway."

140

I rose also. She stared at me and her glad smile settled it.

"One must die some time," said I, "and why not on a Wednesday?"

It was with no little misgiving that I stepped out into the road, and walked beside her towards the village. As we approached White Ladies, a solitary bee sang by us and startled me. My nerves were on edge. I breathed more freely when we had passed the lodge gates. All was very still. The village lay half a mile further on.

Suddenly she caught at my arm. Behind us came from a distance a faint, drowsy hum. Even as we listened, it grew louder.

The next second we were running down the straight white road, hand in hand and hell for leather.

She ran nobly, did the little girl. But all the time the hum was getting more and more distinct.

I wondered if the village would ever come. It seemed as if someone had moved it since the morning.

About the first house was the old Lamb Inn, with its large stable yard. There stood a lonely brougham, horseless with upturned shafts. The yard was deserted.

She slipped on the cobbles, as we turned in, and almost brought me down.

"Go on," she gasped. I'll—"

I picked her up and ran to the brougham. The humming was very loud. To fling open the door and push her in was the work of a moment. Then I stumbled in after her and slammed the door. As I pulled up the window, several bees dashed themselves buzzing against it.

Neither of us spoke for a minute or two. We lay back against the cushions sobbing and gasping for breath, while more bees pattered against the windows.

Presently I stole a glance at my companion. She was leaning back in her comer, still breathing hard with her eyes shut. But she seemed to know I was looking at her, for the soft lips parted in a smile. But she did not open her eyes.

I laid a hand on her arm.

"How's the ankle?" I said. "You turned it, didn't you?"

"Yes, but it's not very bad, thanks. I think you saved my life."

I'm afraid that's putting it rather high. But you might have been stung, so I'm thankful I was there. At the same time, I can't help feeling that it is to my company that you owe this-this unwarrantable assault. It's me they're after. They want to swarm on me. Or else they've recognized one of their enemies. They said, 'That's a beer, one of the beers. Let us slay him, and the intoxicants . . .' Exactly. Of course, Berry and Daphne are dead. It's really very tiresome. With Jill and Jonah both away, I don't know what on earth we shall do about tennis tomorrow."

"I wish we could have some air," said the girl.

I opened the near side window an inch and stood by to close it if necessary. But the bees kept to the other side, where they crawled venomously over the pane.

"What ever are we to do?" she said.

"Wait awhile," said I.

"Excuse me, but you don't happen to have such a thing as a toad on you, have you?"

"I hope not."

"That's a pity," I said thoughtfully.

"Sorry to disappoint you," she said. "Have you lost yours?"

"It's all right," said I. "Toads are with us. They simply hate bees. I'm going to get a pack of toads and hunt them. I shall advertise in the Exchange and Mart tomorrow. How's the ankle?"

"A little stiff."

"Let me rub it, please. It's the only thing."

"Oh, no, thanks." "Don't be ungrateful," I said. "What about my ear?"

She set a small foot on the opposite seat. I tcok off the little shoe. At length:

"I say," she said suddenly, "what about dinner?"

142

"Dinner!" I exclaimed. "Oh, dinner's gone right out. Simply not done in the best circles. Dinner indeed. My dear, you surprise me!"

"Ah, but you see I don't move in the best circles. I'm only very common and vulgar and actually get hungry sometimes. Shocking, isn't it?"

"Never mind," I said encouragingly. "You are still young. If you begin to break off this indecent habit—"

"It seems I have begun. It's a quarter to nine. You know it is awful. If you had told me yesterday that tonight I should be sitting shut up in a horseless brougham at the back of an inn, alone with a strange man massaging my foot, I should have—"

"Of course you would. But there you are, lass, you never know your luck."

She looked at me darkly.

"Needs must when the devil drives," she said.

I looked at her.

"My skin may be thick," said I, "but it's not impenetrable. But you knew that."

With a light laugh she laid a hand on my arm.

"Don't be silly, lad, but put my shoe on again."

As I fitted it on, I heard footsteps in the yard outside. Instinctively we both shrank back into the brougham. It was quite dark now. Then a stable door grated and I heard a horse move.

"Who is it?" she whispered.

"Some ostler, I expect."

"What's he going to do?"

"I forget for the moment," said I. "I ought to know, too," I added reflectively. "Wait a minute, I will consult the oracle."

So saying I made a pass or two and gazed intently into the gloom.

"Idiot," she murmured.

"Hush," I said. "Do not speak to the man at the wheel, and, above all, refrain from disconcerting the beer—I mean seer. What do I see? A man-let him pass for a man-in motion. He moves. Yes," I said excitedly, "yes, it is a stable. The man moves across the stable. Lo, he leads forth a horse. There now." I turned to her triumphantly. "The horse you fancy, madam, will also run, and the-ah-fee is one guinea. You don't fancy any horse, madam? Ah, but you will. Very soon too. Sooner, perhaps, than you—But you can't help it, madam. The crystal cannot lie. Pleasant weather we're having, aren't we? No, I'm afraid I haven't change for a note, but I could send it on, madam. On. On Monday you for instance—"

"Stop, stop," she said, laughing and putting a little hand on my wrist. "Listen. Oh, I say."

A horse was undoubtedly led out of the stable. Breathlessly we heard it come across the yard, and the next moment we felt rather than saw it put between the shafts of our brougham.

My companion uttered a stifled cry and set a hand upon the door handle.

"Sit still, lass," I whispered; "for the love of Heaven, sit still. He's going to drive us away."

"Oh, lad."

"We are in luck."

"But where are we going?"

"Heaven knows. But away from the bees, any way."

The horse was harnessed at last. The lamps were lighted-the while we cowered in the depths of the brougham, the coachman mounted heavily upon the box and we rolled slowly out of the yard.

Round to the left we swung, away from White Ladies, slowly into the village and to the left again. I kept my companion informed as to our whereabouts.

"That's right," I said, "there's the butcher's. Splendid meat he sells-I beg his pardon-purveys. Wears wonderfully well. Always follows the hounds on one of his own saddles. And there's the tobacconist. You should see the plugs he keeps. I've got one I use as a paper-weight. We used to think it was a piece of the original Atlantic cable. I've had it years now, and it's still going strong-very strong. It makes rather a good paperweight, imparts a homely soupcon of farmyard life into one's correspondence, you know. The P.M. had to give up reading my letters-said they made him feel as if he'd gone to the country. Ah, we are now within a stone's throw of the church-a noble edifice, complete with one bell. Hullo! Stand by with that ankle, lass; we're going to the doctor's. You'll like him rather. Incompetent, but genial. Shouldn't wonder if he wants to paint your foot. He is a bit of an artist in his way. When I cut my head open last year, he painted the place all over with some of his stuff. It certainly healed all right, but the way the wasps followed me-I might have been a private view. Now for it. You stand on the steps quite naturally, and I'll manage the driver."

As we drew up to the porch, I opened the door of the vehicle and handed her out. Then I closed the door very carefully and looked at the coachman. His eyes were protruding from his head, and he recoiled as I laid a hand the box.

"How much?" I said carelessly.

A choking sound came from between his lips, and the the next moment he had flung off the opposite side and was peering into the depths of the brougham. When he had felt all over the cushions, he shut the door and came and looked at me over the back of the horse.

"Well, I'm drat—"

"Not yet," I said. "Don't anticipate. How much?"

"Six months' 'ard, I should say," he replied slowly, and let down easy at that, gettin' into a private broom wiv yeller wheels an' frightenin' an honest man out of his blooming life. Look at the perspiration on my forehead."

He took off his hat, and bent his head toward the lamp, that my view might be the better.

"I had already noticed that you were rather hot," I said shortly, "but had in error attributed it to the clemency of the weather. But pray be covered. I would not have your blood also upon my soul. The air strikes cold."

"Go hon," he said with ponderous sarcasm. "Go hon. Hi am all ears."

"No, no," I said hastily, "not all. Do yourself justice, man."

"Justice," he said bitterly. "Justice. I wonder you 'ave the face to—"

"Be thankful that one of us has a face to have," I said shortly. "Among other maladies you suffer from irritation of the palm. Yes?"

He stared at me.

"Don't know about the palm in particular," he said, after a while, "but being so much with the 'orses it do tend to—"

"That'll do," I said hurriedly. "Lo, here is a crown, by the vulgar erroneously denominated a 'dollar'. Take it, and drink the lady's health before you go to bed."

He took the coins greedily, and touched his hat. Then he partially undressed, in the traditional fashion, and put them away, apparently in a wallet next to his skin.

I turned to the girl.

"We'll go in, shall we?" I said. "They'll give us some food, even if they do want to paint us. And we can ring up your people. I expect they'll be getting anxious."

"Oh, no. This morning they went up to town for the day, and they've only just about got back. And, as I was dining out, they won't expect me for another half-hour. But I think—"

"Dining out, lass? Good heavens, I'm afraid you'll have missed the soup, won't you?"

"I thought they'd given up dinner in the best circles."

"Ah, yes. Of course. But what about the auction halma?"

"That's what's worrying me. And so I was going to say if you'll be good enough to tell me where I am, I'll make my way home to where I'm staying."

Before I could reply, a voice that I recognized came through the drawing-room window.

"Ah, how do you do, Mrs. Fletcher. Sorry we've taken to up so much of your husband's time. But he's done us proud. I had fourteen. Just cast your eye-your critical eye-over this arm and take your pick. How do you like them? Penny plain, twopence coloured. Walk up. Damn. I beg your pardon. Has the ambulance arrived?"

The voice was the voice of Berry.

"The cab's here," said another voice. "I can see the horse's nose."

I suddenly realized that Jonah had got the car and was just wondering what was the matter with our own brougham, when:

"That's Daphne," said my companion. "Was it Berry who spoke first?"

I stared at her.

"Was it, lad?" she repeated.

"Yes, witch, it was. But how on earth?"

I admit I'm only your second cousin and haven't seen Daphne for eighteen months, still, after being at school in France together for two years, we ought to have some dim recollection of each other's tones."

"Why," I said, "you're cousin Madrigal, who bit me on the nose, aged four, under the nursery table. Are you sorry, now?"

"I did it in self-defence, lad."

"What was I doing?"

"You tried to kiss me."

I glanced round. The coachman had begun to undress again, and it was very dark.

"That was a long time ago," I said wistfully.

"Once bitten, twice shy," she said.

As I kissed her, the light went up in the hall.

"Put not your faith in proverbs," said I.

Dr. Fletcher opened the door.

"Hullo," said the worthy leech.

"Bring forth your dead," said I.

He laughed heartily.

"Have you come for them?"

"We have. Complete with plague-cart. Allow me introduce my cousin. Dr. Fletcher-Miss Madrigal Stukely. How are the deceased?"

"Flourishing," replied the leech. I took eleven out of your sister."

"And fourteen out of Berry-that's twenty-five. I say, there's no chance of their getting bee hydrophobia, is there? And stinging us, or anything?"

At this moment Daphne appeared, smelling like a consulting room."

"Why, Madrigal darling, so Boy brought you to fetch us back; did he? I'm so awfully sorry Berry and I weren't there for dinner. I hope Boy entertained you properly."

I gasped. Then :

"Madrigal, were you-?

Daphne was staring at me. So our brougham had been sent to fetch . . .

Madrigal laid her band on my arm.

"It's all right, Daphne dear. As I was going home to dress about half-past seven, I met Boy—"

"Hurrying?" said Daphne."

"Now I come to think of it, he was walking rather—"

"A nice brisk pace," said I.

"Be quiet," said Daphne, "or I'll sting you."

"Well," resumed Madrigal, "I met him and he explained—"

"About dinner?"

"About dinner. So we didn't either of us dress. In fact we didn't dine either; we were-er . . ."

"So anxious about you and Berry," I suggested.

My brother-in-law put his head round the door and looked at me.

"I remember," he said slowly, "I remember catching a fleeting glance-a very fleeting glance-of the anxious look upon your face as you cleared the second celery bed. At the time I thought-but never mind. I now realize that the solicitude there portrayed was on our account. Woman, I fear we judged your brother too hastily."

"I was going for assistance," I said.

"And lost your way," said Berry. He turned to his wife: "M'dear, I'm afraid he will always remain a worm. What a thought."

"Make it toads," said I. "It's safer."

CHAPTER IX

A POINT OF HONOUR

"The point is—"I began.

The girl looked up quickly.

"What?"

"This," said I. "Would you be alarmed or offended if I put my services—"

"Such as they are."

"Such as they are, thank you, at your disposal?"

"Is that an offer or a question?"

"Neither," said I. "It's a point."

She knitted her brows.

"What does one do with points?"

"One deals with them."

"M'm. Well, you can see what you can do, if you like. You mustn't be rough with the bag. It's sensitive, for all that it's made of pigskin."

"May I have the alleged key? Thank you. It is not by force, but by persuasion, that I—ahem—gain my points."

"I should think you're an only child."

"I am," I said. "That's why."

We were in a first—class compartment on the London South Western Railway, rushing away from London, down to Dorsetshire, with its heights and woodland and its grey stone walls. There had been some trouble at Waterloo, and it was only at the last moment that an 'engaged' label had been torn off our carriage window and we had been permitted to enter. The other occupant of the carriage—an aged member of the House of Lords—after regarding us with disapproval for ninety miles, had left the train at the last station. Then my lady had turned to her nice new dressing-bag and had sought to open it. In vain she had inserted a key. In vain she had attempted to insert other keys, obviously too large. Therein she had shown her feminism. I love to see a woman do a womanly thing. Finally she had sighed and pushed her dark hair back from her temples with a gesture of annoyance. The time seeming ripe, I had spoken.

Now I turned to the obstructive wards. All she had done was to double-lock it, and I had it open in a moment.

"Thank you so much."

"Not at all. I was brought up as a burglar. What a blessed thing the old earl's left us."

"I suppose it is."

"Thank you so much."

"Not at all."

"You see if I had offered my services-such as they are-in his presence, he would probably have challenged me, and stuck your glove in his hat."

She laughed.

"He looked rather like it, didn't he?"

"And, of course, according to his lights, you should still be endeavouring to pull the alarm cord."

"Instead of which—"

"You are going to put your feet up and smoke one of my cigarettes. It's not a smoking carriage so you'll be able to taste the tobacco."

"Is this another point?" she said, smiling.

"No," said I. "It's a certainty."

Her dark hair was smooth and shining and full of lights and set off her fresh complexion to perfection. This was not at all brown, but her eyes were. Great, big ones these, with a star in each of them for laughter. Her nose turned up ever so slightly, and she had a little way of tilting her

151

dainty chin, as if to keep it company. Red lips. Presently she looked at me through the smoke.

"Are you going to Whinnerley?" she said.

"Yes, please."

"To the Hall?"

"Even as you are."

"How did you know?"

"The sensitive bag had a label."

"Oh, I believe you're one of Berry and Co."

"Look here," I said, "you mustn't judge me by my company. If my relatives and connections by marriage like to make themselves infamous, that is no fault of mine. They have made their beds. Let them lie on them. I will recline upon my humble, but separate couch."

"What have they done?"

"Notorious wrong. Only last week, for instance, they mocked me."

"No?"

"They did, indeed-during the savoury. As part-owner, I craved a seat in the car. They scorned my request. Who was I? Today, they drive from Norfolk to Dorset. But for their swabhood they would have picked me up in London on the way."

"On the what?"

"I admit it would have necessitated a slight deviation, but against that you must set off the tone my presence lends—Forgive me, but there's a wasp on your left leg."

She sat up with a cry.

"Oh, take it off! Take it off!"

"Its taste—"

"Bother its taste. Take it off! Is it crawling—"

"Up? Yes. Don't move. Draw your dress tight."

Obediently, she drew her dress close about her, perhaps half an inch below a knee that Artemis might have been proud to display. I let the wasp reach the dark blue cloth. Then I seized him. As I put him out of the window, he naturally stung me. Before I had time to apologize for the expletive which escaped me, she had caught my hand.

"Which finger is it?"

"The second. South and by east of the nail."

"Here?"

"Yes."

"Shall I press the poison out?"

"You can amputate it and sear the stump if you like. Good heavens, your necklace is undone at the back."

"It isn't?"

"It is really."

"Well, do it up with your left hand. I'll attend to the sting."

It was at this interesting juncture that the door opened and a footman stood in the August afternoon sunshine, touching his cap and staring fixedly down the platform. On a station lamp was 'Whinnerley Bluff'.

How we got out of the train and into the car, neither of us ever knew. When I recovered my senses, she was sitting as far away as possible in an open landaulette, staring at my dressing-case and her bag, and moaning.

"Whatever must they think? Whatever must they think?"

"They can't think we've been married long," said I musingly. "They only do that sort of thing on the honeymoon."

She shivered.

"I wouldn't mind if they thought we were married, but they know we aren't."

"I suppose they do."

"Of course they do. Or they will."

Here some children cheered as we went by. She bowed abstractedly, and I raised my hat, as in a trance.

"What's this village?" I said.

"Oh, Whinnerley, I suppose. No, it isn't."

"Here. Where are we going?" said I.

As I spoke, we swung through lodge gates I had never seen before, while two gardeners and a smiling woman beamed delightedly upon us. We stared at them in return. It was all wrong. This wasn't the Hall, and it wasn't Whinnerley. There was some mistake. The car must have been sent to meet somebody else-somebody like us. And we—

I think we saw the streamer at the same moment. It was a large white one, slung across the curling drive from one tree to another. On it were the words: "Welcome to the Happy Pair."

As we left it behind, we turned and faced one another. It was all as clear as daylight. We were the wrong pair. The right pair had never come. We had travelled in their 'engaged' carriage. We had alighted at their station—Whinnerley Bluff-doubtless some new halt, built since my last visit. We were in their car. We had received cheers and smiles meant for them. We were being greeted by a banner for them set up. And we were on the point of arriving at the house lent to them for their honeymoon. Thank you.

Suddenly my companion's words flashed across my mind.

"I wouldn't mind if they thought we were married." I caught her arm.

"Do you see what has happened?" I said.

She nodded frightenedly.

"They think we're a married couple-married this morning."

She shivered again.

"Let them go on thinking it."

She stared at me.

"Play up," I cried. "You know what you said just now. Well, here's our chance. Only play up for an hour or two. The real ones can't arrive before seven. There isn't a train before then. We can slip away after tea. Whinnerley proper can't be far. Play up, my dear, play up. It's a chance in a lifetime."

A wonderful light came into her eyes.

"Shall we?" she whispered.

"Yes, yes. Say you will."

She looked away suddenly over the sunlit park. Then she spoke very slowly."

"I'm trusting you rather a lot, aren't I?" she said.

"Yes," I said quietly.

"But since you make such a point—"

I took her hand. As I raised it, she turned, and we looked each other full in the eyes.

Said I: "This point is a point of honour."

Then I kissed her small, gloved fingers.

A moment later the car swept out of the avenue, under an old gateway and into a fair courtyard, which I seemed to have seen before in the pages of Country Life. The house was beautiful. There it lay, in the hot sunshine, all grey and warm and peaceful-a perfect specimen of the Tudor period, and about its walls a tattered robe of wisteria. It seemed to be smiling in its sleep. As we drove up to the great stone steps, the studded door was opened and a manservant appeared. The car stopped.

"Oh, I'm afraid," whispered my companion.

"Play up," I whispered back. "It's all right."

"No, no. I'm afraid. I don't know what to say to them."

The footman opened the door, and I got out. As I handed her out, her hand was trembling terribly. Suddenly there was a scrambling noise, and a great black and white Newfoundland came bounding down the steps. When he saw us, he stopped.

"Oh, you darling." said my companion.

The dog looked at her for a moment uncertainly. Then he threw up his head and barked twice, wagging his tail. She put out her hand and stroked his head. The great fellow whined with pleasure. Then he took her hand in his mouth and turned up the steps once more.

"Oh, look!" she cried delightedly. "He's leading me in."

The situation was saved. I followed thankfully. As I entered the hall:

"He has taken to your ladyship," a gentle housekeeper was saying. "It's not many he welcomes like that."

The woman bowed to me, and turned towards the staircase. Mechanically I took the two letters from the salver the footman was holding out. Then I thought of something. I looked at the girl. She was half-way up the stairs.

"Er-darling," I said.

She swung round and stopped, flushing furiously. Then:

"Yes, dear?"

I went to where she was standing. The housekeeper was twenty paces away at the top of the stairs. I spoke as carelessly as I could, and in an undertone.

"They will want to unpack your things. Also they will soon know that there is no luggage. Ours, of course, went on to Whinnerley proper. Say your maid is coming on with it by the next train, and that she will unpack when she comes."

"All right."

I returned to the hall. Not to be outdone by the housekeeper, the footman was most solicitous. He led me to an oak-panelled lavatory, turned on the water, and held a towel ready while I washed. Then he brushed me all over, and flicked the dust from my shoes. With the slightest encouragement, I believe he would have shaved me. Then he led me to the 'reception rooms' in turn. When the tour was over, he brought me cigarettes and asked me if I would like tea served in the garden.

"By all means," I said.

"Tell her ladyship she will find me out of doors."

"Yes, sir."

I passed through the dining-room and on to a great lawn. The garden was in exquisite order. Everywhere there was a profusion of flowers, and on all sides beyond a sunk fence lay the great park. Far in a cool glade I saw some deer browsing. On the left, I could see the drive by which we had come. Lazily I traced its line curling away between the trees. Suddenly something red and moving caught my eye. For a moment the trees hid it from view. Then I saw it again-just a flash of red in the avenue-moving towards the house. I watched it curiously. It approached a small gap. The next second there appeared a telegraph boy upon a red bicycle. Thank you. Instinctively I started to head him off. I had to run to do it, but I prayed that no one was looking. We reached the gate house together.

"Telegram?" said I.

He dismounted and gave it to me like a lamb. It was addressed to Maulfry Tower, Winningly Bluff, and it read: Missed train arrive 7.10 Tagel.

"No answer," said I. Then I remembered the cheering children, and gave him a shilling. He thanked me shyly and sped away to the lodge gates. I turned to see the girl approaching, and went to meet her.

"For him, ginger beer," said I; "for us, tea. For them, when they arrive, the wagonette. They will not send the car for your maid. But, never mind, they have a good time coming. Isn't it all beautiful!"

"Of course," said she, "after this I shall go into a convent-that is, after I have served my term of imprisonment. I can never face the world again."

"Why again?" said I. "You see, my dear, we're not facing it now. If we were, it would be different. But now we're in a backwater. In an hour or two we shall be on the broad stream of Life once more. The current is very strong sometimes. But here there is no current, nor any time, nor action. Only the sun makes shining patches on the water, while now and again dragon-flies dart through the sleepy hum of insect life, like bright thoughts flashing across a reverie. Now, isn't that nice? I really don't know how I do it. But to resume. No one knew of our turning aside-no one will see us return. For us the universe is standing still. And there's the tea. Come, madam wife, sit by my side, and let the world slip; we shall ne'er be younger."

She looked at me critically, bending her brows. Then:

"I should never have married you," she said, "if I had known there was insanity in your family."

Tea was set out under the trees on the lawn, between the house and the drive. On three sides roses and honey-suckle screened the table from view. The fourth lay open to the sinking sun and the park and the distant hills. The footman had been joined by a butler, who bowed at our approach. In silence she poured out the tea. Then:

"Sugar?" she said, without thinking.

"Ahem! Not today, thanks, dear. I had mine in the champagne."

"As the footman handed me the cucumber sandwiches, his hand shook a little. I went on ruthlessly:

"Talking of which, did you notice the detectives?"

"No," she said. "What about them?"

"Wall-eyed, my dear, all of them. Cost me two-and-six extra, but I thought it was worth it. Worries the thieves awfully, you know. They can't tell whether they're watching the fish-slice or the 'Longfellow'. And all the time they're really counting the marron glaces. It's called 'getting the wall-eye.'"

I stooped to straighten my spat. When I looked up, the servants had disappeared. I glanced through the leaves to see them pass into the dining-room.

"Gone?" said the girl. I nodded.

"Thank goodness! And now, who are you? I believe one is supposed to get to know one's husband on the honeymoon."

I took one of the letters the footman had given me out of my pocket.

"I am," said I, "Sir Peter Tagel. That's why you're 'my lady'.

"Is it really? And now, your alias?"

"I'll tell you when we separate. Meanwhile, I do hope I shall make you happy. When the time comes I shall win you bread. To do this I shall, of course, have to leave your side. But that's for after. Till then-but I fear my thoughtless reference to our parting has unnerved you. You are overwrought. Lean upon me. That's what I'm for. I am your man-your husband. Where's that come from?"

"Surrey, I should think."

I frowned at my cigarette. "I don't think you're honouring me enough," I said. "Of course, it's early days yet, but-good heavens! What about the ring?"

"What about it?"

"Well, they'll see you haven't—"

I stopped, for a smile was playing about her lips as she lay back, looking into the elm-tops. Then I caught her cool, left hand. From the third finger a plain gold ring winked at me. I stared at it. Till we arrived at the house, her hands had been gloved. I balanced her hand in my palm, and looked at her.

"There is," I said, "a question."

"Yes?"

"Yes. Are you married?"

"You've been telling me I am for the last half-hour."

"Yes, but are you really?"

"Peter, dear!" This in a tone of gentle rebuke.

I ground my teeth.

"And you're going to win me bread, you know-nice brown bread."

I rose, and stood in front of her. Still the faint smile on the red mouth.

"Look at me," I commanded.

"It wasn't an 'obey' marriage, was it?" This dreamily.

"Was that ring on that finger when we were in the train?"

Slowly she got up and faced me, her eyes six inches from mine, but still looking away over my head, up at the high elms. Then she put her hands on my shoulders.

"Oh, Saint Anthony," I whispered.

The smile deepened. Then:

"I'll tell you when we separate," she said.

For one dear, short half-hour we had wandered in the park. The sunshot glades hung out an invitation it would have been churlish to refuse. And so in and out of the tall bracken, under the spreading oaks, close to the gentle-eyed deer, we had roamed for a while at will, carelessly, letting the world slip. Sir Peter and his lady taking the air.

And now we were back in the gentle garden, facing the old grey house, watching the smoke rise from a tall chimney, a slight, straight wisp against the background of blue. And-the sun was low.

I sighed. Somehow it seemed such a pity. I glanced at my companion. She looked rather wistful.

"Why is everything all wrong?" I said suddenly.

She smiled a little.

"Is it?"

"Of course it is. Haven't we got to slink away and leave all this? My dear, it's all utterly wrong. The time is out of joint-dislocated,"

"It isn't really, Peter."

I looked at her quickly. Her eyes were wide open now, and very bright.

"You're right, lass," said I. "If one goes up a backwater, I suppose one's got to come down again. Only—

"Only it's been a rather short backwater, hasn't it?"

"It has been very sunny, Peter."

A pause, then:

"It was sweet of you to say that," I said. "Thank you." But, as I spoke, I did not look at her. I dared not.

A clock chimed the three-quarters. A quarter to seven. Thank you. A moment later we were arranging our escape.

When retrieved, our impedimenta would consist of her parasol and dressing-bag, and my dressing-case. My stick and gloves were in the hall, and I decided to let them go. Her bag was in a fair bedroom-a little brass knocker upon the door-hard by the top of the staircase. She had heard them put my case in the room adjoining. Very well. She was to sit-loll,

160

if she liked-in the arbour, where tea had been served, while I ventured indoors and secured the luggage. Once across the lawn, I was to drop it over the sunk fence close to the drive. Together we could then stroll towards the lodge gates. I should leave her half-way, come by the wood to the fence, take up our chattels, and join her again somewhere on the verge of the grounds close to the lodge gates. Then we could scramble over the oak palisade into the road.

As I strolled towards the dining-room, wheels crunched on the gravel-drive. I turned to see a wagonette swinging down the avenue.

There was a writing-table in the bedroom window, and before I crept out of the room I sat down and wrote a few lines :

"To THE HOUSEKEEPER—"Lady Pan and I regret the unfortunate confusion for which a certain similarity of name and title has been responsible.

"(SIR) PETER PAN.)

Then I took a five-pound note from my case and slipped it into the envelope. I addressed the latter, and put it with the two letters and the telegram on the dressing-table.

On my way indoors and upstairs I had encountered no one. Incidentally, I should not have minded if I had. But now it was a very different matter. Mentally and physically the luggage embarrassed me. My appearance proclaimed an exodus-suggested a flight. Of course, if I did meet a servant, I should try and bluff my way out; but—There was no doubt about it this was one of the tighter places.

I lighted a cigarette. Then I put the parasol under my arm and opened the door. Not a sound. I picked up her bag and my case, and started.

I am sure there is not another edifice in England with so many creaking boards. They shrieked beneath me at every step. At the top of the stairs I put down the luggage and listened carefully. As yet there were no lights burning, and it was more than dusk in the hall below. I wiped the sweat off my forehead, and began the descent. At the bottom I ran into the footman. He was very nice about it, though I am certain the dressing-case bruised his shin. Then:

"Excuse me, sir," he said, and switched on the light.

And with the light came the brain-wave.

"I want the car at once," I said. "There's been some terrible mistake. This isn't our luggage. I don't know whose it is. The label on this bag says 'Whinnerley Hall', and that's not my dressing-case. I'm not even sure that this is her ladyship's parasol."

"Not-not yours, sir?"

"Certainly not. Beastly things." I flung them down in the hall.

"Never seen them before in my life. Order the car, man; order the car. I want to take them back to the station and find out what's become of our own."

The footman fled. When the housekeeper appeared, breathless, I was sitting on a table, swinging the parasol and smoking angrily.

"Is the car coming?" I demanded.

"Yes, indeed, sir. It'll be round in a moment. What a dreadful thing to have happened, sir. I can't understand—"

"Neither can I, except that they're both something like our things. But look at that label. This isn't Whinnerley Hall, is it?"

"No, indeed, sir."

"Well, have them put in the car. I'll go and find her ladyship. I'm afraid she'll be terribly upset."

I flung out of the house. Thirty seconds later I was explaining things to an open-mouthed girl in the arbour. As I finished, I heard the car coming round from the garage.

"Come along, dear. I glanced at my watch. "With any luck we shall just catch the seven-ten on to Whinnerley. Remember, you're terribly upset and simply frantic about your jewellery, especially the tiara Uncle George gave you. Do you think you could cry? I should have to kiss you then."

Again the faint smile. The next minute we were in the car, rushing down the avenue. There was the white banner, hanging very still now, for the faint breeze had died with the day. As we approached the lodge gates I leaned forward and looked across her-she was on my right-looked away over the park to where the sun had set. The sky was flaming.

"Sic transit," said I.

"Goodbye, backwater," said she.

Her voice was not unsteady, but there was that in her tone that made me look at her. Her lashes were wet.

As the car swung out of the gates, our hands touched. I took hers in mine and held it. Then I started. It was the left hand, but there was no ring upon its fingers. I tightened my hold. So we sat for two minutes or more. Then:

"Do you think they would see?" I said, glancing at the chauffeur and groom.

"I'm afraid they might. But—"

"But what, darling?"

"It wouldn't matter very much if they did, would it?"

We reached the station simultaneously with the seven ten. As the groom opened the door—

"Come along, dear." I handed her out. Turning to the servant, "Bring the bag and the dressing-case," I added. "Quick!"

"Yes, sir."

A small boy waved an implement and uttered a feeble protest about tickets, but we thrust past him on to the platform. There I looked round wildly.

"Where's Delphine?" I cried.

"I don't believe she's come," wailed my companion.

I turned to the groom.

"You'd better go back," I said. "Put those things down and go back to the car, in case we miss her ladyship's maid. Don't let her go off in the wagonette."

"Very good, sir."

He put the luggage on a seat and ran back to the exit. Exactly opposite to where we were standing was a first-class carriage. As the guard's whistle was blown:

"Have you got my bag, Peter?" said a plaintive voice.

"Yes, m'dear," and Sir Peter and Lady Tagel passed down the platform. We watched them greedily.

The train began to move.

"The last lap," said Berry. "Courage, my travel-stained comrades. Where was it we broke down? Oh, yes, Scrota Gruff. Such a sweet name, so full of promise, so—"

Then he took his head in and pulled up the window.

"Fancy you two being in the next carriage all the time," said Daphne. "I expect Boy's introduced himself, Julia dear. Yes, I thought so. Still for what it's worth, my brother-Lady Julia Lory."

Which is why she's 'my lady'. Though she always says it isn't.

CHAPTER X

PRIDE GOETH BEFORE

"Who is Silvia? What is she?
That all her swains commend he.
Holy, fair, and wise is she;
The heaven such grace did lend her,
That she might admired be."

The song and its melody floated out into the night, away and over the sleeping countryside. In no way breaking the silence; rising up out of it, rather. It was as if Nature dreamed as she lay sleeping, a dream clear-cut, melodious. Over all the moon hung full, turning the world to silver. Never had music so fairy a setting.

"Then to Sylvia let us sing,
That Silvia is excelling,
She excels each mortal thing
Upon the dull earth dwelling
To her let us garlands bring"

Half-past eleven o'clock of a fine moonlit night, and I was alone with the car all among the Carinthian Alps. It was for Fladstadt that I was making. That was the Bairlings' nearest town. Their place, St. Martin, lay twenty odd miles from Fladstadt. But in the town people would show me the way. At St. Martin I should find Daphne and the others, newly come from Vienna this afternoon. Friends of Jonah's, the Bairlings. None of us others knew them.

At ten o'clock in the morning I had slid out of Trieste, reckoning to reach Fladstadt in twelve hours. And, till I lost my way, I had come well. I had lost it at half-past nine and only discovered that I had lost it an hour later. It was too late to turn back then. I tried to get on and across by by-roads-always a dangerous game. Just when I was getting desperate I had chanced on a signpost pointing to the town I sought. The next moment one of the tires had gone.

The puncture I did not mind, The car had detachable wheels, and one was all ready, waiting to be used. But when I found that I had no jack . . . Better men than I would have sworn. The imperturbable Jonah would have stamped about the road. As for Berry, with no one there to suffer his satire, suppressed enmity would have brought about a collapse. He would probably have lost his memory.

There was nothing for it, but to drive slowly forward on the flat tire. When I came to a village I could rouse an innkeeper, and if the place did not boast a jack, at least sturdy peasants should raise the car with a stout pole. Accordingly, I had gone on.

For the first five miles I had not lighted on so much as a barn. Then suddenly I had swung round a bend of the road to see a great white mansion right ahead of me. The house stood solitary by the roadside, dark woods rising steep behind. No light came from its windows. Turreted, white-walled, dark-roofed in the moonlight, it might have been the outpost of some fairy town. The building stood upon the left-hand side of the way, and, as I drew slowly alongside, wondering if I dared knock upon its gates for assistance, I found that house and road curled to the left together. Round the bend I had crept, close to the white facade. As I turned, I saw a light above me, shining out over a low balcony of stone. I had stopped the car and the engine, and stepped on tiptoe to the other side of the road. From there I could see the ceiling of a tall, first-floor room, whose wide, open windows led on to the balcony. I saw no figure, no shadow. For a minute or two I had heard no sound. Then, with no warning, had come an exquisite touching of keys and a girl's voice.

"To her let us garlands bring."

The melody faded and ceased. The refrain melted into the silence. For a moment I stood still, my eyes on the balcony above. Then I slipped noiselessly to the car, picked up a rug from the back seat and laid it, folded small, on the edge of the car's back. Half on the padded leather and half on the cape hood, strapped tight, I laid it. Standing upon this perilous perch, I was just able to lay my fingers upon the cold edge of the balcony's floor. With an effort I could grasp one of the stone balusters. An idea occurred to me, and I got carefully down. One of the luggage-carrier's straps was six feet long. I had it loose in a moment. A minute later and I had wheedled it round the baluster I could clutch. Buckled, it made a loop three feet in length that would have supported a bullock. I was about to soar, when I remembered the car. I jumped down once more, turned the key of the switch, and slipped it into my pocket. No one could steal her now. The next second I had my foot in the thong.

I sat on the coping, looking into the room. Broad and lofty it was, its walls hung with a fair blue paper. A handsome tapestry, looped up a little on one side, masked the tall double doors, and in the far corner stood a great tiled stove for burning wood. From the ceiling was hanging a basin of alabaster-an electric fitting, really. The powerful light of its hidden lamps spread, softened, all about the chamber. The blue walls bore a few reproductions of famous pictures. Meisonnier seemed in high favour, while Sir Joshua's Nellie O'Brien surveyed the salon with her quiet, steady gaze. A great bowl of fresh flowers stood on the grand piano.

The girl herself was sitting half on the edge of an old gate-table in the middle of the room. The toe of one rosy slipper touched the polished boards, and her other foot swung gently to and fro. One of her short sleeves she had pushed up to the shoulder and was looking critically at a scratch, which showed red, high up on her round, white arm. A simple evening frock of old-rose colour, dainty old gold slippers to keep her feet. Her skin was wonderfully white, her hair dark and brown. This was cut straight across her forehead in French fashion, and then brought down and away over the ears. Her face was towards me, as she examined her arm. I could see she was very pretty.

"Don't you think you ought to apologize?" she said suddenly.

Her words took me by surprise. For a moment I did not answer.

"Eh?" she said, looking up.

"Yes," I said, "I do. Fact is, I haven't any, and the gardens are all shut now."

"Any what? "she said, letting the sleeve slip back into its place.

"Garlands, Silvia."

She smiled for an instant. Then:

"How dare you come up like this?"

"I wanted to see what Silvia was like."

She stifled a little yawn.

"You heard me say she was holy, fair and wise."

"And excelling, I know. But the second verse asks,

"Is she kind as she is fair?"

"Well?"

"I came up to see if she was."

"And is she?"

"I don't think she is quite."

"Can you get down all right?"

"In fact, I'm sure she isn't," I said. "But then—"

"What?"

"She'd have to be most awfully kind to be that, Silvia. Goodbye."

"I say," said Silvia.

"Yes? I said, with one leg over the balustrade.

"As you're here, if you would like to come in and sit down for a little-I mean, I don't want to seem inhospitable."

"I knew it," said I. "I knew she was, really."

168

"Goodbye, Silvia. Thank you very, very much all the same. I've found out what I wanted to know."

I slipped over the coping and set my foot in the thong. There was a rustle of silk and a quick step on the balcony. Then two soft hands took hold of my wrists. I looked up at the big eyes, the face white in the moonlight, the dark, straight-cut hair.

"Wait!" she said. "Who are you and where do you come from?"

"My name's Valentine," said I. "I am a gentleman of Verona."

The small mouth twitched. "Be serious," she said. I told her my name and spoke of my run from Trieste, adding that I sought Fladstadt and St. Martin. She heard me in silence. Then:

"Are you tired?" she said quietly.

"A little."

"Then I tell you that you may come in and rest for a while. Yes, and talk to me. Presently you can go on. I will show you the way."

She let go my wrists and stood up, clasping her hands behind her head.

"You're very hospit—"

"It isn't a question of hospitality or anything else," she said slowly. "I just tell you that you may come in if you want to."

I gazed at the slim, straight figure, the bare bent arms, the soft white throat. Then I drew myself up and bestrode the coping.

"Of course," I said, "this is a dream. In reality I am fast asleep in the car. Possibly I have met with an accident and am still unconscious. Yet your hands felt warm . . ."

"And your wrists very cold, sir. Come along in and sit down. Even if you are dreaming I suppose you'll be able to drink some coffee if I give it you."

"If you give it me."

I drew up the thong and followed her into the room. She motioned me to sit in a deep chair and put cigarettes by my side. Then she lighted the lamps that were set beneath two little silver coffee-pots, standing on

169

a tray on the gate-table. I watched her in silence. When the lamps were burning, she turned and seated herself on the table as I had seen her first. She regarded me curiously, swinging that little right leg.

"I shouldn't have liked you to think me unkind," she said, with a grave smile.

I rose to my feet.

"Silvia," I said.

"Sir?"

"I do not know what to say. Yet I want to say something. I think you are very gentle, Silvia. If I were old, I think the sight of you would make me feel young again, and if Shakespeare had known you, I think he would have written more sonnets and fewer plays."

Silvia spread out deprecating white arms and bowed low.

"I doubt it," she said. "But I know he would have given me a cigarette."

"I beg your pardon," said I, handing her the box.

When I had given her a light, she turned again to the coffee.

"It ought to be hot enough now, I think. D'you mind using my cup? I don't take sugar."

"It will be a privilege, Silvia."

"Milk?"

"Please."

The hot cafe-au-lait was very grateful. Despite the season, my long drive through the mountain air had left me a little cold. I took my seat on an arm of the deep chair. Outside, somewhere close at hand, a clock struck twelve.

"The witching hour," said I. "How is it you're not in bed and asleep, Silvia?"

"Sleep! What with the noise of passing cars?"

"I forgot," said I. "The continuous roar of the traffic here must be very trying. The congestion between here and Villach is a disgrace. I met three carts in the last forty odd miles myself. Can't something be done about it?"

"-And the curiosity of cold-wristed burglars-By the way, I can't get over your climbing up like that, you know. It's all right, as it happens, and I'm rather glad you did, but this might have been a bedroom or-or anything."

"Or a bathroom. Of course it might. But then, you see, you very seldom find a piano in the bathroom nowadays, Silvia. Incidentally, what a sweet room this is."

"Do you like my pictures?"

"Awfully. Especially the one on the gate-table."

My lady blew smoke out of a faint smile. Then:

"If it comes to that, there's rather a good one on the arm of your chair," she said.

"Yes. By the same artist,too. But the one on the table knocks it. That'll be hung on the line year after year."

"What line?"

"At the Academy of Hearts. I beg your pardon, my dear. It slipped out."

Silvia threw back her dainty head and laughed merrily. Presently:

"But the one on the table's damaged," she said. "Didn't you see the scratch?"

"And the one on the chair wants cleaning badly. In its present state they wouldn't hang it anywhere except at Pentonville. But the scratch. How did you get it?"

"Ah! That was the Marquis. We were by the window, and when you slipped that strap round, he jumped like anything. He was in my arms, you see."

I'm awfully sorry; but do you often embrace nobles, and how do you say goodbye to dukes? I mean to say, I haven't got my patent with me, and my coronet's in the store-I mean, strong room; but anyone who doesn't know me will tell you-Besides, I never scratch."

"The Marquis is a Blue Persian."

"These foreign titles," I murmured scornfully.

"Don't be patronizing," said Silvia. "You know where Pride goes. Besides, I've met some very nice counts."

I leaned forward. "I know. So've I. Barons, too. The last I struck's doing seven years now. But you're English, Silvia. English, d'you hear? I'll bet they're all over you out here. I know them. I'm a fool, but I don't like to think of your-I mean, I'd rather be an English-er—"

"Burglar?"

We both laughed, and I got up. "Silvia," I said, "tell me the best way to Fladstadt and turn me out while there is yet time."

"What do you mean?"

"This. I've already been in love with you for a quarter of an hour. In another ten minutes I shall be sitting at your feet. Half an hour later—"

"You will be just running into Fladstadt. It's straight on. You can't miss the way."

"And St. Martin? Have you ever heard of it?"

She puckered her brows.

"Isn't that where some English people have a place? People called-er-Waring, is it?"

"Bairling," said I.

"Bairling. That's it. Let's see. I'm afraid it's some miles from Fladstadt."

"Twenty, I'm told."

"About that."

"And this is how far?"

"From Fladstadt? About twenty-three."

I groaned. "Forty-three miles to go, and a flat tire," I said.

"Now far's the next village?"

"Why?"

"I want to get another wheel on."

"If you like to wait here a little longer, my brother'll be back with the car. He's on the way from Fladstadt now. That's why I'm sitting up. He'll give you a jack."

"You're awfully good, Silvia. But have you forgotten what I said?"

"About sitting at my feet? No, but I don't think you meant it. If I did, I should have rung long ago."

"Thank you," said I.

"Of course," she went on; "you're only a burglar, but you are-English."

"Yes, Silvia. I mightn't have been, though."

"You mean, I didn't know whether you were English or not, till after you'd climbed up? Nor I did. But one of the men's up, and there's a bell-push under the flap of the table."

She slipped a hand behind her. "I'm touching it now," she added.

"I wondered why you didn't sit in a chair," I said, with a slow smile. A deep flush stole over the girl's features. For a moment she looked at me with no laughter in her eyes. Then she slipped off the table and moved across the room to an open bureau. She seemed to look for something. Then she strolled back to the table and took her seat on its edge once more.

"Is that a car coming? she said suddenly, her dark eyes on the floor.

I listened. "I don't think so," I said, and stepped out on to the balcony.

There was no sound at all. It was the dead of night indeed. I glanced over the balustrade at the car. Her headlights burned steadily, making the moonlit road ahead more bright.

"I can hear nothing," I said, coming back into the boudoir.

"Look," said Silvia, pointing over my shoulder.

As I turned, something struck me on the cheek. I stooped and picked it up. A piece of flexible cord about five inches long. I swung round and looked at the girl. On the table a pair of scissors lay by her side.

"Why have you done this?" I demanded.

She raised her eyebrows by way of answer and reached for a cigarette. As she lighted it, I saw that her hand was trembling.

"Silvia, dear, surely you don't think—"

"Must you go?"

"It was a poor joke of mine, I know; but—"

"It was. I don't think a count or a baron would have said such a rotten thing."

Her eyes flashed and she was trembling all over. From being pretty, she had become beautiful.

"Perhaps not," said I steadily. "But if they had, they would have meant it, Silvia."

"As you did."

I coiled the flexible cord about a finger, loosed it and thrust it into my pocket.

"I'll go now," I said, "as I came."

"Like a thief."

"Like a thief. You have been wonderfully kind, and I-I have spoiled everything. Let's try and forget this evening. For you, a car passed in the night, the hum of its engine swelling up, only to fade again into the silence. For me, I lingered to listen to the words of a song, and when it was done, sped on into the shadows. I wish you hadn't cut that bell, lass."

"Why?"

I walked out on to the balcony and swung myself over the coping.

"Because then I should have asked if I might kiss you."

When I had lowered myself on to the seat of the car, I unbuckled the strap and started to pull it down. But the buckle caught on the baluster, and I had to stand on my old perch to reach and loosen it. I did so, balancing myself with one hand on the balcony's door. As the strap slipped free, there was a burning pain in my fingers. With a cry I tore them away, lost my balance, and fell sideways into the car on to the back of the front seat. I stood up unsteadily. It hurt me to breathe rather, and there was a stabbing pain in my right side.

"Are you hurt?" said a quick voice above me. Dazedly I raised my head. Silvia was leaning over the balcony, one hand to her white throat. I could hear her quick-coming breath.

"No," I said slowly, "I'm not. But until you tell me that you know I did not mean what I said, I will not believe that you did not mean to stand upon my fingers."

"Are you hurt, lad?"

"No. Did you hear what I said?"

Silvia stood up, her hands before her on the coping.

"You know I didn't."

Without a word I stepped carefully out of the car. The pain was intense. It was as if my side was being seared with a hot iron. How I started the car I shall never know. The effort brought me to my knees. Somehow I crept into my seat, took out the clutch and put in the first speed. I was moving. Mechanically I changed into second, third, and top. We were going now, but the trees by the wayside seemed to be closing in on me. The road was really ridiculously narrow. I could see a corner coming. The pain was awful. My head began to swim, and I felt the near wheel rise on the bank. I wrenched the car round, took out the clutch and dragged the lever into neutral. As I jammed on the hand-brake, I seemed to see many lights. Then came the noise of a horn, cries, and the sound of tires tearing at the road. I fell forward and fainted.

I could smell Daphne. Somewhere at hand was my sister's faint perfume: I opened my eyes.

"Hullo, Boy! said Jill, her small, cool hand on my forehead.

"Better, darling?" said Daphne, brushing my cheek with soft lips.

"I'm all right," I said, raising myself on my left elbow. Still the stabbing pain in my right side. "Where are we?"

"In the hall at St. Martin, dear. How did it all happen?"

"How did I get here?" I asked. "And you-I don't understand."

"We nearly ran you down, old chap. Berry's voice. "About a quarter of a mile from here, towards Fladstadt. But why were you driving away?"

I stared at him. "Driving away?" I said slowly. "Then—"

There were quick steps and the rustling of a dress.

Then Silvia spoke. "What is it, Bi11? Tell me. Who's hurt?"

"It's all right, m'dear," said the man's voice. "Mrs. Pleydell's brother's met with an accident. We found him in the road. Don't make a noise. This is my sister, Mrs. Pleydell."

"How d'you do?" said Daphne. "My brother seems—"

"I'm all right," I said suddenly. "I'd lost my way, see? And one of the tires went, just as I was passing a big white house on the left. I stopped under a balcony, I think."

"That's right," said Bill Bairling. "Balcony of Silvia's room."

"I never knew it was St. Martin, though. I must have cut across country somehow. Still. Well, there was no jack on the car so I couldn't do anything. Just as I was getting in again, I heard a noise above me and turned. My foot slipped on the step, and I fell on my side. Couple of ribs gone, I think. I tried to get on to Fladstadt. Is the car all right?"

"And you said you weren't hurt," cried Silvia, sinking on her knees by Jill.

"Was it you who asked me?" I spoke steadily, looking her full in the eyes.

Yes," said Silvia.

"I know I did. But then, you know, I don't always mean what I say. Then the pain surged up once more, and I fainted.

"Is she kind as she is fair?
For beauty lives with kindness.
Love doth to her eyes repair
To help him of his blindness,
And, being helped, inhabits there."

176

The singing was very gentle. Overnight the song had floated into the air, rich, full, vibrant; but now a tender note had crept into the rendering, giving the melody a rare sweetness. I listened pleasedly. My side was very sore and stiff. Also my head ached rather.

"Priceless voice that little girl's got." said Berry in a low voice.

"Isn't she a dear, too?" said Daphne "Fancy giving up her own bedroom, so that we could have the salon next door."

"I know. But I wish she wouldn't keep on reproaching herself so. If a girl likes to step on to her own balcony, it's not her fault if some fellow underneath falls over himself and breaks a couple of ribs. However. When's the comic leech coming back?"

"This afternoon," said my sister. "But he'll wake before then. I don't expect he'll remember much about last night. I'm so thankful it's not more serious."

How soon did he say he'd be up?"

"Inside a week. It's a clean fracture. Of course, he'll be strapped up for some time. Fancy his going on, though."

"Must have been temporarily deranged," said my brother-in-law airily. "Shock of the fall, I expect."

"Rubbish!" said his wife. Just because you'd have lain there, giving directions about your funeral and saying you forgave people, you think anybody's mad for trying to get on. Boy has courage."

"Only that of his convictions," said Berry. "You forget I've got a clean sheet. My discharge from the Navy was marked 'Amazing'. The only stain upon my character is my marriage. As for my escutcheon, I've shaved in it for years."

"Fool!" said his wife.

"I shall turn my face to the wall if you're not careful."

"Don't," said Daphne. "Remember, it's not our house.

"There was a tap at the door. Then:

"May I come in?" said Silvia.

"Of course you may, dear. No. He's still asleep."

"It's nearly twelve," said Silvia. "Won't you go and rest a little, and let me stay here? You must be so tired. I'll call you the moment he wakes.

Daphne hesitated. "It's awfully good of you—"

"But it isn't. I'd love to."

"The truth is, she's afraid to trust you, Miss Bairling," said Berry. "She thinks you're going to steal his sock-suspenders."

"Will you leave the room?" said my sister.

"After you, beloved."

I could hear Silvia's gentle laughter. Then:

"I shall come back about one, dear, if you don't send for me before," said Daphne.

The next moment I heard the door close, and Silvia seated herself on my left by the side of the bed. I opened my off eye. I lay in a fair, grey-papered chamber, darkened, for the green shutters were drawn close about the open windows. Some of their slides were ajar, letting the bright sunshine slant into the room.

"There was once," I said, "a fool." A smothered exclamation close to my left ear. "A fool, who did everything wrong. He lost his way, his heart, his head, and, last of all, his b~balance. In that order. Yet he was proud. But then he was only a fool."

"But he was-English," she murmured.

"Yes," I said.

"And there was another fool," said Silvia. "A much bigger one, really, because, although she never lost her way or her head or her balance, she lost something much more precious. She lost her temper."

"But not her voice," said I. "And the fools went together to Scotland Yard, and there they found the way and the head and the balance and the temper. But not the heart, Silvia."

"Plural," said Silvia, softly. I opened my near eye and turned my head. The first thing I saw was a rosy arm, lying on the edge of my pillow. Within reach.

"I say," I whispered. "Is the bell in this room all right?"

178

CHAPTER XI

THE LOVE SCENE

When I had drawn blood for the third time, I felt that honour was satisfied, so I cleaned the safety razor carefully and put it away.

Quarter of an hour later I entered the dining-room.

"I said so," said Daphne.

"I know," said I, frowning.

"You don't even know what I said."

"I know that some surmise of yours has proved correct, which is enough."

The coffee really was hot. After drinking a little, my smile returned.

"Tell him," said Berry.

"We've been thinking it over," said Daphne, "and we've come to the conclusion that you'd better call."

"On whom? For what?"

"Be call-boy."

I rose to my feet.

"Ladies and gentlemen," I said, "I have to thank you this day-it is meant for a day, isn't it I-for the honour you have done me. Although I can scarcely hope to sustain the role in a manner worthy of the best traditions of—"

"We'd cast you for something else, if it was safe," said Daphne.

"You don't really think I'm going to call, do you?"

"Why not?"

"And have to stand in the wings while you all get crowds of cabbages and things. Not much! I've been relying on this show ever since Berry trod on the big marrow."

"Well, of course, there is Buckingham," said Berry.

"Or the soothsayer," said Jill.

"You are now talking," I said. "Soothsaying is one of my fortes-my Martello tower, in fact. Of course, Hurlingham—"

"Buckingham, stupid!"

"Well, Buckingham, then, has his points. Whom does he espouse?"

"He doesn't espouse anyone."

"Whom does he love, then?"

Berry and Daphne looked uneasily at one another. I turned to Jonah, who was deep in The Sportsman.

"Who's Buckingham in love with, Jonah"

"Down and four to play. What?" said that worthy.

"Oh, Buckingham? He's hanging round the Queen mostly, I think, but he's got two or three other irons in the fire."

"I will play Hurl-Buckingham," said I.

When Berry had finished, I reminded him that he had suggested the part, and that my mind was made up.

After a lengthy argument, in the course of which Berry drew a stage on the table-cloth to show why it was I couldn't act;

"Oh, well, I suppose he'd better play it," said Daphne: "but I scent trouble."

"That's right," I said. "Let me have a copy of the play."

Berry rose and walked towards the door. With his fingers on the handle, he turned.

"If you don't know what some of the hard words mean," he said, "I shall be in the library."

"Why in the library?" said Daphne.

"I'm going to write in another scene."

"Another scene?"

180

"Well, an epilogue, then."

"What's it going to be?"

"Buckingham's murder," said Berry. "I can see it all. It will be hideously realistic. All women and children will have to leave the theatre."

As he went out:

"I expect the Duke will fight desperately," said I.

Berry put his head round the door.

"No," he said, "that's the dastardly part of it. It is from behind that his brains are dashed out with a club."

I stretched out my hand for a roll.

"Do you know how a log falls?" said Berry. "Because, if—"

I could not get Daphne to see that, if Berry had not withdrawn his head, the roll would not have hit the Sargent. However.

The good works of which Daphne is sometimes full occasionally overflow and deluge those in her immediate vicinity. Very well, then. A local institution, whose particular function has for the moment escaped me, suddenly required funds. Perhaps I should say that it was suddenly noised abroad that this was the case, for it was one of the kind that is always in this uncomfortable plight. If one day someone were to present it with a million pounds and four billiard tables, next week we should be asked to subscribe to a fund to buy it a bagatelle board. At any rate, in a burst of generosity, Daphne had undertaken that we would get up a show. When she told us of her involving promise, we were appalled.

"A show?" gasped Jonah.

"Yes," said Berry. "You know, a show-, display. We are to exhibit us to a horrified assembly."

"But, Daphne darling," said Jill. "What have you done?"

"It's all right," said my sister. "We can do a play. A little one, you know, and the Merrows will help."

"Of course," said Berry. "Some telling trifle or other. Can't we dramatize 'The Inchcape Rock'?"

"Excellent," said I. "I should like to play the abbot. It would be rather suitable, too. If you remember, 'they blest the Abbot of Aberbrothok.'"

"Why not?" said Berry. "We could have a very fervent little scene with them all blessing you."

"And perhaps Heath Robinson would paint the scenery.

And so on.

In the end, Berry and Jonah had constructed quite a passable little drama, by dint of drawing largely on Dumas in the first place, and their own imagination in the second. There were one or two strong situations, relieved by some quite creditable light comedy, and all the 'curtains' were good. The village hall, complete with alleged stage, was engaged, and half the county were blackmailed into taking tickets. There were only twelve characters, of which we accounted for five, and it was arranged that we should all twelve foregather four days beforehand, to rehearse properly. The other seven artists were to stay with us at White Ladies for the rehearsals and performance, and generally till the affair had blown over.

It was ten days before the date of the production that I was cast for Buckingham. Six days to become word perfect. When three of them had gone, I explained to the others that, for all their jealousy, they would find that I should succeed in getting into the skin of the part, and that, as it was impossible to polish my study of George Villiers in the teeth of interference which refused to respect the privacy even of my own bedroom, I should go apart with Pomfret, and perfect my rendering in the shelter of the countryside.

"Have pity upon our animal life!" cried Berry, when I made known my intention. "Consider the flora and fauna of our happy shire!"

"Hush, brother," said I. "You know not what you say. I shall not seek the fields. Rather—"

"That's something. We don't want you hauled up for sheep-worrying just now."

"-shall I repair to some sequestered grove. There, when I shall commune with myself, Nature will go astray. Springtime will come again. Trees will break forth into blossom, meadows will blow anew, and the voice of the turtle—"

"If you don't ring off," said Berry. "I'll set George at you."

George is our gorgonzola, which brings me back to Pomfret. Pomfret is a little two-seater. I got him because I thought he'd be so useful just to run to and fro when the car was out. And he is. We made friends at Olympia, and I took to him at once. A fortnight later, Jill was driving him delightedly round and round in front of the house. After watching her for a while, Berry got in and sat down by her side.

"Not that I want a drive," he explained carefully; but I want to see if my dressing-case will be able to stand it as far as the station."

"If you think" I began, but the next moment Jill had turned down the drive, and I watched the three go curling out of sight.

When they returned, half an hour later, Berry unreservedly withdrew his remark about the dressing-case, and the next day, when Daphne suggested that Pomfret should bear a small basket of grapes to the vicarage, he told her she ought to be ashamed of herself.

From that day Pomfret was one of us.

And now, with three days left to learn my words, and a copy of the play in my pocket, I drove forth into the countryside. When I had idly covered about twenty miles, I turned down a little lane and pulled up by the side of a still wood. I stopped the engine and listened. Not a sound. I left the road and strolled in among the trees till I came to where one lay felled, making a little space. It was a sunshiny morning in October, and summer was dying hard. For the most part, the soft colourings of autumn were absent, and, as if loyal to their old mistress, the woods yet wore the dear green livery, faded a little, perhaps, but the more grateful because it should so soon be laid aside. The pleasant place suited my purpose well, and for twenty minutes I wrestled with the powerful little scene Jonah had written between the Queen and Buckingham. By the end of that time I knew it fairly well, so I left it for a while and stealthily entered the old oak chamber-Act III, Scene I-by the secret door behind the arras. After bringing down the curtain with two ugly looks, four steps, and a sneer, I sat down on the fallen beech-tree, lighted a cigarette, and wondered why I had rejected the post of call-boy. Then I started on the love-scene again.

"'Madam, it is said that I am a harsh man. I am not harsh to every one. Better for me, perhaps, if I were; yet so God made me.'"

"When do you open?"

"That's wrong, said I." 'Can you be gentle, then?' comes after that. Now, however, that you have shattered the atmosphere I had created-of course, I think you're absolutely beautiful, and, if you'll wait a second, I'll get Pomfret's rug."

"I don't know what you mean, but thanks all the same, and if Pomfret doesn't mind, this tree is rather grubby."

I got the rug and spread it on the fallen trunk for her. She was what the Irish are popularly believed to call 'a shlip of a ghirl,' clad in a dark blue riding-habit that fitted her slim figure beautifully. No hat covered her thick, blue-black hair, which was parted in the middle and loosely knotted behind. Here and there a wisp of it was in the act of escaping. I watched them greedily. Merry grey eyes and the softest colouring, with a small red mouth, ready to join the eyes in their laughter if its owner listed. She was wearing natty little patent-leather boots, and her hunting hat and crop lay on the log by her side. She sat down and began to pull the gloves off a pair of small brown hands.

"Do you know if cats ever drink water?" she said musingly.

"From what I remember of last year's statistics, there was, I believe, a marked decrease in the number of alcoholism cases reported as occurring amongst that species. I'm speaking off-hand, you know."

"Never mind that: it's very good hearing."

"I know, and, talking of tight-ropes, Alice, have you seen the March Hare lately?"

184

She threw her head back and laughed merrily. Then—

"We are fools, you know," she said.

"Perhaps. Still, a little folly—"

"Is a dangerous thing. And, now, when do you open?"

"Tomorrow week. And, owing to the iniquitous provisions of the new Shops Act, foisted by a reckless Government upon a—"

"You can cut that bit."

"Thank you. We close the same night."

"Positively for one performance only?"

"Exactly. And that's why I shall only just be able to get you a seat."

"You needn't trouble."

"What! Don't you want to come?"

"Is it going to be very good?"

"Good? My dear Alice, we shall that night light such a candle as shall never be put out. Electric light is doomed. The knell of acetylene gas has sounded."

"You've only got a few lines, I suppose?"

I looked at her sorrowfully.

"Whose rug is she sitting on?" I said.

"Pomfret's."

"Pomfret is but the bailee of the rug, Alice."

"Oh," she cried, "he's going to be a barrister!"

"Talking of cats," I said stiffly, "and speaking as counsel of five years' standing—"

I stopped, for she was on her feet now, facing me, and standing very close, with her hands behind her and a tilted chin, looking into my eyes.

"Talking of what, did you say?"

For a second I hesitated. Then:

"Gnats," I said.

She turned and resumed her place on the fallen tree. "Now you're going on with your rehearsal," she announced. "I'll hear you."

"Will you read the cues?"

"Give me the book."

I showed her the point I had reached when she entered.

"You are the Queen," I said. "It's rather confusing, because I had thought you were Alice; but it can't be helped. Besides, you came on just before you did, really, and you've spoken twice before you opened your small red mouth."

"Is that how it describes the Queen?" This suspiciously.

"I was really thinking of Alice, but—"

"But what?"

"The Queen has got a delicate, white throat. It says so."

"How can you tell? I've got a stock on."

"I said the Queen had. Besides, when you put your face up to mine just now—"

"Hush! Besides, you were looking me in the eyes all the time, so—"

"And, if I was, do you blame me?"

"I'm not in the witness-box now, counsel."

"No, but you're sitting on Pomfret's rug, and Pomfret is but the-"She began to laugh helplessly.

"Come along, Alice," I said. "'Yet so God made me. Now you say, 'Can you be gentle, then?' and give me the glad eye.

"It only says 'archly' here, in brackets."

"Same thing," said I

"'Can you be gentle, then?'"

A pause. Then:

"Go on," she said.

"I'm waiting for my cue."

"I've said it-Hare."

"John or March?"

"March, of course. John is an actor."

"Thank you, Alice, dear. I repeat, I await my cue, the which you incontinently withhold. Selah!"

She tried not to laugh.

"I've given it, you silly man."

"My dear, I come in on the eye. It's most important. You must give it to me, because I've got to give it back to you in a second or two."

She gave it me exquisitely.

"'There are with whom I can be more than gentle, madam.'"

Here I returned the eye with vigour.

"'What manner of men are these you favour?'"

"'They are not men, madam. Neither are they favoured of me.

"'Of whom, then?'"

"'Of Heaven, madam, and at birth. I mean fair women.'"

"Such as—"

"'Such as you, madam.'"

The way she said 'Hush!' at that was a flash of genius. It was indescribably eloquent. She forbade and invited in the same breath. It was wonderful, and it made me Buckingham. And Buckingham it brought to her feet. Little wonder. It would have brought a cardinal. In the passionate rhetoric of my lines I wooed her, sitting there on the tree trunk, her head thrown back, eyes closed, lips parted, and always the faint smile that sends a man mad. I never had to tell her to rise. To the line she swayed towards me. To the line she slipped into my arms. She even raised her lips to mine at the last. Then, as I stooped for the kiss, she placed her two small hands firmly on my face and pushed me away.

"Very nice, indeed," she said. "You know your lines well, and you know how to speak them. Hare, I think you're going to be rather good."

I wiped the perspiration off my forehead.

"You made me good, then. I shall never give such a show again."

"Of course you will."

"Never! Never, Alice! But you-you're wonderful. Good Heavens, lass, this might be the two hundredth night you'd played the part. Are you some great one I've not recognized? And will you sign a picture-postcard for our second housemaid-the one who saw 'Buzz-Buzz' eighteen times?"

"What! Not the one with fair hair?"

187

"And flat feet? The very one. Junket, her name is. By Curds out of Season. My mistake. I was thinking of our beagle. Don't think I'm quite mad. I'm only drunk. You're the wine."

"The Queen is, you mean."

"No, no-you, Alice."

She looked at her wrist-watch.

"Oh, all right," I said. "The Queen's the wine, the play's the thing. Anything you like. Only I'm tired of play-acting, and I only want to talk to Alice. Come and let me introduce Pomfret."

"He hasn't been here all the time?"

"Waiting in the road."

"Oh, he's a horse."

I laughed by way of answer, and we walked to where Pomfret stood, patient, immobile. I introduced him elaborately. My lady swept him a curtsey.

"I have to thank you for lending me your rug, Pomfret," she said.

I replied for the little chap:

"It's not my rug; I am but the bail—"

"That's all right. Is your master nice to you?"

"But yes, lady. Don't you like him?"

"He seems to mean well."

"Isn't that rather unkind?" said Pomfret.

"I'm not in the witness-box now."

"Then there's no reason why you shouldn't tell the truth."

"Really, Pomfret!"

"Forgive me, Alice. I'm only a young car, and sometimes, when the petrol gets into my tank—"

"I hope you don't take more than you should."

"I'm sober enough to see you've got a fine pair of headlights."

"I'm afraid you're of rather a coming-on disposition, Pomfret."

"Oh, I can do my thirty-five. His licence will show you that.

"Oh, Pomfret, did you get it endorsed?"

"It was his own fault. Kept egging me on all the time, and then, when we were stopped, tells the police that it's a physical impossibility for me to do more than fifteen. And I had to stand there and hear him say it! He told me afterwards that it was only a facon de parler, but I was angry. I simply shook with anger, the radiator was boiling, too, and one of the tires burst with rage."

"And I suppose the petrol pipe was choked with emotion."

"And the engine almost throttled in consequence. But that is another story. And now, won't you let me take you for a little run? My clutch is not at all fierce."

My companion leaned against Pomfret's hood and laughed.

"He's a bit of a nut, isn't he?" said I.

"Do you think he's quite safe?"

"Rather! Besides, I shall be with you."

"That's not saying much."

"Thank you. And talking of gurnats—"

"Where will you take me?"

"Whithersoever she listed."

"Is it far from here to Tendon Harrow?"

"About sixteen miles."

"Would you mind, Hare?"

"You know I'd love it."

I started up Pomfret, and we settled ourselves in the car. As luck would have it, I had a second coat with me, and she said she was quite warm and comfortable.

Presently she told me all that had happened. In the morning she had ridden alone to hounds. The meet had been at Will Cross. The mare was keen, and for a few miles all went well. Then the hounds had split. Most of the field had followed the master, but she and a few others had followed the huntsman. After a while she had dropped a little behind. Then there had been a check. She had seized upon the opportunity it afforded her to slip off and tighten her girths.

"Wasn't there any man there to—"

"Wait. The next second the hounds picked up the scent again, and, before I knew where I was, the mare had jerked the bridle out of my hand and was half-way across the first field."

"And didn't anyone catch her?"

"The man who caught her is a brute. He would have wanted to tighten my girths for me, and that's why I dropped behind. I felt it would be him, so I slid out of sight behind a hedge, and when I saw it was him coming back with her, I didn't want his smile, so I just ran into the woods and started to walk home."

"Did he see you?"

"No. He may be there still, for all I know."

"He must have been having a roaring time leading the mare about all day."

"I hope it'll teach him not to pester a girl again."

I sighed. "Some of us are brutes, aren't we?"

"Yes."

A pause. Then:

"But some men have been very nice to me."

"The devil they have!" said I.

Here, as certain of our own writers say and have said, a gurgle of delight escaped her. I leaned forward and grabbed at something, caught and handed it to her. She stared at my empty palm.

"Your gurgle, I think."

"Oh," she said, laughing, "you are mad. But I like you. Now, why is that?"

"Personal charm," said I. "The palmist who sits where the draughts are in the Brown Park Hotel, West Central, said I had a magnetism of my own."

"There you are. I never believed in palmistry."

"She also told me to beware of lifts, and a fellow trod on one of my spats in the one at Dover Street the very next morning. Hullo!"

Pomfret slowed gradually down and stopped. I turned to the girl.

"This is what we pay the boy sixteen shillings a week for."

"What's the matter?"

"Petrol's run out. I'm awfully sorry. The silly serf must have forgotten to fill up before I started."

"My dear Hare, what shall we do?"

I made a rapid calculation.

"We can't be more than a quarter of a mile from Fell. In fact, I'm almost sure it's at the foot of the next hill. Yes, I know it is. And if we can get Pomfret to the crest of this rise, it's all down-hill from there to the village. Shall we try, Alice?"

"Rather!"

She got out, and I followed. Fortunately the slope was a gentle one, and, without much of the harder labour, we managed to top the rise. Then we got in again, and began to descend the hill. When the brakes failed, one after another, I was, if possible, more pained than surprised. I rebuked Pomfret and turned to my companion:

"Do you mind making ready to die?" I said. "I'm sorry, but if we don't take the next corner, I'm afraid we shall be what is called 'found later'.

We took it on two wheels, and I then ran Pomfret's near front wheel on to the low bank by the side of the road.

"Put your arms round my neck," I cried.

She did so, and the next moment we plunged into the bushes. I heard a wing snap, and the car seemed to mount a little into the air; then we stopped at a nasty angle, for the off hind wheel was yet in the channel. I breathed a sigh of relief. Then, still grasping the wheel, I looked down at my left shoulder.

I love Harris tweeds," said the girl quietly. "It's just as well, isn't it?"

All things considered, it was. Her nose was embedded in the cloth about two inches above my left breast-pocket. In silence I kissed her hair four times. Then:

"I confess," I said, that the real blue-black hair has always been a weakness of mine.

At that she struggled to rise, but the angle was against her, and, honestly, I couldn't do much. The next minute she had found the edge of the wind-screen-fortunately open at the time of the accident-and had pulled herself off me.

"My hair must have been—"

"Almost in my mouth," I said. "Exactly. I have been—"

"What?"

"Licking it, my dear. It's awfully good for hair, you know-imparts a gloss-like and silky appearance. Besides, since—"

"Idiot!"

I climbed gingerly out of the car, and then helped her into the bushes.

"Suffering from shock, Alice? I'm really devilish sorry."

"Not a bit. It wasn't your fault. Between you and me, Hare, I think you managed it wonderfully."

"Thank you, Alice. That's very sweet of you."

"I hope Pomfret isn't much hurt."

"The little brute. Only a wing, I think. Look here, if we walk into the village, you can have some lunch-you must want it-at the inn, while I get some help to get him out."

Just at the foot of the hill we came upon 'The Old Drum,' its timbered walls showing white behind the red screen of its Virginia creeper. When I had escorted my lady into the little parlour, I sought the kitchen. I could hardly believe my ears when the comfortable mistress of the house told me that at that very moment a toothsome duck was roasting, and that it would and should be placed before us in a quarter of an hour. Without waiting to inquire whom we were about to deprive of their succulent dish, I hastened with the good news to my companion.

"Splendid!" she said.

"You don't mind waiting?"

"I should have waited for you, anyway. Now go and retrieve Pomfret; you've just got time."

To the two husbandmen I found in the bar, the idea of earning twopence a minute for a quarter of an hour appealed so strongly that they did not wait to finish the ale I had ordered for them, and the feats of strength they performed in persuading Pomfret to return to the path from which he had strayed made me ache all over. The result was that the car was in the yard before the duck had left the oven, and I was able to have a wash at the pump before luncheon was served. Pomfret had come off very lightly, on the whole. Except for the broken wing, a fair complement of scratches, and the total wreck of one of the lamps, he seemed to have taken no hurt.

So it happened that Alice and I lunched together. I think we were both glad of the food. When it was over, I lighted her cigarette, and drew her attention to the oleograph, which pictured Gideon's astonishment at the condition of what, on examination, proved to be a large fleece. Out of perspective in the background a youth staggered under a pile of first-fruits.

"No wayside inn parlour is complete without one such picture," said I. "As a rule, we are misled about Moses. This, however, is of a later school. Besides, this is really something out of the common."

"Why?"

"Well, that's not Gideon really, but Garrick as Gideon. Very rare. And that with the first-fruits is Kean as—

"Yes?"

"As Ever," I went on hurriedly; "Gideon's great pal, you know, brother of Always. And Mrs. Siddons—"

"Who made her debut six years after Garrick's farewell . . . And you're all wrong about Kean. But don't let me stop you. Which is Nell Gwynne?"

"Nelly? Ah, no, she isn't in the picture. But she stopped here once-for lunch-quite by chance and unattended, save for a poor fool she had found in the forest. Hunting she had been, and had lost her horse, and he brought her on her way on a pillion. Be sure he rode with his chin on his shoulder all the time. She never said who she was, but he knew her for some great lady, for all his dullness. Ah, Nell, you-she was very sweet to him: let him see the stars in her eyes, let him mark the blue cloud of her hair, suffered him to sit by her side at their meal, gave him of her fair company, and-and, like them all, he loved her. All the time, too-from the moment when he turned and saw her standing there by the fallen tree in the forest, with her loose hair scrambling over her temples-scrambling to see the stars in her eyes. The day passed, and then another; and then the weeks and months, and presently the years, very slowly. But always the fool saw her standing there in the sunshine, with the dear, faint smile on her lips, and the bright memory of her eyes lighted his path when the way was dark, and he might have stumbled, always, always."

I stopped. She was looking away out of the latticed window up at the clear blue sky-looking with the look that is blind and seeth nothing. I came round to the back of her chair and put my hands on her shoulders.

"We never finished our scene," I said gently.

"No?"

"No. You pushed me away."

"Did I?"

A pause. Then:

"May I finish it now?" I said.

"I expect," she said slowly, "I expect you know that bit all right."

"I shall cut it on the night of the performance."

She leaned right back in her chair and looked steadily up into my eyes. I bent over her.

"You'll do nothing of the sort," she said firmly. "She may be—"

"A goddess. But she won't be you."

"No?" she smiled.

"Never, Alice."

"Promise me you'll not cut it on the night."

I groaned.

"But-"I faltered.

"Promise."

"Oh, all right! But I shall hate it, Alice, hate—"

"A present for a good Hare," she said softly, and raised her lips to mine.

On examination Pomfret proved to be practically unhurt, and I was able to get some petrol in the village; but naturally I didn't dare to drive him without seeing to the brakes. It was impossible for my companion to wait while I rectified the trouble, but we managed to raise what had once been a dog-cart, and in that she left for Tendon Harrow. She left, I say, for she would not let me come with her. She was so firm. I implored her, but it was no good. She simply would not be entreated, and I had to content myself with putting her carefully in and watching her drive away in the care of a blushing half-boots, half-ostler, who could not have been more than eighteen.

I got home about six.

"Where on earth have you been?" said Daphne, as I entered the smoking-room.

"Ask Pomfret," said I. "He's in disgrace."

"You haven't hurt him?"

"He nearly killed me."

"What happened"

"Lost his temper just because the petrol ran out. Believe me, a horrid exhibition. Absolutely let himself go. In other words, the brakes failed, and I had to run him into the bushes. One lamp and one wing broken, otherwise unhurt. To adjusting brakes-materials, nil; labour, three hours at a drink an hour, three pints ale. Oh, rotten, my dear, rotten!"

I sank into a chair.

"Meanwhile, we've had to entertain the Wilson crowd. I suppose you forgot they were coming?"

"I was with you in spirit."

"In beer, you mean," said Berry. "Look here, I knew you when you were seven, before you had put off the white mantle of innocence and assumed the cloak of depravity. It has been my unhappy lot to be frequently in your company ever since, and, speaking from a long and distasteful experience of you and your ways, I am quite satisfied that, if you did meet with some slight contretemps, you made no whole-hearted effort to rejoin us in time to degrade your intellect by discussing the sort of topics which appeal to that genus of hopeless wasters which the Wilsons adorn."

"Was it very bad?" said I.

"Bad?" said Jonah. "Bad? When a woman with six male children leads off by telling you that she keeps a book in which she has faithfully recorded all the amusing sayings of her produce up to the age of seven, it's pretty bad, isn't it?"

"Not really?"

"Fact," said Berry. "She quoted a lot of them. One of the more nutty was a contribution from Albert on seeing his father smoking for the first time. 'Mother, is daddy on fire' Now, that really happened. We had about half an hour of the book. Jonah asked her why she didn't publish it, and she nearly kissed him. It was terrible."

"To make things worse," said Jonah, "they brought Baldwin and Arthur with them, as specimens of what they could do in the child line."

"How awful!" said I

"It was rather trying," said Berry. "But they were all right as soon as we turned them on to the typewriter."

"What!" I gasped.

"Oh, we had little or no trouble with them after that."

"Quiet as mice," said Jonah.

"Do you know that machine cost me twenty-five pounds?" I cried.

"The jam'll wash off," said Berry. "You don't know how easily jam comes off. Why, I've known"

"If I thought you really had turned them on to the typewriter, I should never forgive you."

"You oughtn't to say a thing like that, even in jest," said Berry; "it isn't Christian. I tell you for your good."

"Seriously, you didn't do such a wicked thing? Hullo, where is it?"

"They're going to bring it back on Wednesday. I said they couldn't have it more than a week."

I glanced at Jill, who was standing by the window. Her left eyelid flickered, and I knew it was all right.

"Well, I can't help it," I said, sinking back into my chair and lighting a cigarette.

"Poor old chap!" said Daphne. "I believe you thought we had done you down."

"Of course I didn't. Is it tomorrow you've got to go up to Town, Jill?"

"Yes, Boy. Are you going up, too?"

"Must. I'll give you lunch at the Berkeley if you like, dear."

Jill came across and laid her cheek against mine.

"I always like Boy, because he's grateful," she said gently.

Three days later our fellow-mummers began to arrive. A deep melancholy had settled upon me. I cursed the play, I cursed the players, I cursed my part, and most of all I cursed the day which had seen me cast for Buckingham. Whenever I picked up the book, I saw my queen, Alice, standing there by the fallen tree or sitting looking up at me as I bent over her chair in the parlour of 'The Old Drum'. And now her place was to be taken, usurped by another-a Miss Tanyon-whom I hated terribly, though I didn't know her, and the very idea of whom was enough to kill any dramatic instinct I once seemed to possess. Whenever I remembered my promise to Alice, I writhed. So odious are comparisons.

When Daphne announced that the wretched woman was coming by the five-fourteen, and that she should go with the car to meet her, and added that I had better come, too, I refused point-blank.

"I don't know what's the matter with you," said my sister. "Don't you want to see the girl you'll have to play the love-scene with?"

This about finished me, and I laughed bitterly.

"No," I said, "I'm damned if I do."

When Daphne pressed her point as only Daphne can, I felt really too timid and bored with the whole affair to argue about it, so I gave way. Accordingly, at ten minutes past five, I stood moodily on the platform by my sister's side. The train steamed in, and the passengers began to alight. Daphne scanned them eagerly.

"I don't see her," she said half to herself.

We were standing half-way down the platform, and I turned and looked listlessly towards the front of the train. That end of the platform was empty except for two people. One was a stoker who had stepped off the foot-plate. The other was Alice. She was in blue still-a blue coat and skirt, with a fox fur about her shoulders. A small, blue felt hat was somewhat shading her eyes, but I could see she was looking at me and smiling. I forgot all about Miss Tanyon-she simply didn't matter now.

Involuntarily :

"Why. there's the Queen!" I cried, and started towards her.

"Where?" said Daphne.

"Here," I flung over my shoulder.

A four-wheeled truck of luggage, propelled by a porter across my bows, blocked my way for a moment, and Daphne overtook me.

"So it is," she said. "But how did you know?"

CHAPTER XII

THE ORDER OF THE BATH

Berry blotted the letter with maddening precision. Then he picked it up tenderly and handed it to me.

"How will that do?"

"Read it aloud," said Daphne.

I did so.

"Dear Sir,-In the interests of personal cleanliness, we have-not without considerable hesitation-decided to install a fourth bathroom at our historic home, 'White Ladies'. This decision will necessitate the loss or conversion of one of the dressing-rooms, a fact which fills us with the gravest misgivings, since there are only eleven in the whole mansion. At the same time, thee conventions of a prudish age make it undesirable that a second bath should be installed in one of the rooms already existing for that purpose. We think the fourth room on your right, as you leave the back stairs, going south. This is locally known as the Green Room and takes its name, not, as you may imagine, from the fact that the late Sir Henry Irving once slept there, but from the hue of the rodents, said there frequently to have been observed by the fourth Earl. Please execute the work with your customary diligence. We should like to pay on the hire system, i.e., so much a month, extending over a period of two years. The great strides, recently made in the perilous art of aviation, suggest to us that the windows should be of ground glass. Yours faithfully, etc. P.S.—If your men drop the bath on the stairs, the second footman will at once apply for a warrant for their arrest."

Jill buried her face in the sofa-cushions and gave way to unrestrained merriment. Jonah laughed openly. I set my teeth and tried not to smile. For an instant the corners of Daphne's mouth twitched. Then:

"Wretched ass," she said.

"The truth is," said her husband, "you don't know literature when you see it. Now that letter—"

"I suppose I shall have to write to the man," said I.

"There you are," said Berry. "Insults at every turn. I was about to say that I regarded that letter as one of the brightest jewels in an already crowded diadem."

"Give me the writing-block," I said shortly, producing my fountain-pen. I turned to Daphne. "What sort of a bath d'you want?"

"Porcelain-enamel, they call it, don't they?" she replied vaguely, subjecting a box of chocolates to a searching cross-examination.

Berry rose to his feet and cleared his throat. Then he sang lustily :

"What of the bath?" The bath was made of porcelain, Of true ware, of good ware, The ware that won't come off"

A large cushion sailed into his face. As it fell to the ground, Berry seized it and held it at arm's length.

"Ha," he said rapturously. "A floral tribute. They recognize my talent."

"Not at all," said Jonah. "I only threw that, because the dead cats haven't come."

"Exactly," said I. "We all know you ought to be understudying at the Hoxton Empire, but that's no reason why we should be subjected—"

"Did you notice the remarkable compass of my voice?" said Berry, sinking into a chair.

"I did," said I. "I should box it, if I were you, brother. Bottle it, if you prefer."

"Poor fool," said my brother-in-law. "For the trumpet notes, to which it has just been your privilege to listen, there is a great future. In short, my voice is futurist. The moment they hear it, the few who have paid for their seats will realize what the box-office will say when they demand the return of their money."

"And those who have not paid?" said I.

"Oh, they will understand why they were given tickets."

"Suppose you write that letter," said Daphne wearily.

I bent over the writing-block.

"You know," said Berry, "I don't think this bath's at all necessary."

At this there was a great uproar. At length:

"Besides," said my sister, "we all decided that we must have another bath ages ago. The only question there's ever been was where to put it."

"Of course," said I. "If we don't, where are we going to dip the sheep?"

"Well, I think it's a shame to pull the old place about like this. If we're so awfully dirty, we'd better find another house that's got four bathrooms already, and sell White Ladies."

"Sell White Ladies?" cried Jill.

Berry nodded.

"Not only lock and stock, but barrel too. Yes," he added bitterly, "the old water-butt must go."

"Look here," said I. "It occurs to me that this isn't a case for a letter. We ought to go and choose a bath properly."

"That's rather an idea," said Daphne.

"Simply sparkling," said her husband. "Personally, I've got something better to do than to burst down to South London, and stagger round floor after floor, staring at baths."

"You needn't worry," said Daphne coolly. "I wouldn't go with you for a hundred pounds."

Berry turned to us others.

"Yet we love one another," he said, with a leer in his wife's direction. "In reality I am the light of her eyes. The acetylene gas, as it were, of her existence. Well, well." He rose and stretched himself. "I wash my hands of the whole matter. Note the appropriate simile. Install what cistern you please. If approached properly, I may consent to test the work when complete. Mind you spare no expense."

"We don't propose to," said Daphne.

Berry regarded her sorrowfully.

"I suppose," he said, "I suppose you know what word will be found at the post-mortem graven upon my heart?"

"What?" said Daphne, stifling a yawn.

"Plunge."

It was quite a good day to choose a bath. True, it was winter. But then the sun was shining out of a clear, blue sky, there was a rare freshness in the London air, and beneath me-for I was crossing Westminster Bridge-old Thames marched all a-glitter. I watched his passage gratefully. It was that of a never-ending band. Playing all the way, too, but silently. Yet, the music was there. The pity was that one could not hear it. The pomp, the swagger, the swing of the Guards, the shifting movement, the bright array-all these were unmistakable. The very lilt of the air made itself felt. Very cheery. Certainly, the river was en fete.

It had been arranged that the selection of an appropriate bath should be made by Daphne, Jonah, and me. When I came down to breakfast to find that Jonah had already left for Huntercombe, I was more hurt than surprised. But, when Daphne appeared during the marmalade, clad in a new riding-habit, I made haste to empty my mouth.

"You can't ride there," I said. "The traffic's too heavy. Besides, the tram-lines—"

"You don't want me, old chap," said my sister, stooping to lay her soft cheek against mine, as she passed to her place.

I drank some coffee with an injured air. Then:

"This," I said, "is low down. Not nice. I don't like it in you. It argues—"

"-the confidence we repose in your judgment," said Daphne.

"Yes, brother," said Berry, looking up from The Sportsman. "The bath-dressing-gown has fallen upon your rounded shoulders. Ill though it becomes you, I trust that—"

"Enough," said I. "Alone I will select a bath. Doubtless you will all deplore my choice as bitterly as you will fight with one another for the privilege of using it. However. When I am dead, you will regret—"

No, we shan't," said my brother-in-law. "We shall just bury you under another name and try to keep the obituary notices out of the papers."

I sat back in my chair and frowned. "Be good enough to pass the rolls," said I.

"You've only had four, said Berry, pushing them across. "Mind you get a good lunch at Lambeth. I'm told they do you very well at 'The Three Balls.'

"When I'm choosing a bath," said I, "I always lunch at 'The Rising Spray.' And now, here I was, afoot upon Westminster Bridge bound for the warehouse of the firm we proposed to honour with our patronage.

I passed on into the roar of the crowded streets, and a quarter of an hour later I reached the place I sought.

Almost immediately the office-boy took me for a commercial traveller and refused point-blank to announce my arrival. I told him that I had an appointment.

"Yes," he said pleasantly. "They all 'as."

"Friend," said I, "I see that you are bent on gaining the feathered fowl. In other words, if I'm kept waiting much longer you'll get the bird."

"I don't think," he replied somewhat uneasily.

"That," said I, "is what I complain of."

I seated myself on a table and lighted a cigarette. Then:

"I wonder how he'll like his new place," I said, apostrophizing the skylight.

A pause. Then:

"Of corse, the guv'nor might be in," said the youth. "Yer never knows."

"Speak for yourself," said I. "At the same time, you appear to be doing what you conceive to be your duty. And for those who do their duty, there is always a shilling in the left-hand trouser-pocket—"

But the boy was half-way upstairs. I had proved my identity.

Five minutes later one of the partners was conducting me in the direction of the baths.

Now he had twice begged me to be careful not to hit my head, for he led me through divers dark, low-pitched corridors. Especially divers. I remembered his warning about a fifth of a second too late.

When we at length emerged again into the broad light of day, I contemplated my new bowler in some annoyance. It was bashed in properly. A large dent-in shape somewhat resembling the Empire of India-leered at me, its edges generously defined with whitewash. Very trying.

My good host was greatly concerned, and begged to be allowed to take the damaged headgear away and have it brushed. After a little I consented, promising to walk round and look at the baths while he was gone. The next moment he had disappeared.

I laid my stick and gloves on a glass-topped table and looked about me. Never before had I seen so many baths gathered together. Large and small, deep and shallow, normal and abnormal, they stood orderly in long lines. The more elaborate ones, fitted with screens and showers, douches, etc., stood a little apart upon a baize-covered dais, bright with their glistening pipes and rows of taps. And in an alcove, all glorious, electric light burning above its gold-lacquered fittings, reposed the bath of baths, a veritable monarch, with his attendant basin, marble-topped table, gilded towel-rails, etc., etc.

Attracted by the aristocracy upon the dais, I was proceeding to stroll humbly in their direction, when I heard the sound of footsteps. The next moment a girl stepped lightly between great sliding iron doors, which led obviously from an adjoining chamber on the same floor.

Very smart she was, in a black cloth coat with ermine collar and cuffs. On her head was a trim black hat from which a fine brooch was blazing. Save that she was fair, and that her feet flashed as she walked, I could see little more.

For a moment the new-comer hesitated, looking about her. Then she came towards me.

"Oh," she said. "I want to choose a bath."

For an instant I looked at her. Then I remembered that I was hatless, stickless, gloveless.

I bowed.

"Certainly, madam. What sort of bath do you require?"

She was looking at me now-narrowly rather. Quickly she swung round and glanced about the great hall. Then she spoke, somewhat uneasily.

"Er-if you would show me some baths with showers and things, please—"

"With pleasure, madam. Will you come this way?"

I preceded her in the direction of the great ones.

"Now this," I said, laying my hand familiarly on the smooth edge of one of the grandes dames, "this is 'The Duchess.' Very popular, madam. She may not exactly figure in Society, but I can assure you that every morning half Society figures in her." I glanced at the girl to see an amused smile struggling with grave suspicion in her eyes. I went on hurriedly. "We've been selling a great number lately."

"Have you?" she said slowly.

"Yes, indeed, madam. Only this morning we received an order for fourteen from Madagascar." I turned to another patrician. "Here again is a first-class bath. 'The Nobleman.' A great feature is the glass screen. The enamel, too, is of the very best quality. Nickelplated fittings, stream line body, detachable whee-er-that is, the waste also is constructed on a most ingenious principle: we call it the 'Want-Not' pattern."

"Ah," she said quietly. "And what's the price of this-er-paragon?"

I glanced at the ticket, knitting my brows.

"Well, it's listed at 'AWK/-', but to you, madam, the price is—"

I looked at her, smiling.

"Yes?" she said, with her grey eyes on mine. Her eyebrows were raised a little, and the soft lips had taken on the curve that tells of laughter hardly controlled.

"Another look like that," said I, "and I'll give it you and pay the carriage."

She broke into a long ripple of delight. Then she took her seat upon 'The Nobleman's' broad edge and regarded me mischievously.

"I think you ought to apologize," she said severely.

"Who took me for a salesman?" said I.

"I never did that. You see, I've been looking at basins over there"- she pointed in the direction of the iron doors-"and they said if I came through here, I should find one of the partners. Besides, I wasn't a bit sure when I first spoke, but, as you had no hat-And then you led me on. Still, I beg your pardon."

"Not at all. The partner's a very nice chap. And the mischief is reparable. I mean—"

"Where is the partner?"

"At the present moment I believe he's engaged in trying to efface the Indian Empire. Bit of a Socialist, you know," I added. "May I smoke?"

"What d'you mean?"

"Doesn't she know the word? Smoke, my dear. Draw into and expel from the mouth the fumes of burning tobac—"

"Idiot! About the Little Englander."

I explained.

"And now," I said, with a wave of my cigarette, "behold me once more at your service. The gentle art of bathing, madam, is of considerable antiquity. In classical times the bath played a very prominent part in the everyday existence of the cleanly nut. Then came a dead period in the

206

history of personal irrigation. Recently, however, the bath-rate has once more gone up, immersion is again in vogue, and today in the best circles scarcely a month passes without—"And these"-she swept the nobility with a glance-"are the upper ten!"

"Precisely. You can tell that from their polish."

"Rather exclusive, aren't they?"

"Collectively, yes, madam. Individually, they will receive you with open arms. Only last night an order arrived from"

"I know. Madagascar. You're no good as a sales-man.

I drew myself up. "From Honolulu, for twenty-two 'God-sends.'" I said icily. "Madagascar's request was for 'Duchesses.'"

That, over there, is a 'Wallsend,'-I mean 'God-send.'"

"And I suppose you've supplied Cochin China for years'"

"One of our oldest clients," said I.

"You know," said she, "when I look round, I feel as if I had never seen a bath before."

"I know. I felt just like that at first. And yet I have," I added thoughtfully; "they had one at a hotel I stayed at last Easter. At Biarritz, that was."

"I wish you'd be serious," she said, laughing. "Then you might be of some use."

"I don't think you're at all kind," said I, leaning against the screen of 'The Duchess' with a dejected air.

"Excuse me," she said, "but is that the Slinker Slouch I've heard of? Your attitude, I mean?"

"No," I said shortly. "It's the Leicester Lounge. But, to return to your unkindness. I want a bath just as much as you do."

She recoiled. "You know what I mean. I'm a customer, like you. We're both in the same ba-boat. And I have been doing my best to indicate the merits of-er-of—"

"The idle rich," she said, smiling. "Yes, but you see you shouldn't have. When you saw me coming you ought to have—"

"Dodged behind a pillar, picked up my stick and gloves, and kept about ten bath-lengths away, until the partner reappeared? No doubt. But, then, you shouldn't have looked so priceless, or worn your sense of humour on your sleeve. You shouldn't have had a small, straight nose or a mouth like a red flower. You shouldn't have walked like a thoroughbred, or carried your clothes as if they were worth wearing. You shouldn't have had eyes I could see to read by, if the light failed."

"Finished?"

"No. But listen. I think I hear the partner coming-the genuine article, this time." There was no sound.

"Anyway," I went on, "he'll be back in a moment; and so, as I'm afraid I didn't consider you just now, I'll try and make up for it. Goodbye."

"But what about your bath? Have you seen one you like?"

"Yes," said I. "I have. One. Not a bath, though. But I can easily come another day."

I turned resolutely away.

"I say," said the girl quietly.

I swung round and looked at her. She still sat upon the edge of 'The Nobleman,' her little gloved hands gripping the rim on either side of her. Her face was raised a little, but she was looking down. One slight leg thrust out from under the blue frock, its dainty instep gleaming under the silk stocking. The ankle above it, very slender; the bucked shoe literally beaming with pride.

"Yes?" I said.

"I haven't seen a bath I like, either," she said simply.

At this moment the partner came bustling back, full of apologies. Stifling a desire to strangle him, I congratulated the good man upon the condition of my hat, and turned to the girl.

"Then, as we both want to see some baths, perhaps we might look at some together?" I said.

"I think so."

"If you please, madam," said the partner. He turned to 'The Duchess.' "Now, this is a first-class bath. One of our very latest models. Only this morning we received an order from Ceylon . . ."

Fortunately, we were both a little behind him.

No one can say that we did not weigh the merits of the various baths carefully. We passed from one to another, asking questions, receiving information, examining, criticizing, discussing for over an hour. Four times, to our great joy, the excellent partner actually climbed into a bath, the more satisfactorily to emphasize its advantages. As he sat there, faithfully reproducing the various movements of the arms, universally, I suppose, employed in the process of ablution, the living picture which he presented, put an obviously severe strain upon the gravity of my companion. And when, in response to a daringly ingenuous thirst for intelligence on my part, he proceeded to demonstrate the comparative ease with which a left-handed bather, suffering from sciatica, could manipulate the taps from the wrong end of the bath, the girl hurriedly sought the shelter of a convenient pillar to hide her open merriment. We had a great time.

Finally, we each gave an order for a 'Pompadour, which seemed, on the whole, to merit the palm. It was certainly the last word in the bath line.

While she was giving her name and the address of the home, which her new bath was to adorn, I strolled a little apart, thinking. When she had finished, the partner turned to me.

"I think I have the address, sir. The same as before?"

"That's right," said I. "I'm going down there on Tuesday. Could you send a man down that day to see the room and take the measurements? I'd like to be there myself."

"Certainly, sir.

"Very well. He'd better come by the nine-thirty, which'll get him down in two hours. I'll send to meet him. I'm going down by car myself."

"Thank you, sir." He turned to the girl inquiringly. "Perhaps Tuesday would suit you, too, madam? I don't think you mentioned any particular day, and as it's the same station for both houses, madam—"

He broke off. She and I were staring at one another. Then:

"How awfully strange," we said in unison.

The partner being there, there was no more to be said.

"Tuesday will do very well," she said, turning to him.

Together he conducted us to the street. Then, might he send for a taxi? There was a rank . . . The idea of sending for two taxis never seemed to enter his head. A good fellow, that partner. But, no thank you, my lady would walk. Would pick up a cab presently.

"May I have the pleasure of seeing you to a taxi?" said I, naturally enough.

"Thank you very much."

We bade the partner goodbye and turned in the direction of Westminster.

"You're sure it's not taking you out of your way?" said my companion with an innocent look.

"Out of my way," said I. "D'you think I live at Tooting?"

She broke into a little laugh. I went on:

"And if I did. If I lived at Hither Green and was just going to miss the last tram, don't you think I'd er-miss it?"

"You're very kind," she said quietly.

"Not at all," said I, with a glance downward. "The small bright shoe is on the other exquisite-er-foot. It's very good of you to let me walk with you, especially in view of my recent scandalous behaviour all among the baths."

"Which reminds me, you were awful. I thought I should die, when you asked that poor man—"

"A wholesome thirst for knowledge, my dear. Talking of which, d'you know it's getting on for half-past one?"

"Is it really?"

210

"It is, indeed. Time tears away sometimes, doesn't he?"

"Sometimes."

"You are sweet," said I. "However. About Time. He's a mocker of men, you know: very contrary. When he can serve, not he. When he cannot, he is willing enough. Beg him to hasten, he'll cock his hat and stroll with an air of leisure that makes us dance. Cry him to tarry, he is already gone, the wind panting behind him. Bid him return, he is at once all sympathy-grave sympathy: 'He may not. Otherwise he would have been so pleased . . . Sorry. Rather like my brother-in-law. You'll meet him at White Ladies."

"Is that where the bath's going?"

"Certainly. We shall be there in the spring. Will you come to our bath-warming?"

"Perhaps."

We came to the bridge and the sunshine and the marching river, and beyond these to Bridge Street and the green square. At the corner she hesitated.

"I think I'd better say goodbye now."

"I'm going to see a fellow," said I. "I wish you'd come with me."

A quick look of surprise. Then:

"Do I know him?"

"I think so. He's one of the Times. Lunch Time he's called; brother of Half Time. Both sons of the old man."

She smiled.

"Ah," she said. "I've an appointment with him, too. Only mine's at home. I must be going. I'm keeping him waiting now."

She held out her hand. I looked at it.

"You've made a mistake," I said. "I know for a fact he's going to be at the Carlton."

"No good! I know the family. The father taught them all the trick of being able to be in more than one place at the same time."

"All of them?"

"Yes."

"My dear, you're wrong. You've forgotten Mean. He's got a place at Greenwich, you know, and never leaves it. Well, I won't bother her, for she's been awfully sweet. Shall I call her a taxi?"

She nodded. "I don't think we ought to stand here any longer: the atmospheric pressure of the Labour party is already affecting my breathing. Besides, any moment I might be mistaken for a Cabinet Minister. I know a salesman's pretty bad, but I must draw the line somewhere."

With that I hailed a taxi. As it was coming to the kerb:

"You're a dear C.B.," I said. "But I would have loved to have given you lunch."

She smiled gently.

"Would you?"

"You know I would, lass. Well, I shall look forward to you and the spring."

The cab drew up, and I opened the door. She stepped in.

"Where shall I tell him to go?"

For a moment she hesitated. Then she spoke slowly:

"Was it the Carlton you said?"

An hour later I stood once more at a taxi's door. Our luncheon was over, and I was saying farewell.

"You've been awfully kind," said the girl.

"Goodbye," said I. "I shall look forward to you at White Ladies."

"And to the spring."

I bowed.

"My dear, the terms are synonymous."

The smile deepened.

"If this wasn't the Haymarket," said I . . .

She was gone, her eyes full of laughter.

I turned to see Berry three paces away.

212

"Helping the porter?" he said pleasantly. "I wondered where you got that two shillings from last week. But oughtn't you to be in uniform? I should have thought Nathans—"

"I've chosen a bath," I said, seeking to divert his thoughts. After all he might not have seen. "Fine big place. Stacks of baths, you know. By the way, the office-boy took me for a commercial traveller, I added.

"Naturally. And the girl? Who did she take you for?"

I drew myself up.

"She's a C.B. too," I said loftily. "What more natural than that we should—"

"C.B.?" said Berry scornfully. "Now, if you had said K.G.—"

I cut him short.

"You needn't tell the others," I said.

A fat grin stole into his face. He sighed.

"The call of duty, brother, however distasteful—"

"Look here," said I. "You know those new cigars at the club?"

"Yes," he said eagerly. "The half-a-crown ones."

"They're not new," I said uneasily.

"Never mind," he said airily, taking my arm. "I feel sure a half-a-crown cigar would affect my memory. And a dry Martini would probably finish it."

I groaned.

"This is sheer blackmail," said I.

"Take it or leave it," said Berry, with the air of one who has the whip-hand.

"All right," I said wearily.

"I should think so, my son. And cheap at the price, too."

On the whole I think it was.

CHAPTER XIII

A LUCID INTERVAL

"Ausgang verboten!" said the guard.

"Yes," said Berry. "You look it."

"Hush!" said Daphne.

"Hush yourself," replied her husband. "The man is ill. I would minister to him."

We got him away somehbw and bore him towards a taxi. Before we could stop him, he had congratulated the driver in excellent French on his recovery from the accident "which had so painfully disfigured him," and had asked for the name and address of the man who had designed the body of his cab. This was too much for Daphne, and she and Jonah called another taxi, and said they would see us at the hotel. Satisfied that the conductor of the hotel omnibus was collecting our luggage, I followed Jill and Berry into the cab, and we drove out of the station.

When we reached the hotel, Berry told the porter that he need not uncover, as he was travelling incognito, and asked if Mrs. Pleydel had arrived. Receiving a negative answer, he gave the man five marks and asked him to be very careful as to the way he lifted the cat's basket out of his wife's cab. Then he suffered himself to be conducted to the sitting-room which I had engaged on the first floor.

Five minutes later Daphne burst into the room.

"What on earth's the matter with the people here?" she demanded. "Half the staff are feeling all over the inside of our cab, and the porter

214

keeps asking me if I'm sure the cat was put in at the station. Is this some of your doing?"

"Possibly some idle banter—"

"I knew it," said Daphne. If this is how you begin, we shan't get out of Munich alive."

Why we had chosen Munich is not very easy to tell. Of course, we ought to have gone to Biarritz and taken the car, but they wouldn't have that. Everybody had wanted to go to a different place. Berry's choice was Minsk, because, he said, he wanted to rub up his Hebrew. Such a suggestion is characteristic of Berry. Then Munich was mentioned, and as no one had seemed very keen, no one had taken the trouble to be very rude about it. Consequently, Munich won. A day or two after our arrival, one of Wagner's triumphs was to be given at the Opera House, and, amid a scene of great excitement, Berry secured four tickets. I say four because I mean four. I have never appreciated opera, and was all along reluctant to go. But when I found that the show began at half-past four, I put my foot down and reminded the others of the Daylight Saving Bill. With gusto they retorted that I had been to more matinees than they cared to remember. I replied that for a theatre to begin at half-past four was out of all order and convenience, and that, as an Englishman and a member of a conservative club, I was not prepared to subscribe to such an unnatural arrangement.

"Brother," said Berry, "I weep for you. Not now, but in the privacy of my chamber I often weep great tears."

"Friend," said I, "your plain but honest face belies your words. You don't want to see the opera any more than I do, and now you're jealous because tomorrow I shall sit down to dinner comfortably while you are trying to remember which of the sandwiches have mustard, and praying that the lights won't go up till your mouth's empty."

To the consternation of the assistants in the library, Berry covered his face with his hands.

"He thinks it decent to revile me," he said weakly. "Where is my wife, my helpmeet?"

But Daphne had already retired. As I left the shop, an American lady approached Berry and told him the way to the English chemist.

At five the next day it began to rain. I was in Maximilian Street at the time, admiring the proportions of the thoroughfare and ready for anything. The rain suggested to me that I should take a taxi to the Rumpelmayer's of Munich. A closed one was crawling by the kerb opposite to me, on the far side of the road. I put up my stick, and it slowed down. I crossed to it, spoke to the driver, who scowled at me, seemingly because I approached him from the road and not from the pavement-Munich is very particular-and got in. As I sat back in the dark corner, the opposite door opened. The light of the offside lamps showed me two big, brown eyes, a dear, puzzled face, half wondering, half wanting to laugh, and a row of white teeth catching a red upper lip that trembled in a smile. The next moment their owner stepped quickly in, the driver let in his clutch with a jerk, and my unwitting companion was projected heavily into the corner-not mine-she had been about to occupy.

She swore gently.

"That's right," said I.

She jumped properly.

"Good Heavens!"

"I'm so sorry, but I'm all right," said I, "I assure you. Young man of gentlemanly appearance. Harrow and Oxford, terms moderate, bathroom and domestic offices, possession early in June—"

"Get out of my cab at once."

"-will send photograph if required. Whose cab?"

"Well, I engaged it."

"So did I."

"When?"

"Just now."

"How awfully funny."

216

"Isn't it? I'm so glad. I'm English, too, you know. I can prove that by my German. And—"

"But you don't want to go where I do."

"But I do."

"Don't be silly! You know what I mean."

At this moment the off hind wheel of a big limousine, which was passing us, caught our near front wheel. The steering-wheel was knocked out of the cabman's hands, and we landed up against a lamp-post with a crash that flung my companion and myself on to the floor of the taxi. The girl cried out, put her small hand into my mouth, and sat up.

I spoke into her glove.

"Are you hurt?"

"No, but I think I'm going to cry."

"Don't, my dear. It's all right. All the same, it's an outrage and a casus belli. Where does the British Ambassador live?"

Here the door was opened. The girl released me to adjust her hat, and I rolled on to the step and sat looking at a tall footman, who raised his hat and said something in German. The next minute a lady appeared. She began to speak in German, then:

"Oh, you are English," she said. I rose and bowed stiffly.

"Yes, madame, I have that honour."

"I am so very sorry. I do hope you are not hurt."

"I am only shaken, thank you."

She looked into the cab. "My dear," she purred, "I am so terribly sorry. I hope you were not hurt either. I cannot say—"

"No, I'm all right, thank you. I'll get out."

Then she fainted. I caught her and carried her to the limousine. When I had set her on the deep seat, I turned to the lady.

"I do not know where she lives," I said. "We have only met casually."

"A physician?" she queried. "Had she better—"

"I don't think it is a case for a doctor. She has only fainted. Perhaps you—"

"I will attend to her, and when we get to the Opera House, my maid—"

She turned to the footman and seemed to tell him to stay behind and see to the cabman and the police, who had come up. Then she stepped into the car, and a moment later we were slipping silently up the street. By the lights in the car, I could see that our friend was a handsome woman of perhaps thirty-eight. She was almost entirely enveloped in a magnificent sable coat: her head was bare. The great thing about her was her exquisite voice. While her fingers were busy about the girl's hat and throat, the latter opened her eyes. Then she sat up and put her hand to her head.

"No, lean back, my dear," said our hostess. "I will spray you."

She sprayed her with eau-de-Cologne.

"That's lovely," said the girl, with closed eyes. "Thank you so much."

The other stopped for a moment to take off the jaunty little hat and lightly push the dark hair away from the white temples.

The girl thanked her with a smile. Then she started up again. "Oh, but where is—"

She saw me, and stopped, colouring.

"He is here, in the car."

She closed her eyes once more, and the colour had faded from her cheeks before she spoke again. "Where are we going?" she said.

"To the Opera House, dear. You see, I am singing there. I would take you home, but I am late now. My maid, she will make you comfortable. I have nice rooms at the theatre, quite an apartment." She turned to me.

"And you will come, too, please. There is plenty of room. Besides she is in your charge."

"Of course," said I. "Thank you very much."

As she had said, a regular little suite had been allotted to our hostess at the Opera House. As well as the dressingroom, there was a bathroom and a large sitting-room, with flowers everywhere, and beautifully furnished. Here I waited, wondering a little. The others had passed into the dressing-room.

Presently Yvonne, the French maid, entered the room.

"Mademoiselle recovers, monsieur," she said, with a smile. "Also she dines here, and monsieur with her. It is all arranged.

"If you please," said I. It seemed about the best thing to say.

Very swiftly she laid the table for two-a cold chicken, some salad, rolls, and a bottle of champagne. Thank you.

"It is not much," said Yvonne apologetically. "Now at Madame's house—"

"Yvonne!" came from the dressing-room.

"Pardon, monsieur."

Yvonne disappeared. Five minutes later a telephone bell rang. Then the dressing-room door opened, and Madame came forth robed, and the girl with her, looking as right as rain.

"That was my call," said our hostess. "I go to sing now. By the time you have finished, I shall be back, and then, later, if you would like to sit in a box for a little while, it will be quiet for you both. Come, Yvonne."

She swept out of the room. Yvonne closed the door behind her.

"I like her," said I.

"She's a dear," said my companion.

"I like you, too," said I.

She swept me a curtsey.

"It was silly of me to faint."

"You did it so sweetly."

"This'll teach you not to take other people's taxis."

"On the contrary—

"Would you like to give me some chicken?"

"I should like—"

"Yes?"

She looked at me straight in the eyes.

I walked to the table and took up the knife and fork.

"Yes?"

I looked at her, smiling gloriously now.

"Oh, I'd like Berry to see us now.

She came across and laid a hand on my shoulder.

"I like you, too," she said.

We had a great meal. She didn't want to drink any champagne, but I persuaded her to take a little.

"And who's Berry?" she said, pushing back her chair.

"A mistake," said I. A great mistake. That's what he is."

She laughed.

"Who made him?"

"My sister. She married him, you see."

"Of course, I shall get confused in a moment."

"Well, things have got a move on in the last hour and a quarter, haven't they? I mean to say, at five o'clock you found a stranger in your taxi. Five minutes later you were smashed up. Now you're in a prima donna's room at the Opera House, eating a cold collation. Collation is good, isn't it?"

"Awfully? Where did you hear it?"

I frowned. "I came out top in dictation last term."

"Indeed? Genius and madness do go together, don't they? You are mad, aren't you?"

"Raving, my dear. I've been certified for two years come Ember. Out on licence under the new Cock and Bull Bill. You know, 'And your petitioners will ever Pray—'"

"I suppose you do have lucid intervals?"

"Only on third Tuesdays."

"Such as today."

"By Jove, so it is. I thought one was about due. Now I come to think of it, I nearly had one just now."

"When?"

"When you asked me what I should like."

In silence she traced a pattern upon the white cloth with a small pink finger. I watched it, and wondered whether her eyes were smiling. I couldn't see them, but her mouth looked as if it wanted to. Then:

"I think you'd better tell me when the interval's coming," she said quietly. "One usually goes out—"

"You're thinking of Plays," said I. "Between Acts II and III ten minutes and the safety curtain. But with Life and fools it's different. You don't go out in these intervals."

"No?"

"No," I said. "On the contrary, it's where you come in."

She looked up, smiling, at that. I addressed her eyes. "You see, in Life it's just the intervals that count-those rare hours when, though the band's not playing, there's music in the air; though the world's standing still, and no one's looking on, there's most afoot; though the—"

Here the door opened, and Madame came in, Yvonne at her heels.

"It is the interval," she explained. Thank you.

Oh, but she was in fine fettle, was Madame.

My voice is good tonight. It is you two that have helped me. You are so young and goodly. And I have a box, the Royal box-they are not using it, you see-if you would like to hear the rest of the opera. Yes? But you must come back and say 'Good night' to me aiterwards."

Our murmured thanks she would have none of. Supper and a box was little enough. Had she not nearly killed us both an hour ago?

"But now I shall sing to you, and you will forgive me. I am in voice tonight. Is it not so, Yvonne?"

"But, Madame!"

The ecstasy of Yvonne was almost pathetic.

The ceremony with which we were installed in the Royal box was worthy of the Regent himself. But then Madame was a very great lady. The lights in the house did not go down for a minute, and I peered over the rim of the balcony to see if I could locate Berry and Co. Suddenly I saw Jill, and Berry next to her. He was staring straight at the Royal box, and his face was a study. He must have seen me come in. Then the lights died, and the curtain went up.

The singing of Madame I cannot describe. It was not of this world. And we knew her. We were her friends. She was our hostess. To the house she was the great artiste-a name to whisper, a figurehead to bow before. For us, we were listening to the song of a friend. As she had promised, she sang to us. There was no mistaking it. And the great charm of her welled out in that wonderful voice. All the spirit of melody danced in her notes. When she was singing, there seemed to be none but us in the theatre, and soon no theatre-only us in the world. We two only stepped by her side, walked with her, understood.

Actually the girl and I sat spellbound, smiling down as she smiled up from the stage. We knew afterwards that we had been sitting hand-in-hand, as children do.

At the end of it all the house rose at her. Never was there such a scene. We rose, too, and stood smiling. Somehow we did not applaud. She just smiled back.

"Shall we go?" said I.

"Yes."

As I turned to the door, I caught sight of four faces looking earnestly up from the stalls. I bowed gravely. An attendant was waiting in the corridor, and we were escorted through the iron door the way we had come.

Madame sat in a deep arm-chair in the sitting-room, her hair all about her shoulders. She looked tired. Virtue had gone out of her.

"Ah, my dears," she said. My companion kneeled by her side and put her arms round her neck. Then she spoke and kissed her. I do not know what she said. The other held her very close for a moment, then looked at me and smiled. I raised her hand to my lips.

"I cannot say anything, Madame."

"It is all said. We have spoken together for the last half-hour. Is it not so?"

"It is so, Madame."

After a little, my companion said we must be going.

"He will see me to my hotel," she said."

I do not like letting you go," said our hostess, "but I take long to dress. My car shall carry you home and return for me. Yvonne, see to that. Yes, there will be plenty of time. Besides, you have driven enough in taxis for today. What have you lost, my dear?"

The girl was looking about her.

"I think I must have left it in the box-my chain bag. How silly!"

"My dear, I leave everything everywhere"

"I will get it," said I. Yvonne had gone for the car. Besides, I wanted to go.

"Oh, thank you. It's quite a small gold—"

"I know it," said I, smiling.

"Can you find your way?" said Madame. "The house will be almost in darkness."

"Oh, yes, Madame."

A moment later I was in the corridor beyond the iron door. It was quite dark, but twenty paces away a faint suggestion of light showed where the door of the Royal box stood open. When I reached it, I saw that a solitary lamp was burning on the far side of the stalls. After glancing at it, the darkness of the box seemed more impenetrable. I felt for the little gold bag-on the balcony, on the chair, on the floor. It was nowhere. I stood up and peered into the great, dim auditorium, wondering whether I dared strike a match. Fearing that there might be a fireman somewhere in the darkness, I abandoned the idea. The sudden flash might be seen, and then people would come running, and there would have to be explanations. I went down on my hands and knees, and felt round her chair and then mine, and then all over the box. Just as I got up, my right hand encountered something hard and shiny. Clearly it wasn't what I was looking for, but out of curiosity I stooped to feel it again. I groped in vain for a moment; then I put my hand full on the buckle of a patent-leather shoe. As my fingers closed about a warm ankle:

"Pardon, monsieur!" came a quick whisper.

I let go. "Is that you, Yvonne?"

"Si, monsieur."

"I never heard you come in."

"I have come this moment, and did not see monsieur in the dark. Madame has sent me. Monsieur cannot find that little bag?"

"No. Do you think I might strike a match?"

"Ah, no, monsieur, not in the Opera House, They are so particular."

"I see-at least, I don't, and that's the trouble. However—"

I felt over the balcony again. No good.

"Where did mademoiselle sit, monsieur?"

"Where are you?"

I groped in the direction of the whisper and found an arm.

"In that chair there," I said, guiding her to it.

"Here, monsieur?"

"Yes, that's right."

I heard her hands groping about the chair and turned to try the floor on the other side again.

"I have it, monsieur."

"Well," said I, "I could have sworn I'd felt everywhere round that chair."

She chinked the bag by way of answer.

"Anyway, we've got it," said I. "Come on." And I made for the door. Then I stopped to take one more look at the great house. As I did so, a woman appeared on the far side of the stalls. She paused for a second to glance at herself in a mirror immediately under the solitary electric light. I recognized Yvonne. Then she passed on. Neither of us spoke for a moment. Then:

"Why did you say you were Yvonne?" said I.

"Yvonne is my name, too."

224

"Were you afraid I might have a lucid interval?"

"Perhaps."

"Your fears are realized. I have-I'm having one now."

"How awful!"

"Isn't it? And now we've found your bag, would you mind if I looked for something else?"

"Something of yours or mine?"

"Something of yours?"

"Can I help you?" she said slowly.

"Materially."

With a little half laugh, half sob, a warm arm slid round my neck.

"Here they are!" she whispered.

Madame would not let us go till Yvonne had returned from the manager's office with the offer of a box for Thursday.

"So it is not 'Goodbye' and you will come and see me again. I sing then for the last time in Munich. I fear you cannot have your own box, though. The Regent is coming that night. It is too bad."

We laughed and bade her farewell.

As the car slowed down at my companion's hotel, the footman slid off the front seat and opened the door. I got up and out of the car. As I turned, I saw the girl pick up her gloves and leave the precious bag on the seat.

"My dear, your bag—"

But, as she got out, the bag left the seat with her. By the lights in the car I saw that it was attached to a chain about her neck; and the chain lay beneath her dress. I handed her out thoughtfully.

"Till Thursday, then," she said.

"Till tomorrow morning," said I.

She laughed.

"I think there ought to be an interval."

"Isn't that just what I'm saying? What about a luncheon interval tomorrow?"

"Well, it mustn't be a lucid one"

"All right. I'll bring Jonah and Daphne."

"Mayn't I see the mistake?"

"If I can find him."

"Goodbye"

"Goodbye. I say—"

She turned, one small foot on the steps.

"I love your feet," I said.

"Anything else?"

"Yes. Do you always unfasten that chain and take off the bag when you go to the theatre?"

She looked down at the little foot in its shining shoe. Then:

"Only on third Tuesdays," she said.

When I reached my hotel, I passed quickly upstairs to the sitting-room.

"Here he is," said Daphne "Come along, darling, and have some supper, and tell us all about it."

"Supper!" said Berry. "Woman, you forget yourself. You are no longer on the joy-wheel. My lord has dined."

"As a matter of fact, I have," said I. "Madame gave me some dinner at the Opera House."

"Of course," said Berry.

"What did I say? We grovelling worms can gnaw our sandwiches the while he cracks bottles of-champagne, was it?"

I nodded.

Berry rose to his feet, and in a voice broken with emotion, called such shades of his ancestors "as are on night duty" to witness. "Hencefifth," he said, "I intend to lead a wicked life

"Blackpool-Conservative; no change," said Jonah.

Berry ignored the interruption. "Virtue may have its own cakes and ale. I dare say it has. What of it? I never see any of them. Vice is more generous. Its patrons actually wallow in champagne. For me, the most beastly sandwiches I ever ate, and an expensive stall. For him, dinner with the prima donna and the Royal box. By the way, who did the girl mistake you for? One of the attendants or the business manager?"

"Who was she?" said Jill.

"I don't know."

"Rot!" said Jonah.

"It's the truth."

"She looked rather a dear," said Daphne.

"She is. You'll meet her tomorrow. And Berry-she wants to meet Berry. She said so."

"There you are," said my brother-in-law. "Is my tie straight?"

I lighted a cigarette to conceal a smile.

CHAPTER XIV

A PRIVATE VIEW

When I had adjusted the cushions, I sank into the chair and sighed.

"What's that for?" said Daphne

"Sin," said I.

"Whose?"

"That of him who packed for me at the Blahs this morning. A sin of omission rather than commission, though he did put my sponge-bag into my collarcase," I added musingly. "They're both round, you see. Still, I pass that by."

"But what do you really complain of?" said Jill. "He's left my dressing-gown out."

"I expect he thought it was a loose cover," said Jonah. "It'll be sent on all right," said Daphne "That's nothing. What about my fan? You're not a bit sorry for me about that."

"I have already been sorry about it. I was sorry for you on Friday just by the sideboard. I remember it perfectly. All the same, if you will waste Berry's substance at places of entertainment in the West End, and then fling a priceless heirloom down in the hall of the theatre, you mustn't be surprised if some flat-footed seeker after pleasure treads on it."

"He was a very nice man, and his feet weren't a bit flat."

"I believe you did it on purpose to get into conversation with him. Where's Berry?"

At that moment the gentleman in question walked across the lawn towards us.

"Thank Heaven!" he said when he saw me. "I'm so glad you're back. I've run out of your cigarettes."

I handed him my case in silence.

"It's curious," he said, "how used one can get to inferior tobacco."

Tea appeared in serial form. After depositing the three-storied cake dish holder-or whatever the thing is called-with a to-be-completed air, the footman disappeared, to return a moment later with the teapot and hot water. As he turned to go:

"Bring me the tray that's on the billiard-table," said Berry. "Carry it carefully."

"Yes, sir.

"Without moving, we all observed one another, the eyes looking sideways. You see, the tray bore a jig-saw. When I had left on the previous Saturday for a week-end visit, we had done the top right-hand corner and half what looked as if it must be the left side. Most of this we had done on Friday evening; but artificial light is inclined to militate against the labourer, and at eleven o'clock Berry had sworn twice, shown us which pieces were missing, and related the true history of poor Agatha Glynde, who spent more than a fortnight over 'David Copperfield' before she found out that the pieces had been mixed up with those of Constable's 'Hay Wain.' This upset us so much that Jonah said he should try and get a question asked in the House about it, and we decided to send the thing back the next day and demand the return of the money.

On the way up to bed, Daphne had asked me if I thought we could get "damages, or compensation, or something," and I had replied that, if we could prove malice, they had undoubtedly brought themselves within the pale of the criminal law.

The next morning Jill had done nearly two more square inches before breakfast, and I missed the midday train to town.

"Hullo, you have got on!" I said, as the man set the tray and its precious burden gingerly on the grass in our midst.

"Aha, my friend," said Berry, "I thought you'd sit up! Yes, sir, the tract already developed represents no less an area than thirty-six square inches-coldly calculated by me this afternoon during that fair hour which succeeds the sleep of repletion and the just-but the vast possibilities which lie hidden beneath the surface of the undeveloped expanse of picture are almost frightening. A land rich in minerals, teeming with virgin soil-a very Canaan of today. Does it not call you, brother?"

"It does," said I. "I wish it didn't, because it's wicked waste of time, but it does."

I kneeled down that I might the better appreciate their industry. The jig-saw was called 'A Young Diana' and was alleged to be a reproduction of the picture of that name which had appeared in the Academy the year before. I hardly remembered it. I gazed admiringly at the two clouds drifting alone at the top right-hand corner, the solitary hoof planted upon a slice of green sward, the ragged suggestion of forest land in the distance, and a ladder of enormous length, which appeared to possess something of that spirit of independence which distinguished Mahomet's coffin. In other words, it was self-supporting. After a careful scrutiny, I rose to my feet, took a pace or two backwards, and put my head on one side. Then:

"I like it," I said. "I like it. Some people might say it looked a little crude or unfinished; but, to my mind, that but preserves, as it were, the spirit of barbarism which the title suggests."

"Suggestion as opposed to realization," said Berry, "is the rule by which we work. To the jaded appet-imagination the hoof suggests a horse. It is up to you to imagine the horse. We have, as it were, with an effort set in motion the long unused machinery of your brain. It is for you, brother, to carry on the good work. Please pass out quietly. There will be collection plates at both doors."

"You're not to touch it yet," said Daphne. "I want to talk about abroad first. If we're really going, we must settle things."

"Of course we're going," said Berry. "I ordered a yachting cap yesterday."

"What's that for?" said Jill.

"Well, we're not going to fly across the Channel, are we?

Besides that, supposing we go to Lucerne part of the time?"

"What about taking the car?" said Daphne.

"It's expensive," said Berry moodily, "but I don't see how else we can satisfactorily sustain the flow of bloated plutocracy which at present oozes from us."

We all agreed that the car must come. Then arose the burning question of where to go. In a rash moment Jill murmured something about Montenegro.

"Montenegro?" said Berry, with a carelessness that should have put her on her guard.

"Yes," said Jill. "I heard someone talking about it when I was dining with the Bedells. It sounded priceless. I had a sort of idea it was quite small, and had a prince, but it's really quite big, and it's got a king over it, and they all wear the old picturesque dress, and the scenery's gorgeous. And, if it was wet, we could go to the-the—"

"Kursaal," said Berry. "No, not Kursaal. It's like that, though."

"Casino?"

"That's it-Casino. And then we could go on to Nice and Cannes, and—"

"You're going too fast, aren't you? Servia comes before Cannes, doesn't it?"

"Well, Servia, too."

"All right," said Berry. "I was going to suggest that we joined the Danube at Limoges, went up as far as Milan, where the falls are, and then struck off to Toledo, taking Warsaw on the way, but—"

"That'd be rather a long way round, wouldn't it?" said Jill, all seriousness in her grey eyes.

"Ah, I mean the Spanish Toledo, not the one in the States."

"Oh, I see—"

She checked herself suddenly and looked round. "He's laughing at me," she said. "What have I said wrong?"

"If anyone asked me where we should be without our Jill," said Berry, "I couldn't tell them."

When we began to discuss the tour in good earnest, the argument proper began. I had suggested that we should make for Frankfort, to start with, and Daphne and Jonah rather favoured Germany. Berry, however, wanted to go to Austria. It was after a casual enough remark of Jonah's that the roads in Germany were very good that Berry really got going.

"The roads good?" he said. "That settles it-say no more. The survey, which is, after all, the object of our holiday (sic), will be able to be made with success. If we start at once, we shall be able to get the book published by Christmas: 'Road Surfaces in Germany,' by a Hog."

"The old German towns are fascinating," said Daphne.

"Nothing like them," said Berry. "I can smell some of them now. Can you not hear the cheerful din of the iron tires upon the cobbled streets? Can you not see the grateful smile spreading over the beer-sodden features of the cathedral verger, as he pockets the money we pay for the privilege of following an objectionable rabble round an edifice, which we shall remember more for the biting chill of its atmosphere than anything else? And then the musty quiet of the museums, and the miles we shall cover in the picture galleries, halting now and then to do a brief gloat in front of one of Van Stunk's masterpieces . . .

My heart leaps up when I behold a Van Stunk on the wall. Wordsworth knew his Englishman, didn't he?"

"Oh, well, if you're so dead against it—"

"Against it, dear. How can I be against it? Why, we may even be arrested as spies! There"-he looked round triumphantly-"who shall say that the age of romance is dead? Let us go forth and languish in a German gaol. Think of the notices we shall get in the papers! We'll give our photographs to The Daily Glass before we start. I expect we shall see one another in the chapel on Sundays, and I shall write to you in blood every day, darling, on a piece of my mattress. The letters will always be in the top left-hand corner of the steak pudding. Don't say I didn't tell you where to look."

"We shall be able to talk," said I-"by rapping on the wall, I mean."

"Certainly. Once for the letter A, twice for the chambermaid, three times for the boots. In the meantime, Jonah and you will each have removed a large stone from the floor of your cells by means of a nail which he found in his soup. Say you work sixteen hours out of the twenty-four you ought to have burrowed outside the gates in about five years."

Jill shuddered. "Austria would be rather nice, just now, wouldn't it?" she ventured.

"We could go high up if it got hot, of course," said Daphne slowly, "and the air's nice—"

I'll find out what we do about shipping the car on Friday," said Berry.

I must have been tired, for I never heard the tea-things taken away. When I opened my eyes, Berry and Co. had gone. I looked at the jig-saw and began to wonder what had waked me.

"First of all," said a quiet voice, "I take five and three-quarters. Do you think you can remember that?"

"I'll try. Long ones, of course."

"Yes, please. Not the ordinary white kid: I like the fawn suede ones."

"With pleasure."

"And now, please, can I be shown over the house?"

I turned and regarded her. Sitting easily in a chair to my right, and a little behind me, she was holding out to me a slip of paper. I took it mechanically but I did not look at it.

"Don't move for a minute or two," I said. "You look absolutely splendid like that."

She smiled. I rather think her frock was of linen-at any rate, it was blue. Her large straw hat was blue, too, and so were her smart French gloves and her dainty shoes; her ankles were very pretty, but her complexion was the thing: She had one of the clearest skins I have ever seen, and the delicate bloom of her cheeks was a wonder in itself. I could not well see her eyes, for she was sitting with her head thrown back-her gloved right hand behind it holding down the brim of her hat-and as she was looking at me and not up into the sky, they were almost hidden by their lids. Her left arm lay carelessly along the arm of the chair, and, her sleeve being loose and open, I could see half a dozen inches of warm pink arm. I just looked at her.

"Done?" she said.

"Not quite." I have said before, and I say again, that girls of this type ought not to be allowed to raise their eyebrows and smile faintly at the same moment. It amounts to a technical assault. I fancy she saw me set my teeth, for the next moment she put up her left hand and bent the broad blue rim over her face.

"Early closing day," she said. I contemplated her ankles in silence. After a minute:

"Well?" said my companion from behind the brim.

"I hate it when the blinds are down," said I, "but—"

"But what?"

"Happily, they are only short blinds. In other words, just as the ostrich, when pursued, is said to thrust its head into the sand, believing—"

"And now please can I be shown over the house?"

I glanced at the order-to-view which she had handed me. It referred to The Grange, which stood in its own grounds about half a mile away. Its lodge gates were rather like ours. The same mistake had been made before.

"The agent at Bettshanger gave me that today, and I motored over this afternoon. The car's outside. I was walking up the drive-how pretty it all is!-when I saw you asleep here. I suppose I ought to have gone up to the house really, but it looked so nice and cool here that I came and sat down instead and waited for you to wake."

"I'm so glad you did."

"Why?"

"Well, you see, they're rather a queer lot up there at the house-might have said you couldn't see over, or something."

She opened her big eyes.

"But I've got an order."

"That's the worst of it. They'll take orders from no one. Once they'd caught sight of it, you would have been blindfolded and led back to the village by a circuitous route."

"Nonsense!"

"It's a fact. But I'll show you round, all right. Anything I can tell you about the place before we move?"

She regarded me suspiciously. Then:

"Is there a billiard-room?" she said.

"Certainly. And a table complete with three balls, one of latest models—slate bed, pneumatic cushions. Be careful of the top one; it bust the other day. The butler had pumped it up too tight."

"Servants' hall?"

"Every time. All the domestic offices are noble."

"Telephone?"

"Of course. In case of fire, call 'Fire Brigade.' No number required. Speak direct to fire-station. Give address of fire."

"That's useful."

"Rather! You'll have them up under the hour, if they can get the horses."

"All the same, I don't think we shall come here. You see, I didn't know it was an asylum."

"It's very cheap," said I. "I can do it at ten guineas a week-without the inspection-pit, that is."

She leaned forward and laughed. "Oh dear!" she said, "what a thing it is to be really silly sometimes!"

She got up and smoothed down her dress.

"And now, please, can I be shown over the house?"

"With pleasure," I said, getting up. "That is, unless you'd rather see The Grange first."

She stared at me for a moment, then she snatched the order out of my hand. "What's this place?" she demanded.

"White Ladies."

"Are you trying to let it?"

"Well, we haven't thought—"

"And you've let me sit here all this time making a fool of myself, when you knew perfectly well—"

"Five and three-quarters, was it?"

She stamped her foot.

"Dear pretty Girl Blue, don't be angry."

"You ought to be ashamed of yourself!"

"I know, but I'm so busy just now that it's done for me. My sister is ashamed of me every evening at eight-fifteen. Matinees on Wednesdays at two. Could you come one day?"

She laughed in spite of herself. Then:

"And now where is this Grange place?"

"Next but one on the right, but it looks rotten in the evening."

"It's only just five."

"Besides, they had measles there last May-stacks of them."

"Stacks of what?"

"Measles. One of them escaped one day and was brought back by the village corner-boy. He said he'd have kept it, only he hadn't got a dog licence."

"But The Grange has got a ghost, hasn't it? And I love ghosts."

"The Grey Lady? My dear, she's gone. Always used to walk the back stairs on third Fridays, and one night the servants left the lights on. She gave notice the next day. Wanted a change, I think. You see, she'd been in one place nearly two hundred years. Besides, the stairs were bad."

"It's a nice house, isn't it?"

"Pretty well. But it hasn't got a priest's hole."

"What does that matter?"

"Well, where are you going to keep the gorgonzolas?"

She leaned on the back of a chair and began to laugh helplessly. Presently:

"You wretched man!" she said. "I'm really awfully angry with you."

"I knew it."

"Be quiet. You've wasted my time here until it's too late for me to see The Grange, and what on earth I shall tell father I don't know."

"He's not outside?"

"In the car? You don't think I should still be here if he was? No, I came over alone."

"That's all right. Now you'll be able to help me with this jig-saw."

She gave rather a good gasp at that.

"Girl Blue, please. You've heaps of time, because, if you'd gone to The Grange, you wouldn't have got away yet. And it's a nice jig-saw, quite one of the family."

"Eats out of your hand, I suppose?"

"Rather. And sits up and barks for Baldwin and all the rest of it. 'A Young Diana' it's called. Appeared in last year's Academy, and—"

But she was down on her knees on the lawn, staring at the tray by now. I joined her, wondering a little.

"That's a bit of Merrylegs," she said, picking up one of the pieces, "and there's another. That's a bit of her dear nose, and there's her white stocking. Look here, we'll do her first."

I sat down on the turf and looked at her. "Either," I said slowly-"either you're a witch, and that isn't allowed, or else you've had to learn this picture some time as a punishment."

She laughed. "I sat for it," she explained. "That's all."

It was my turn to gasp.

"It's hanging in the dining-room at home now. Come along. There's a bit of my habit. Keep it with Merrylegs. I'll fit them together in a minute."

I took off my coat, kneeled down beside her, and began to receive Merrylegs piecemeal. When she had picked out all of the mare, she cleared a little space, and began fitting the bits together at a rate that was astonishing. Then she turned her attention to the background. Laid upon its side, the mysterious ladder became a distant fence, and little by little a landscape grew into being under her small fingers. Suddenly she caught my arm.

"Somebody's coming!" she whispered.

I heard footsteps crunch on a path's gravel, then all was silent again. Whoever it was, was coming towards us over the lawn. A clump of rhododendrons hid us from them, and them from us.

"Behind there!" I whispered, pointing to three tall elms at our back, which grew so close together that they formed a giant screen. She was out of sight in a second, and I had just time to throw my coat over the jig-saw and sit down upon the glove she had dropped before Berry appeared.

"Hullo!" he said.

"Hullo!" said I.

"What are you doing?"

"Doing?"

"Yes, you know-executing, performing, carrying out?"

"Go away!" I said. "You are trespassing upon a private reverie. Didn't you see the notice?"

He shook his head. "You have, as it were, burst rudely open the door of the brown study in which I am communing with Nature and one or

238

two of my imagination's friends. Kindly apologize and withdraw, closing the door as you go."

"All right, Omar. Where's your Thou?"

"You frightened her away."

Berry grinned. "Heard the pattering of my little feet, I suppose!"

"Yes. She wouldn't believe it was only footsteps, but let that pass. If she were to hear the same noise-forgive me-retreating, she would probably return."

"Really think so?"

"That is my steadfast conviction."

"Well, you go indoors, and we'll see. If I don't follow you in five minutes, you'll know you're right."

"Friend," said I, "the indecency of your suggestion is almost grotesque. To impose upon a timid, trusting Thou is either base or dastardly-I forget which. I am glad none of the others were here to hear what I feel sure to have been but a thoughtless, idle word. I shan't say anything about it, so no one, except you and me, will ever know; and even if I cannot ever forget, I shall come to forgive it in years to come."

"Time will heal the wound, brother. Till then, where's the jig-saw?"

"An evil beast hath devoured it. It is, without doubt, rent in pieces."

"In which case I shall prefer a bill of indictment against you as accessory for mutilation next autumn assize. I warn you."

"Thanks! I shall see you at dinner, shan't I? Not that I want to, but I just shall."

Berry sighed. "From your manner, more than from what you say, anyone would think you wanted me to go, old chap. Of course, I know you, so it doesn't matter; but you ought to be more careful. No, I've not taken offence, because I know none was meant; but I'm going to go just to teach you a lesson. Yes, I am. Give my love to Thou, won't you?"

"Certainly not! She's had one shock already this afternoon."

"Oh, was today the first time she'd seen you?"

He strolled back to the house. When I heard his footsteps on the gravel again, I got up and peered through the rhododendrons. I watched him go indoors, and turned to see the girl once more on her knees by the jig-saw. I kneeled opposite her and watched her at work. After a moment she glanced up and met my eyes.

"You'll see the picture better from this side," she said.

"Which picture?"

"Round you come!"

I crawled to her side with a sigh. On she went at a wonderful pace. Old elms rose up in the background, a splash of red and brown resolved itself into a sunny farm, and four pieces which Berry had recognized as water went to make up a sheltered haystack. When it was nearly finished, she leaned across me and looked at my wrist-watch.

"I'll just have time," she whispered half to herself.

"Only just?"

"Only just. Did you speak?"

"Yes, I did. I said 'Damn!' And I'll say it again."

She leaned on my shoulder and laughed for a second. Then:

"I'm sure you wouldn't find that in the Rubaiyat."

"Perhaps Thou didn't have to be back in time for dinner."

She fell to work again, but I could see she was smiling. The loose pieces left were very few now. A tuft of grass fell into place, a wisp of smoke stole out of the farmhouse chimney, a quick-set hedge sprang up in the distance, landscape and sky merged on the horizon, and the thing was done.

She sat back on her heels and regarded it for a moment. Then she slipped sideways on to the lawn, smoothed down her frock, and looked at me.

"Not bad, is it?" she said.

"It's sweet!"

"You ought to see the original."

"I have. That's why I love it. I shall have it framed and keep it in memory of this private view."

"Sentiment, with a vengeance."

"What if it is, Girl Blue?"

For answer, she began to pull on her gloves. I watched her in silence. When they were both on, she rose, and so did I.

"I'll go as I came," she said. "Don't come with me to the gate."

I bowed. She put out her hand. I bent over it.

"Goodbye," I said.

"Goodbye, and-and thanks for—"

"For what, Girl Blue?"

"For not asking any questions."

I smiled and turned away. Then I kneeled down suddenly and kissed the face that looked up out of the picture, the face that would have meant nothing two hours before, the face that looked out into the clear breeze and over the open country, the face that—

"As this is quite a private view," said the original, speaking very slowly, "and as tomorrow you won't be able to—"

I didn't hear the rest of the sentence.

Before I had finished my second cigarette, Berry, Daphne, and Jill came round the bank of rhododendrons.

"Why, Boy," said Jill, "have you been here all the time?"

A cry from Daphne interrupted her.

The next moment they were all down on their knees poring over my late companion's handiwork. A moment later, as with one consent, they all looked up and stared at me. I looked away and smoked with careless deliberation.

"How on earth have you done it?" gasped Daphne.

"Done what?" said I. "Oh, that? Oh, it wasn't very hard!"

"You must be better at them than you were on Saturday," said Jill. "Have you been practising at the Blahs?"

I felt Berry was looking at me, and waited.

"Then it was a glove you were sitting on," he said slowly. Berry's a nut—every time.

It was the first week in October, and we were back in town. They were all out but me. Sunday afternoon it was, and I was alone in the library finishing a little work. I do work sometimes. Suddenly the telephone went. I picked up the receiver.

"Is that the garage?" said Girl Blue.

"No, dear. It's me. How are you?"

"Why, it's you!"

"I know. I said so just now. You're looking splendid. Oh, I am glad! I've waited such a long time!"

"You must thank the Exchange, not me."

"Don't rub it in!"

"Well, goodbye."

"I don't think you're very kind, Girl Blue."

"No?"

"No, I don't! I've got the gloves, by the way."

"Thank you."

"I'll send them to you, care of Charing Cross Post Office, if you like, unless you'd rather I buried them six paces due east of the fourteenth lamp-post on the west side of Edgware Road."

"I think," she said slowly, "I think I may as well take them with me."

"Certainly, madam. Sign, please! But when, dear?"

"Well, I shall be at the Albert Hall next Friday."

"Girl Blue!"

"I don't suppose you're going, but perhaps you could send them by someone who—"

"Under what symbol shall I meet her?"

"Wait a moment! You shall have the seventh waltz—"

"Only seven? Where is he? What is his name?"

"You heard what I said. And we'll meet under—oh, under—"

"Mistletoe," said I. "Goodbye!"

242

"Goodbye! Oh, Girl Blue, I forgot to say—"

"Number, please!" said Exchange.

"You've cut me off!" I roared.

"Sorry."

A pause. Then:

"Here you are."

"Hullo, dear!" I said.

"Is that the cab rank?" said a man's fat voice.

"No, it isn't," said I. "And you've got an ugly face and flat feet, and I hate you!"

Then I rang off.

CHAPTER XV

ALL FOUND

I had seen her but once before, and that was at the Savoy on New Year's Eve. She had been with her party at one table, and I with mine at another. And in the midst of the reveling I had chanced to look up and into one of the great mirrors which made a panel upon the wall. There I had seen the girl, sitting back in her chair, smiling and fresh and white-shouldered, in a dress of black and gold, her fingers about the stem of her goblet. Not talking, listening, rather, to the words of a man at her side, whose eyes were watching her smiling lips somewhat greedily. He had red hair, I remember, and a moustache brushed up to hide a long upper lip. And, as I looked, she also had looked up, and our eyes had met. There and then I had raised my wine and toasted her-her of the looking-glass. The smile had deepened. Then she had raised her glass, and drunk to me in return. That was all. And when Berry had leaned across the table and asked:

"Who's your friend?"

"I wish I knew."

"Pshaw!" said my brother-in-law. "I say it deliberately."

"I drank to a thought," said I. "Believe me. "After all, a thought is a reflection. And now here she was, sitting in the grass by the wayside.

"She's brown, isn't she?" said I.

"As a berry. I like his breeches."

I bowed. "Thank you. And for you,'picturesque' is the word-one of the words. Shall I compare you to a summer's day?"

"I'd rather you collected that cow. She's getting too near the river for my liking. I'm looking after the dears."

"Are you?" said I. "But—"

"But what?"

"'Quis custodiet—'"

The apple she threw passed over my shoulder.

Mountains and valleys, swift rivers and curling roads, here and there a village shining in the hot sun, and once in a while a castle in the woods, white-walled, red-roofed, peaceful enough now in its old age, but hinting at wild oats sown and reaped when it was young. Hinting broadly, too. At nights shaken with the flare of torches and the clash of arms, at oaths and laughter and the tinkle of spurs on the worn steps, at threats and bloodlettings and all the good old ways, now dead, out of date, and less indebted to memory than imagination. And then at galleries with creaking floors, at arras and the rustle of a dress; whisperings, too, and the proud flash of eyes, hands lily-white, whose fingers men must kiss and in the eyes mirror themselves. But these things are not dead. Old-fashioned wrath is over-gone to its long home: love is not even wrinkled. Yet again it was before wrath . . .

I set out to describe the province of Krain, and now I have strayed from the highway up one of those curling roads to one of those white castles, only to lose myself in the thicket of Romance beyond. Perhaps it does not matter. Anyway, it was on the slope of a green meadow all among the mountains of Krain that the girl was sitting, herself unminded, minding her cows. And out of the woods above her a round, white tower proclaimed a chateau set on the shoulder of a hill.

Her dress was that of the country, and yet, perhaps, rather such as Croatian peasants wear. All white linen, embroidered ever so richly, cut low and round at the neck, and with the skirt falling some four inches below her knee: short sleeves, a small, white apron, and over her thick, fair hair a bright red kerchief. But her stockings were of white silk, and small, black buckled slippers kept the little feet. Clear, blue eyes hers, and a small merry mouth, and a skin after the sun's own heart. It was so brown-such an even, delicate brown. Brown cheeks and temples, brown arms and hands, brown throat. Oh, very picturesque.

I rounded up the cow errant, returned to my lady, and took my seat by her side.

"Thank you," she said. "And now, who are you and what do you want?"

"My name," said I, "is Norval. And I want to know the way to the pageant-ground, and when does your scene come on?"

"It is a nice dress, isn't it?"

She rose and stood smoothing her frock and apron.

"Sweet. Only you ought to have bare brown legs."

"My dear man, this isn't the Garden of Eden."

"No? Some other Paradise, I suppose. Old Omar's, perhaps. Besides, I forgot. Dolls never go barefoot, do they?"

"Dolls?"

"Yes. Aren't you the 'great big beautiful doll' they sing of?"

She threw back her head, and laughed at that, pleasedly. Then she began to sing softly:

"Oh, you beautiful doll, You great big beautiful doll . . ."

We finished the verse together, the cows watching us with big eyes.

"I think we're rather good," said I, when it was over.

"I know we're both mad," said she. "And I don't feel a bit like singing really, either."

"Oh, great and beautiful one," said I, "what is the matter? Indicate to me the fly that dares to lurk in this fair bowl of ointment."

She looked away over the river. Then:

"After all, it's nothing to do with you."

"Nothing whatever." said I.

"Then why do you ask?"

"Something to say, I suppose. Is not the clemency of the weather delightful?"

"Yes, but those cows belong to me."

I laughed scornfully. Then:

"My aunt has four eggs," I said simply.

She turned away, ostensibly to pick a flower, but I saw her shoulders shaking. At length:

"There is a pig in the grass," she said. "Its name is Norval."

"The doll is on its hind legs," I replied, getting up. "As for me, is it not that I shall have been about to go? Adieu, mademoiselle."

"Er-au revoir, monsieur."

"That's better," said I. "And now, what's the trouble, my dear?"

Well, it was about the chauffeur. You see, she was spending the summer here in the chateau. Yes, the chateau above us, white on the hillside. She and a companion-a girl-alone, with a household of their own, very happy, very comfortable . . .

"We are really, you know. Don't think we're suffragists. Truth is, I'd got about sick of men, and thought I'd take a rest. I heard of this old place to be let furnished, came to see if it was half as nice as it sounded, and never even went back to England to collect Betty. Just couldn't leave it. Betty followed post-haste with the servants and heavy luggage, and-and—"

"And the parrot?" I hazarded.

"No. Oh, the linen and everything. I'd got the car with me. We've been here nearly two months now, and I love it more every day. Don't miss men a bit, either."

This last in an inimitable tone, half nonchalant, half defiant.

"I expect they do most of the missing."

"Thanks, awfully. However, I may tell you the family's been rather narky—"

"I beg your pardon?"

"Narky. Like a nark."

"Of course. How stupid of me! Same root as 'snirksome.' As you were."

"Well, rather ratty about it all. Said it was all ridiculous and unheard of."

"Did they use the word 'proceeding'?"

"They did."

"Ah!"

"The one thing that sort of stopped them from really doing anything was the fact that Betty was with me. Betty's dear, and they all know it. And her being here, I suppose, seemed to save it from being what's called an 'impossible position.' Well, a week ago comes a letter from the Brethes-that's my uncle and aunt-saying they're motoring through Austria to Italy, and are going to stay a night at Laipnik on the way. Would like to run over and see me, as they understand Savavic-that's me-is only thirty miles away. All very nice."

"Sweet of them." I agreed.

"Isn't it! Only, three days ago Betty gets a wire to say her mother's ill, and she has to bolt for the night train to Paris."

"Yes. So that uncle dear mustn't come to Savavic at any price. If he does, Betty's absence becomes apparent, and the good old 'impossible position' arises at once. Consequently, I send a nice letter to the one hotel at Laipnik 'to await arrival,' saying the road's so bad and hard to find that I'll come over to them instead of their coming here."

"Much as you would have loved them to see Savavic."

"Exactly. You're rather intelligent."

"Oh, I'm often like that. It's in the blood. Grandpa got his B.A.," I explained. "We've loaned his hood to the Wallace Collection. Go on."

"Well, that all sounds very nice and easy, doesn't it? Then, to put the lid on, my chauffeur breaks his arm yesterday afternoon."

"And the uncle's due when?"

"Slept at Laipnik last night. I was to have lunched with them today. Oh, the fat's in the fire all right this time. I may expect them any time after three." I reflected a moment. Then:

"I'll drive you to Laipnik," said I. "I'm as safe as a house at the wheel."

"You're awfully good and kind," said the girl, shaking her head, "but it's no good. Think. How on earth would I explain you?"

"It is unnecessary to explain a chauffeur."

"Oh, but you can't—"

"Certainly I can. At any rate, I'm going to. Come along and get changed, mistress."

I scrambled to my feet.

"If you'll show me the way to the garage, I'll be looking over the car. What is she, by the way? And where does your late chauffeur keep his boots?"

"Are you an angel?" said the girl, getting up.

"Who told you?" said I.

The boots were much too big and the gaiters a little small. Still, they did. A long dust-coat came down over the tops of the gaiters, making the uniform unnecessary. I took the cap to wear when we reached the town. Gloves, near enough. It was a big, open car, and all the way to Laipnik the girl, looking priceless in a fawn-coloured dress, sat by my side. We went like the wind. After a while:

"He drives well," said my companion, half to herself.

"Thank you, beautiful doll-I should say madam. Is that right?"

"Quite, thanks. How are the boots?"

"A bit spacious. I'm afraid I've lost one of my toes already."

"You poor man. Which one?"

"Baldwin," said I. "He's got separated from the others, you know. I'll be able to look for him when we get to Laipnik. Told them to keep together, too," I added bitterly.

She gave a little peal of laughter. Then:

"How tiresome" she said. "And I'm afraid your calves weren't made for those gaiters."

"I admit they don't fit as well as your stockings, but—"

"Norval."

"Madam?"

"Behave yourself."

"Very good, madam. By the way, what about my wages?"

"What do you suggest? I shan't object to anything reasonable."

"No? Well, I was getting eleven-three a yar-day in my last place, and all found-especially all."

"'All found''s rather a dangerous phrase."

"Not at all. It only means washing and beer and the English papers, when you've done with them, and meat on Sundays. A smile, too, when I'm tired, and a word of thanks after seventy miles in the rain with a head wind."

"It might cover a multitude of sins, Norval."

Here I saved a dog's life and passed two wagons before their drivers had had time to inspire the horses with the terror they felt themselves. Then:

"'All found''s all right, if you know your man," said I.

"But I don't."

I caught her laughing eyes in the windscreen, and straightway drank to them from an imaginary wine-glass. She smiled gently, and the eyes looked away with the look that sees at once not at all and yet farthest. She was gazing down the vista of memory.

"Then it's a compact," I said quietly. "Sealed with a drink."

"I never drank to you this time, Norval."

"Yes, you did," said I. "Only with thine eyes, doll beautiful."

"You forget yourself."

"I remember you. You were wearing a black and gold dress. Sweet you looked."

She turned away and pointed to a church we were leaving on our right.

"That," she said, "is a church."

"You amaze me. I thought it was a swimming-bath."

She bit the lip that wanted to smile.

"To return to you, who are my mutton, I wish this road wasn't so narrow. I can't look at you except in the screen."

"We first met in a looking-glass."

"True. But now I want something more-more tangible."

"Indeed?"

I glanced down. "At any rate, I've got your feet, bless them. I shall compose a sonnet to them, beautiful doll."

"And I'll write an epic about yours."

Five minutes passed. "How's the epic going?" said I.

"I've only done four lines."

"Let's have them."

"The beetling beetle-crushing baulks of boots Crashed on their thunderous way, while men-at-arms, Who knew no fear, shuddered and crossed themselves, And little children whimpered with a fright Too fierce for tears."

"Very good," said I. "Now you shall have mine.

I thought they were stars, And I know they were shining, But so brightly. The daintiest things that were ever created. They danced on my heart from the moment I saw them, But so lightly That while they were there my heart became lighter, Yet on it they made an enduring impression, Lasting and deep. Fairies' steps may be slighter, But so slightly. You'll think I am mad, but I'm only a blighter. I thought they were stars, And I know they were shining."

"Thank you very much. I didn't know you were a poet."

"Nor was I till I entered your service," said I.

So presently we came to Laipnik. I stopped outside the little town, put on my cap, and settled the girl on the back seat. Five minutes later we rolled up to the hotel.

On the steps stood a stout man with a serious face, looking suspiciously at the cigar he had just lighted.

"Hullo, Uncle Dick," said my mistress.

"My dear child, I am glad you've come. You aunt's upstairs rather tired, but wild to see you. We're going to stay another night here and go on early tomorrow."

"Are you? I'll come up at once."

I opened the door of the car and handed her out. She kissed her relative and turned to me.

"Er-will you-er—"

I coughed.

"You will get your own lunch, Norval, and come to the office for orders at half-past two."

"Very good, madam."

As I raised my cap:

"Oh, I feel such a beast," she murmured.

I never gave Berry and the others a thought till I had eaten my lunch and was musing over my coffee with a cigarette. They were coming in the car from Salzburg, and were going to join me this evening at a farm called Poganec, where I had slept last night and where we were all going to stay. We had told people we were going to fish. I think Jonah meant it. We others were going to sleep and watch him and sleep again. Now, Poganec and Savavic were only seven miles apart, and were served by the same post office. In fact, they were at opposite ends of the same valley, in the midst of which, half-way between the two, our common village slept in the hot sun. It was in the course of my first walk that I had come upon Savavic. And now, instead of being at Poganec to welcome them this afternoon, here was I at Laipnik pretending to be a chauffeur. What did it matter? I should be back that evening. Only seven miles . . .

At half-past two I was at the office, and at twenty-nine minutes to three my lady appeared in the hall. I went to her, cap in hand. She turned and walked to a little lounge-place out of sight of the office. I followed her there. For a moment she did not speak. Then:

"Oh, I feel such a beast!" she said passionately. "Such a beast! Don't take your cap off to me. Put it on. For heaven's sake, put it on! And sit down. Sprawl about. Light a cigarette. Shake me. Kiss me, if you like. Anything to show you're my own class and not a servant." She stopped and passed a hand over her eyes. Then she spoke hopelessly. "And all the time it's no good. You've got to take us out for a drive, and I've got to treat you-you like a servant. And you've got to say 'Yes, madam,' and 'No, madam,' and have your tea alone, and-Oh, what on earth did I do it for?"

She was on the verge of tears. I put my hands on her shoulders and looked into her eyes.

"My dear beautiful doll, don't take it all so seriously. It's only a game. We're both play-acting. You've just got to keep it up and order me about in the most monstrously imperious manner this afternoon, and then in the evening we're going to drive home together. And I'm going to get some of my own back then, I don't mind telling you. I'll sprawl and smoke cigarettes and shake you, and-What else was it you said? I haven't forgotten that you agreed to 'all found,' you know. You wait. And I think your eyes are absolutely wonderful. How did it go?

'I thought they were stars,
And I know they were shining.'"

She looked me full in the eyes now, and a grand smile swept into her face. Then she put her arms round my neck and kissed me. The next moment she was half-way up the broad stairs.

Ten minutes later I brought the car round to the door. Niece and uncle and aunt all sat together on the back seat. As I shut the door:

"We don't want to go too far, Norval, or too fast. Lady Brethe is rather tired. I think about twenty miles out and twenty back will do. About two hours altogether."

"Yes, madam. Shall I go towards Savavic?"

"Yes, I think so."

We had done our twenty miles out, and I was looking for a place to turn the car, when I caught sight of Poganec below us in the valley, by road some three or four miles away. Then suddenly for the first time a terrible thought flashed into my mind. We were on the very road which Berry and the others must take, coming from Salzburg. Supposing we met them . . .

Here the road broadened, so I slowed down and, in response to a nod from my mistress, proceeded to turn round. I accomplished the manoeuvre as in a dream, and ended by stopping the engine. This brought me to my senses. As we started off again, I became cooler. After all, very likely we should not meet them. The chances were against it. And if we did, I could accelerate and push by them before they knew where they were. Again—

Here we swung round a corner, and there, fifty paces away, by the side of the road in the hot afternoon sun, stood our car, my car, Berry and Co.'s car. The bonnet was open, and Jonah's head and hands were inside it. Daphne sat still on the back seat, while Jill was sitting on the bank, a posy of wild flowers in her hand. Berry leaned easily against the side of the car, his hat over his eyes, watching Jonah at work. From his attitude he appeared to be offering idiotic advice. So I saw them for less than a second, for the instant they heard us coming, all four started and looked up. I was wondering whether I dared accelerate and dash by like a madman. I dare say the girl was thinking the same. But her uncle settled it.

"Hullo," he said. "Fellow-motorists in trouble? English, apparently, too. Wonder if we-"And the worthy aunt put the lid on.

"Why," she said, "if it isn't those nice children we met at the Europe at Salzburg, Dick."

There was nothing to be done now. I just slowed down. Very slowly we drew abreast, and all the time, till we stopped, I leaned forward and gazed at the four in turn-open-mouthed they were-bending my brows into the fiercest frown and laying my fingers on my lips. Then:

"How d'ye do?" said Lord Brethe.

Berry swallowed, said "Er-oh, how d'ye do?" and took off his hat.

The next moment he had himself in hand. Daphne got out of the car, and Jonah and Jill came up. Greetings were exchanged between them and the Brethes, and my mistress was introduced. I sat as one in a trance. Then I heard the girl saying nervously: "I don't know whether my chauffeur can be of any assistance." I pulled myself together and got out of the car.

There never was such a situation. The Brethes knew nothing and thought nothing. The girl, unaware that these were my own people, saw me being used and treated as a chauffeur by four strangers, while she looked on and got the thanks; and the thought made her writhe. Berry and the others found me about to call them "Sir" and "Madam" and to serve them by mending my own car in the capacity of chauffeur to somebody they had never seen. And I wanted to burst out into hysterical laughter, swear, kick Berry, and hide in the woods. Instead of which, I went up to Jonah, who had gone back to the engine.

"What's the trouble, sir?"

Jonah put his head into the bonnet and exploded with silent laughter. I put my head in, too, and swore at him in a whisper. Then:

"One of the cylinders has been missing since Krainbach," he said. "I think that's the seat of the trouble. But I've only just—"

"I think it's the carburettor, sir," said I, with a finger on the float. "There's practically no petrol in it."

I tried the pressure pump, but it was no good. The petrol pipe was stopped up properly.

"You'll have to have the pipe down, sir. It's the only way."

"How long will that take?" said Lord Brethe, who was standing on the other side of the car, talking to Berry.

"It's half-an-hour's job at least, my lord."

"Oh, well, you'd better do it. Hadn't he, Dolly? We aren't pressed for time, are we, my dear?"

"Oh, no. That is-I mean, of course. Please do everything you can, Norval."

"Very good, madam."

I got some tools out of the tool-box and began to take the pipe down."

Hadn't you better take your dust-coat off, man?" said Berry.

"No, thank you, sir.

Berry turned to Lord Brethe, who had come to watch the operation. "All this comes through~letting my young brother-in-law play about with the car," he explained airily.

"No, really?" said Lord Brethe.

"Yes," said Berry. "He's done more damage, the few times he's driven it, than a skilled chauffeur would do in five years."

"Dear me," said the other. "Knows nothing of the mechanism, I suppose?"

"Doesn't know the difference between the carburettor and the er-exhaust."

Lord Brethe laughed. "Dear, dear. These young men," he said.

Here the spanner I was using slipped off a nut.

"Gently, my man, gently," said Berry pleasantly.

"Yes," said Lord Brethe, "be careful of the paint."

I almost choked.

"Won't you two come and talk to us?" the girl called from the other side of the road.

"I always like watching a repair, dear," replied her uncle. "And Mr. Pleydel is an expert."

"I think I'd better be here just to supervise," said Berry. "Er-have you your cotton-waste handy, man?"

"It's on the step, sir," I said with an effort. "Do you want it?"

"No, no. But you should always keep it by you."

256

I wiped the sweat off my forehead.

"Will you smoke?" said Lord Brethe, producing a cigar-case.

"Ah, thanks," said Berry. With the tail of my eye I saw that it was a Corona Corona. By this time I had taken the pipe down. It was choked with a regular wad of dirt. I remembered bitterly that, when I left them at Strasburg, I had begged them never to fill up without a filter.

"So that was the obstruction?" said his lordship.

I straightened my back.

"Comes of not using a filter, my lord."

Berry's brows contracted. He touched the wad with his foot. "No," he said loftily. "This has clearly worked in from the engine. It is a piece of valve-packing."

I sighed. Heaven only knows what he thought he meant. But old Brethe lapped it up. Heavily I began to replace the pipe. As I unscrewed them, I put the nuts on the step. Now one was missing. It had rolled off.

"Lost something?" said Berry.

"A nut, sir. I shall see it directly."

"Never put anything where it can roll off, man. When you are executing a repair, always lay your tools on the ground and mark the place. It's quicker in the long run. Found it?"

"Yes, sir."

"Wipe it carefully before replacing it."

He turned to Lord Brethe. "You'll excuse me, but you can't be too careful, can you?"

"No, indeed. Quite right, quite right," said the old fool. "We're none of us too old to learn."

The repair was finished at last. I started up the engine, just to make sure she was all right, put away the tools, wiped my hands on a piece of cotton-waste, and resumed my seat in my lady's car without a word.

The girl, looking flushed and anxious, followed her aunt into the car. Lord Brethe climbed in after them. The others stood round.

"It's been awfully kind of you to lend us your chauffeur like this," said Daphne. "I don't know—"

"Oh-er-that's all right," stammered the girl.

"Only too glad," said Lord Brethe. "Mr. Pleydel's been very good and given him several wrinkles well worth having."

"Don't mention it," said Berry, with a smirk.

"Here you are, my man. "I took the crown he offered me in silence and raised my hat. A crown is worth ten pence. As I was letting in the clutch, I heard Jill's voice on my left.

"Thank you very much indeed for helping us so beautifully," she said, and laid her posy of wild flowers on the seat by my side.

"Thank you, madam."

As we moved off:

"What a queer child!" said Lady Brethe.

Two hours later the girl and I slipped once more out of Laipnik. When we were clear of the town, I stopped for a moment, and she took her old seat by my side. For a minute or two neither of us spoke. Then she reached up and took off my cap and pitched it behind into the car. I laughed.

"I wanted to do that a dozen times this afternoon," she said. "And I'd have done it, too, if I'd had the courage of a field-mouse."

"You know what I've wanted to do a dozen times this afternoon, don't you?"

"And these odious people. Will you ever forgive me? If it's any consolation to you, I nearly died of shame."

"And I nearly punched Berry's head and spoiled it all."

"Berry's?"

I explained. When I had finished:

"It was nice of Jill to give you those flowers," she said. "Dear of her. But I shall never forgive Berry."

"He's only human," said I. "And he really was awfully funny."

"I shall tell him what I think of him."

"We've all done that once a week for five years. My dear, he's quite hopeless. Besides, he gave me a whole crown."

"And uncle gave you five. I saw him. I nearly cried, it made me so angry."

"Six altogether," said I. "I bought you some carnations with them. They're in the hood."

"Sweet of you, Norval. Coals of fire?"

"No, dear. Only malmaisons. Isn't that beautiful?"

We had climbed until we were at the top of a pass. Over the mountains the sun was going down. The great valley was already in shadow, but the light on the high woods was wonderful. Away on the top of a hill a little white shrine stood up like a candlestick against the sky. A rosy flush lay on the distant snow mountains, and the heavens themselves were filled with a great red glory. The same thought occurred to both of us.

"Who wouldn't be a day?" said I. It's worth living only twelve hours to die a death like that."

We reached Savavic about half-past seven. I drove straight to the garage. She watched me put the car away and waited while I slipped into my brogues. Then:

"Now I must be off to Poganec," said I. "So endeth the first day's service."

"And the last."

I drew myself up.

"Am I dismissed, then?"

"Oh, well—"

"Of course, if you're not satisfied, madam—"

"But I am, only—"

"Then," said I, "I'll stop on. Good night, beautiful Doll."

"Dolly."

"Dolly, then."

I swept off my hat and turned to go.

"Don't you want to-er-shake me?" said Dolly.

I reached Poganec just as they were finishing dinner. As I entered the room:

"Hullo," said Berry. "This your night out?"

"That'll do." said I. "You had your show this afternoon."

"My show? My humiliation," said my brother-in-law. "Think of it. My wife's brother in service. How can I ever hold up this noble head again? And this after all my years of striving to elevate. But there! Can the leopard change his spots, or the chauffeur his boots? By the way, how did you get into them? Rather a tight fit, wasn't it? You don't look very penitent. I suppose you know I'm bowed with grief?"

"I see you're gorged with food," said I. "Haven't you any dinner for me?"

"It's in a red handkerchief by the coach-house door," said Berry. "Now you can go. I shan't want you any more tonight. Don't forget the-ah-wrinkle I gave you about the cotton-waste."

"Fancy Boy earning some money!" said Daphne. "What wages d'you get?"

"Six-and-tenpence-farthing a week," said I, "and all found."

"That's a dangerous phrase," said Jonah. "Might mean anything."

"Exactly," said Berry. "It includes boots, we know. What else besides boots?"

"Depends on the man," said I.

"It does," said Daphne. "And that's why you've got to give notice at once."

"Notice?"

I felt Jill's hand pushing my hair back from my forehead. She was standing behind my chair.

"Yes," she said, "and come back to us. Fact is, Boy, we can't spare you."

Lightning Source UK Ltd.
Milton Keynes UK
UKHW050847160223
416721UK00008B/410